Strebor ON THE Streetz

BORN DYING

A NOVEL

STREBOR ON THE STREETZ

BORN
DYING

A NOVEL

HAROLD L. TURLEY II

SBI

STREBOR BOOKS

NEW YORK LONDON TORONTO SYDNEY

Strebor Books
P.O. Box 6505
Largo, MD 20792
http://www.streborbooks.com

ISBN-13 978-1-59309-143-9
ISBN-10   1-59309-143-5
LCCN 2007924153

First Strebor Books trade paperback edition February 2008

Cover design: www.mariondesigns.com

10   9   8   7   6   5   4   3   2   1

Manufactured in the United States of America

For information regarding special discounts for bulk purchases, please contact Simon & Schuster Special Sales at 1-800-456-6798 or business@simonandschuster.com

ACKNOWLEDGMENTS

I want to switch things up this time with my acknowledgements and thank the people in my life who made me the man I am today and stopped me from being one of the Money Greens or O'Neals in the world. A man and a woman can give birth to a child, but it truly takes a village to raise him. Without my village, I know I'd either be in jail or possibly dead by now.

First and foremost, I have to thank my Lord and Savior for blessing me with a vivid imagination and the gift to express it through written word. I am a living testimony that through You, ALL things are possible.

I have to thank my mother, Anna Stroman, for being not only my mother but also my friend. I can write a book in itself for all that you've done for me and will continue to do. I would be lost in this world without you.

I want to thank my father, Harold L. Turley Sr. It has been a long time since we've had a father-son relationship but at least I'm lucky enough to say that you made your presence known and I had a father who was a part of my life.

To DeArthur & Lillian Milner, there isn't a day that goes by that I don't think about either of you. The two of you set the perfect example of what a family should be.

To all my aunts and uncles, Aunt Ona, Uncle Butch and Aunt Linda, Uncle Arve and Aunt Bonnie, Uncle Ro, Aunt Nadine and Uncle Fella, and finally Uncle Bobby and Aunt Sia. Without all of you, I would have been lost by the wayside.

To my little brother and little sister, JD and Ashante, though there is a gap between us in age it never created a gap in the love that I share for both of you. Whenever you need anything, you don't even have to ask and it's yours. Unless you are asking for some money, I owe everyone. I haven't forgotten you, Uncle Butch!

To my cousins, there are too many of you to list so if I can't list you all, then I'm not listing any of you. Sike, naw, I want to especially thank Marc, Little Fella, Dytrea, Shamee, Poopee, Lisa, Bo, Nick, Robbie, Chanita, Lil Ro, Stacy, Nicole, Skeeta, and Nikki. Though I have more cousins to list, I was around most of you growing up. And each of you in your own little way shaped me into the man I am today.

To my niggas and niggettes from around the way, Reggie, Rome, Greg, Ray, Ace, Smiley, Lil Dawg, Big Antwain, Neno, Black, White Mike, Kenny, Sam, Black O, Antwan, Big Reds, Buck, and lil Peanut... I'll always treasure the childhood memories we shared. It's sad that after twenty years, we are still tough and going strong. Always know, you have a friend in me for LIPHE!

To my man James, I didn't put you in the cousin or friend category because you are more than that to me. You are like a brother to me. We've always been close and you've always supported me in everything I've done. I know that, that will never change until the day we die. WE NIGGAS FOR LIPHE!

To the friends I've made along the way, Eddie and Nicolle (Hi, Nicolle) and Reggie Clark (get that Madden game up), I'm not the best at making friends but all of you made it extremely easy.

To my sisters from other mothers, Taledia, Vonita, and JoAnna, though I don't talk to all of you as often as others, please don't think I've ever forgotten any of you. All of you carry a special place within my heart. Thank you for all the advice, long talks, and countless support. I know whenever there comes a time I doubt myself, you are always there to pick my spirits back up.

I have to thank two people who along the way had a major impact on my life, Levi Franklin and Bill Lee. Though you were my basketball coaches, you were more like distant uncles. You treated me like family and taught me about more than basketball, but about life. I will never truly be able to repay either of you for keeping me off the streets and doing dirt! Thanks!

To the women who loved me the most but yet I probably hurt the most, Tomeka, Candace, and Teresa. Each one of you taught me different things about the man I was and the man I needed to be. You showed me how to love, how to be a friend, and how to be a companion. In the end, you showed me just what type of man I need to be in order to treat a woman the way she deserves to be treated. Though it didn't work out between us, I thank you for being a part of my life. Each of you will always hold a special place in my heart.

To the women who loved me as if I was their son, Vanessa Greene, Elisa Scott, and Jenith Dekle. Thank you for all that you've done for me and will continue to do for me in the future.

Every time I thank the special lady in my life, when the new book comes out, she is no longer a part of my life. So, I'm not going to jinx anything. I'll just say that each day you show me more and more about life and the things that I need to value most. When I first saw you, I knew it was something special about you. And although I don't know what the future will hold, I do know that I want you and Niya a part of mine. Hopefully by the time this book is released, you won't still be playing hard to get. And don't worry, I won't tell anyone how you acted on the Tea Cup ride at Sesame Place. It's okay for a grown woman to cover her eyes and scream. Oops, did I put that in here?

I want to thank my children for just being the joy in my life, Harold L. Turley III, RaShawn Turley, Malik Brown, and Yhanae Turley. I work so hard so that one day none of you will have to. Everything I do in life is for you. I love you more than I love myself. You are the true definition of unconditional love. Each day you show me how blessed I truly am.

To my literary family, I have to start with Zane. You've given me the platform to follow my dream. I will always be thankful for all that you've done. Charmaine Parker, man, you are the hardest-working woman in show business. The entire Strebor family thanks you. Darrien Lee, Tina Brooks McKinney, Allison Hobbs, and Shelley Halima, I can't wait until we all meet up again and just have a good ole time. The Strebor Family, we are going to take this world by storm. I'm a strong believer in that.

I have to thank Nikki Turner, thanks for always answering the phone when I call. I know at times I get on your nerves but it's all love!

If I have forgotten you, please do not blame my heart or even my mind, after writing a damn novel, working a regular 9-5, and being a full-time dad, I'm lucky I remember my own damn name. I know excuses are nothing but examples of incompetence but, still... There are so many people who have affected my life and who I thank, that I honestly could write an entire book just listing all of you. So, here I want to go ahead and thank _____ for all that you do. Without you, I wouldn't be the man I am today. (You'd better not have written your name in my damn book!) J

Finally I want this book to be for all the niggas still caught in the struggle and who believe that being on the corner, or cooking that coke, is the only way. Hopefully it will show you, that there are so many other avenues you can go because this one only has two guaranteed endings.

Today, let's make a stand. Today, let's make a difference!

THE MAKING OF
MONEY GREEN

CHAPTER 1

"Nate," a woman yelled from the other room in the house. "Nate, get up! You are going to be late for school!"

Nate was dead tired from the night before and school was the last thought on his mind. He didn't feel like budging. Usually his mother would give him a courtesy wake-up call, and then she would head straight for her bedroom where the comfort of her bed awaited her after a long night at work.

Working ten-hour shifts for Telnex Wireless will do that to the average person. However, Nate's mother realized she couldn't be average when it came to her son, especially after she found out about his newfound habit to skip school. At that point, average could no longer be a part of her title.

She was determined to make sure he was where he was supposed to be when he was supposed to be, whether it meant missing a couple of minutes or hours of sleep per day. She didn't care. Nate was her number one priority.

"Nathaniel Donte Rodgers, if you do not get your skinny ass out of that damn bed, you will be wearing those same sheets to your funeral next week," she said as she shook his bed to make sure he'd get up.

"Damn, Ma, I'm up!"

"Excuse you? Who the hell do you think you are talking to? You want to cuss in this house, then you need to go through nine months of pregnancy, forty-six hours of labor, and pay the household bills by yourself. When you do all that, then you can cuss in this house. Other than that you will respect me and my house or I will knock your ass on the floor. Are we clear?"

The smirk that painted Nate's face showed that he understood his mother completely but also took part of what was said as a joke. His mother never had a problem playing tough, but when it came time to lay down the law physically, she was nothing but a pussycat.

"Boy, if you don't wipe that damn smirk off your face…"

Nate cut her off, "I know, I know. You are going to knock me into the middle of next week."

He couldn't help but laugh after repeating a saying his mother said over and over again.

"I'm sorry, Ma, it will never happen again. I was half asleep."

"What have I told you about saying you are sorry? I didn't have a 'sorry' child."

"Excuse me, I meant, I apologize. Now if you don't mind, Mother, can you excuse me so I can get dressed?"

"Boy, please, I've seen what you have. I'm the one who diapered that little thing of yours."

"Ma, there is nothing *little* about my thing."

Now she'd found something to be amused about. She broke out into laughter.

"Child, please, at fourteen years old, everything is little on you but your heart. That is the only thing big a fourteen-year-old can have. Now let's get ready for school so you can continue to expand your mind."

He started to get out of the bed.

"I'll let your little comment slide since you are my mother and I love you, but don't let it happen again. I know a couple of girls who would disagree with you, though."

That caught Nate's mother off guard and now she was intrigued.

"Oh really, is that right? You keep digging yourself a hole deeper and deeper and you don't even know it. Sooner or later, it's going to be so deep you'll never get out of it. "

"It was a joke, Ma. I didn't mean anything by it. I was just pushing your buttons."

She wasn't buying it. "I bet. I know if you are dumb enough to be poking that thing around you need to be at least smart enough to know you need to be wearing a condom as well. Kids these days want to grow up so fast but when they have to face consequences for their actions, then that's when they want to be kids again."

"Ma, come on! It's really not that serious. It was a joke."

"Don't 'come on, Ma' me and don't brush off what I'm saying, either. I'm serious. It's too much shit traveling around out here in these streets and I don't need you bringing it into this house. It used to be all you had to worry about was getting a woman pregnant, but now you have to worry about saving your life."

Nate knew the only way this conversation would ever end would be if he ignored her. He couldn't assure her that he was using protection because then she'd want to know more about his sex life such as when, where, and with whom. If he said he wasn't using protection she'd question as to why not, run down all the possible diseases he could contract, then would start up with the when, where, and with who.

There was no way she'd buy he wasn't sexually active. Then she'd go into her "don't lie to me" speech and the morning would become even longer. Nate decided to do the only thing he could, get ready for school. He just looked at her with his hazel eyes and kept his mouth closed.

"Do you hear me talking to you?" she questioned.

He nodded trying not to be totally disrespectful.

She became frustrated. "It's too early in the morning to be going through this and I'm too tired. Get your ass up and get ready for school."

Nate knew that wasn't the last of that conversation but at least it was for today. His mother finally left the room. Nate decided to make a mental note to get an alarm clock later that day to make sure she didn't have to wake him up anymore and to avoid these types of talks. He thought it was cool being able to talk to your mother, but you didn't want to talk to her about every damn thing. He headed for his closet to pull out an outfit to wear to school. He grabbed a pair of blue jeans and a white T-shirt, nothing special. Nate never saw fit to be flashy. It only brought more attention to yourself.

By the time he got out of the shower and dressed, his mother was fast asleep. He walked into her room and put the covers over top of her, then gave her a kiss on the forehead. He made sure to put two hundred in her purse and hoped she would use it for something regarding the house.

Nate made it a habit to slip money into his mother's purse. He just made sure to put it in the middle of whatever cash she had in her wallet so it didn't stand out. It obviously was working because up to date, she had never questioned him about anything. He knew if she had any clue about what he was doing, then she would have questioned him to the end trying to find out where the money came from. However, those were answers that he knew she would never be ready to deal with.

CHAPTER 2

Nate walked into Oxon Hill High School in Oxon Hill, Maryland, and headed straight for his locker. His day began with English, geometry, and finally Spanish before lunch. He couldn't stand his class schedule. If it were up to him, PE would have been stuck somewhere in between that load.

To his surprise, O'Neal was standing at his locker waiting for Nate. O'Neal and Nate went back since pee-wee football. They were best friends and business partners. He was never real big on school so whenever anyone saw him there, it was shocking. O'Neal was a year older but because of his lack of enthusiasm for education, he was held back and they both were in the same grade.

"Are you ready to break out?" he asked.

"We don't have a job?"

"What's your point, Nate?"

"My point is I can't mess with it today. It's one thing to roll and make some extra change. But it's a whole different ball game to fuck up in school, cause my mother to get suspicious to what I'm doing, and eventually mess with my paper trail, all because I wanted to do was break camp just for the hell of it."

"Keep your pager on then because you know how Chico is. When work needs to be put in, he doesn't factor your English test into consideration." O'Neal extended his hand to give Nate some dap. "I might stick around for a few to try to catch up with the shortie we bumped in to last night. If not, I'll just catch up with you around the way."

"That sounds like a plan."

Nate grabbed his books out of his locker and headed to class. School really was just something to do to pass time to him. He always felt as if there was nothing being taught to him that he'd use in the future. Only the school of hard knocks provided you with the lesson that would be needed for the streets.

Nate was a momma's boy, though and an education was to please her so he did. He'd do anything to make that woman happy. She took things very hard when she lost Nate's father to drugs in the '80s. Nate didn't want to put his mother through that horror again.

Instead, he did whatever it took to make sure he got acceptable grades. He didn't want to overdo things and stand out, either. If so, then the bar would be raised and his mother would grow to expect it. So he made sure to sprinkle in a couple of A's or B's along with a few D's on there as well. That way, there was always something he could improve upon in her eyes.

Nate walked into the cafeteria after his brutal morning schedule ready to relax. To his surprise, O'Neal was still at school. There was no way he'd ever leave and come back all in one day. If he was out, you wouldn't see him anymore until you met up with him after school around the neighborhood.

There was only one thing that could have kept him at school and she was standing right next to him as he was trying to throw on the charm. Nate walked over to the back of the cafeteria where they were standing. O'Neal was in prime form. Pussy was always on his mind. That, if not his temper, would be his biggest downfall.

"What's good? I thought you were breaking camp earlier. Why the sudden change of heart?" Nate asked O'Neal even though he knew the answer. O'Neal shot him a look as if to say, *Stop frontin' like you don't already know.*

"I had some things I needed to take care of first. Have you met Nikki?"

"Naw, not formally, but I've seen her around before. You live in Forest Heights, right?"

"Damn, you stalking me or something?" she said defensively.

Nate quickly became defensive too. She was cute but far from his taste. Part of him took her remark as an insult. What need would he have to stalk her?

"Bitch, please! Don't flatter yourself because it's definitely not that serious!" Nate snapped back.

O'Neal put his hand over his head knowing the conversation from that point on was going nowhere but downhill.

"Who the fuck are you calling a bitch?"

"Calm down, boo! He didn't mean it like that," O'Neal said, trying to defuse the situation.

"Y'all niggas must have me twisted if you think I'm just going to sit here and let you talk to me any ole way. You best believe someone will be addressing this shit later on," she said, then stormed off before either of them could reply.

They both knew what she meant but it wasn't fazing either of them. The damage had already been done and when it came time to bump heads with them Forest Heights niggas, they'd be more than ready.

"Damn, nigga, when are you going to learn to control your mouth? You can't just say whatever comes to mind, especially when it's going to interfere with my action."

Nate couldn't help but laugh. O'Neal never let anything come between him and some action unless it was money.

"My bad. I didn't mean to throw a monkey wrench in your plans, seriously. But Slim came out the mouth wrong with that dumb shit and she needed to be put in her place quick. Don't fake! What do I look like stalking somebody, let alone her ass of all people?"

O'Neal found that very funny. "I was stalking her ass, though. Why didn't you tell me last night you knew where Slim stayed? I could have used that information."

"For what? I knew you'd find a way to catch up with her on your own and not look like you were pressed. Be honest, how does it look, you are never around Forest Heights, you don't live around there, but just happened to be around there to get at Slim out of the blue. That's some pressed shit. There is nothing original about that. Naw, you needed to catch up with her at school or wherever and then play your hand."

"Yeah, you right. Damn, it's about that time, though. We need to get up out of here."

"For what? I know you aren't tripping off that bullshit-ass threat."

"Come on now, you should know me better than that. When have I ever run from a fight? We have to be out because we have a meeting with Chico. He hit me up this morning."

Nate was dumbfounded but knew not to ask any questions. Chico was the one putting money in his pockets so if he called a meeting, Nate was definitely going to be in attendance.

"Did he say what it was about?"

"No, and I really didn't want to know, either. The only thing I needed to know was bread and he will be providing that, so I'm good."

O'Neal turned toward the double doors leading outside and headed through them. Nate wasn't too far behind him. The way the school was built, the cafeteria was at the front of the school and led straight to the parking lot where the school buses dropped off and picked up students.

Usually there were security guards out there but they were only there as props. They broke up the occasional fight here and there but that was about it. They didn't give a damn who left school early nor why. Half the time, they were trying to get the high school girls to leave early with them for some lunchtime fun.

Chico's black Lincoln Town Car pulled up at the bottom of the steps in the parking lot. We headed straight for it.

"What's going on, Chico?" O'Neal said the minute he got in the car.

"Hurry up and close the door. I have business to attend to."

Nate cut straight through the chase.

"How do we factor into these business plans?"

Chico found Nate's bluntness amusing.

"Always the straight shooter, huh, Nate? I like that."

Chico was a small-time dealer under the Cardoza crime family umbrella. Anyone who knew anything knew Mario Cardoza was the man to know in these streets. He held the power in D.C., and Chico was Nate's steppingstone up the ladder to the main man. O'Neal was only along for the small-time paper they were making.

To a couple of fourteen- and sixteen-year-olds, six hundred a week was a lot of money, especially to only be runners. Nate wasn't satisfied with that, though. No, he had bigger plans. He just needed the right avenue to make them happen. He was a firm believer that time and patience would open all the doors to anything they desired. You just had to wait your full course and that was something he was determined to do.

"Chico, my style will never change. I'm always going to be about that paper."

"Well, little homie, if you handle this job right, you will do just that. I've got something new for the both of you. Are you game?"

"Is money green?"

"My man! That is exactly what I wanted to hear. Okay, Nate there is a bag underneath my seat, so before you get out of the car, I want you to slide over and get it. Don't be all obvious, either. Just make your way over to my side before I get to Eastover and then just get out on my side of the car. O'Neal, there is a pistol under your seat. Make sure you reach under and get that as well.

"I'm sure I don't have to school you on how to keep a piece on you. You make sure nothing happens to that damn bag. Now, I'm going to drop both of you off at Eastover, then this is what I want you to do. You need to take the bag to Wayne Place in Southeast. It's not that far of a walk from Eastover but it's not like it's right up the street. Look at it as some much needed exercise.

"When you get on Wayne, ask for Tony. I'm sure someone out there will point you in the right direction. Once you catch up with Tony, let him know you have his weekly delivery. He'll have another bag to give you. I'll meet the both of you back where I drop you off in an hour and a half. If you are late, that is your ass. If anything is missing from either bag, that is your ass.

"If you have any problems, O'Neal, do not hesitate to use that pistol or that will be your ass. Notice I said *use* and not *pull*. This is not show and tell. If it comes out, there better be a bang following right behind it too. I don't care which one but make sure your ass is back here with either bag. We can always do the deal at a later time if need be. You got that?"

By the tone of Chico's voice, this wasn't the normal run. They had moved up to something more serious than the one or two pounds of marijuana Chico had them dropping off at the normal hot spots. Now he had them crossing the D.C. line; before they were restricted to Maryland only. One thing bothered Nate about the whole situation and it was something that needed to be addressed.

"What's Tony's price? I don't like not knowing that, especially when it's my ass on the line. You telling us to make sure nothing is missing from either bag but if this nigga shorts us, how we going to know if we don't even know what short is? I'm not feeling that. I want to make sure every dollar is in there before I head out of that spot."

Chico could see the problem that was facing them. Though he doubted Tony would ever try to go up against the family, anything was possible. Especially if all he had to do was say he gave Nate and O'Neal the regular payment and they were the ones with the sticky hands. Then it would turn into some "he said, she said" shit that would get everyone killed.

"Good point, lil' homie, very good point. It would be smart if you counted the money before you rolled to make sure we aren't being stiffed. Respect is everything so make sure he understands it's for precautionary reasons only and not out of disrespect. This is a business. There should be fourteen thousand in the bag. Anything under that, you walk your ass up out of there with our product in hand. Is that clear?"

"Crystal!"

CHAPTER 3

Chico dropped them off in front of the Midas Brake Shop next to the Popeyes in the Eastover Shopping Center located in Oxon Hill, Maryland. It was at the border of the Southeast, D.C. line. Before Nate got out of the car, he made sure to look and see what time the clock read in Chico's car. It was 1:22 p.m. He set his watch to 1:24 p.m. to give them a two-minute cushion. It didn't make sense to risk getting an ass whipping, shot, or worst, all because he was five minutes late. It wasn't going down like that. No, he was going to make sure they were back by 2:45 p.m.

Nate knew exactly how to get to Wayne Place so that was the easy part. O'Neal had an idea of where to find Tony. The walk to their destination was a quiet one. They both were nervous as hell. The unexpected would do that to you. It played games with your mind trying to figure out what would or could possibly happen.

The bottom line was neither of them knew these niggas. You always heard about drug deals that went bad all the time, and the ones usually doing the drop-off were the same ones who you saw on the news being zipped up in the body bags. Nate kept replaying every possible scenario in his head to avoid that from happening.

Once they reached Wayne Place, their nerves were at full tilt. Nate looked at his watch to check the time and it was 1:47

p.m. That was good to know. It only took them twenty-three minutes to get there so with the same amount of time going back they needed to be leaving by no later than 2:22 p.m. They had good time to spare. Nate stopped walking.

"What's wrong?" O'Neal questioned.

"Nothing, look when we get there let me do all the talking. When I go to count the money, I'm going to give you this bag to hold until everything is peachy. Make sure you keep your eyes and ears open at all times. You are the only nigga I trust with my life in this world so you better make damn sure I leave this place with it."

"Champ, from the cradle to the grave. You know I have your back."

"Okay, we have about fifteen minutes to be in and out. Hopefully they don't try to hit us with no bullshit because of our ages."

"Fuck them!"

They walked up the block to a building that read "3915." There were four men on the front stoop playing craps. That's when it kicked in to them… the easy time they were hoping for wasn't going to happen.

"I'm looking for Tony," Nate said.

A short but stocky light-skinned brother broke away from the game. He looked both of them over quickly and assumed they must have been fiends or something.

"You'll find what you need across the street."

"If Tony isn't over there, then I won't find shit. Now if you're not Tony, can you do us both a favor and point me in the right direction?"

He cracked a brief smile on his face.

"Listen to this little muthafucka. Who do you think you are talking to? Do you even know where your ass is at?"

O'Neal started to become a little anxious and was easing his hand toward the pistol. Nate gave him a calming look to assure him that everything was cool.

"Man, fuck all that, I have business with the man. How about this, when you see him you let him know his weekly delivery came by but you told the little muthafucka to head across the street instead." Nate turned to O'Neal and said, "Come on, we out!"

"Hold up!" Nate heard someone say from behind them. They both turned back around to face whoever it was.

A tall, brown skinny brother with cornrows was now standing up. From the looks of the cash in his hand, he was cleaning house in the crap game.

"Chico sent you?" he asked.

"I don't know who that is, just like I don't know who you are, either. Y'all fellas have a good day."

Nate tapped O'Neal on the shoulder and they both turned to leave again.

"Okay, lil' man. You made your point. I'm Tony."

"Then you are the man I came to see; now can we get to business, please? I have other shit to do with my time."

The short stocky guy cut him off.

"What the fuck does your little ass have to do?"

Nate just ignored him and looked Tony dead in his eyes.

"After you," Nate replied.

"No problem, your boy can wait down here with the fellas."

"We'll pass. No disrespect, but again, I don't know y'all. Where I go, he goes."

Nate looked at his watch to check the time. It was already 2:01 p.m. Time was flying by. By him looking at his watch, it gave the illusion that his time was precious and they were running out of it if they wanted to make the deal happen. Though that wasn't what Nate was really trying to portray, it did the trick to speed things along.

"Okay, come on," he agreed.

They followed Tony into the building and up the stairs. O'Neal was looking over his shoulder the whole time. You could tell he didn't like that the same one with all the damn mouth and attitude downstairs was following behind him up the steps. This whole situation was nerve-wracking but an experience. Tony stopped at Apt B2 and knocked twice.

A dark-skinned guy opened the door and let them in. At a quick glimpse, you could tell that they weren't where the product was usually stored. Nate started to get a little nervous because everything pointed to signs of a set-up. The guy who opened the door headed straight for the couch to take a seat and finished watching Jerry Springer on TV. Tony went into the back room. Once he came out, he had a small black bag in his hand. Nate wasn't an expert on what fourteen thousand looked like up close and personal but that bag seemed a little too small to be carrying it.

"Do you mind if I count it first?"

"This little nigga has balls," the stocky dude said.

Nate could see he needed to do something to ease the tension. They were halfway home and he didn't need the deal going sour because Tony felt like he was being bullied by a kid.

"Again, I don't mean any disrespect, but the people I work for will have my ass if it's not fourteen in this bag."

"Moe, chill out! Little man, it's no problem. I'd want to count it too if I were you. You can't trust anyone in this business."

Tony handed Nate the bag after he handed the product to O'Neal to hold so the money could be counted. Nate was sure all three of them had pistols on them or in the apartment somewhere. They'd felt comfortable they wouldn't try to run out with the money and the product. He didn't waste any time. He quickly counted the 140 one hundred-dollar bills. Nate looked at O'Neal.

"We good."

He handed Tony the product. Tony opened the bag and pulled out what seemed to be a key of cocaine. Tony gave the bag to the dark-skinned guy so he could verify the product was good. Once he gave Tony the nod everything was cool, O'Neal and Nate were out the door.

They made sure to stick to the main roads the entire way back to Eastover which took them a little longer. Nate was extremely cautious and his antennas were straight up in the air. Nate didn't trust the nigga Moe no further than he could throw him. His gut kept telling him he would try to find a way to get over on them and hit their heads for the fourteen they'd just got up off them. Everything about him said he was a scheming-type dude.

The way Nate saw it, Moe was either doing one of two things. Either he was following them back trying to find the right time to run up on them or he'd put the word out on the street that they were out with that type of cash. Tony didn't come off as the type for a set-up. He seemed more like a man who didn't want to mess up a good thing. However, if it came down to it, he could always deny knowing anything about robbing O'Neal and Nate, pocket the cash, and the key he was sold. Chico had made it clear what the repercussions would be if they didn't come back with either the product or the cash.

Once they made it back to Eastover, they still had a good ten minutes to spare so they sat inside the Popeyes chicken spot and waited. It was next to the Midas Brake Shop and the parking lot was in plain view so if Chico pulled up, they wouldn't miss him.

Like clockwork, Chico pulled up in the parking lot at 2:45 p.m. The minute they spotted the Lincoln, Nate headed out to meet Chico while O'Neal waited inside. By the time he reached the car, the trunk was already popped. He quickly opened it, placed the bag inside the trunk, and then closed it. Chico backed out of the parking spot he was occupying and then drove off and that was that. The transaction was finally completed.

CHAPTER 4

O'Neal and Nate grabbed a quick bite to eat while they were at Popeyes. Neither of them had eaten anything that day and figured then was as good as any time to catch a quick bite. There was still plenty of time before school would let out and Nate had to be home. As long as Nate walked in the house at his normal time, his mother wouldn't get suspicious.

O'Neal, on the other hand, was heading back to the school. He'd left his car parked there. After that, he'd probably head home and they would meet up later that evening once his mother left to go to work.

The entire walk home Nate couldn't help but think about Chico and his newfound promotion in the game. Moving coke in Southeast was a big step up from a few pounds of marijuana in Oxon Hill. Nate couldn't but wonder who would slide into Chico's old spot and territory or if was being vacated and left as an open market. Either way, opportunity was knocking on Nate's door and it was time he answered the call.

The only problem was how he was going to play the situation out. The first rule in this business was trust. That could never be understated, trust is everything. What was hurting Nate's chances was that he was a trustworthy runner. That was the hardest thing to find. Nate knew Chico would fight letting either him or O'Neal go. Chico trusted them like family and in a sense that is how he looked at them.

O'Neal and Nate had met Chico through his younger brother Francis. They all played Pop Warner football together for the Oxon Hill Boys and Girls Club. That's actually how all of them had met, instantly bonded and became the best of friends. Once Chico got his foot in the door, he quickly reached out to family for help. Since Francis was younger than him, he didn't look at him like an equal and wouldn't bring him in to help him run his share of the business. Instead, he went to Francis to see if he'd be a runner for him. Who better to trust than your own little brother?

Francis had other plans for his life though and running drugs or money wasn't a part of them. He ate, drank, and slept football and had the skills to achieve it. Football came natural to him. He could do things on the field at an early age that grown men dreamed of. He was the type of kid that you knew football would take Francis somewhere and it was out of the Maryland and Washington, D.C. metropolitan area. That was for sure.

Without a runner, Chico's reign of the business would end fast. There was no way he'd deliver his own product. That was suicide and a sure way to get busted. That pushed Nate and O'Neal to the next available in line and both of them jumped at the opportunity.

To them, money is what made their world go round. They were ignorant to the things life could afford them. In their eyes, hustling was the only way they saw to make serious paper. It didn't matter if there was no retirement plan, no 401K, or medical benefits. Being the next kingpin was more attractive than anything.

The dollar signs were the only think Nate saw. He knew there were only two guaranteed ways out: either a jail cell or a six-by-nine-foot box. But it didn't matter. He, like others before him, figured they were the exception to the rule. He felt as if he was too smart and ahead of the game.

Nate walked into the house and to his surprise, his mother was already gone. That was shocking since it was only 4:42 p.m. and she usually didn't leave the house for work until close to six p.m. She tried to make it a habit to make sure she was home when Nate arrived from school. Nate knew there was only one reason why she wouldn't be there—overtime.

If she was doing overtime, then the bills had to be piling up again. He knew she'd never confided in him about them. He was the child, why would she. His mother would work until she couldn't work anymore to provide for him. He checked the refrigerator to make sure his presumption was correct and it was. His dinner was neatly wrapped and on the top shelf waiting for him.

A part of him was at ease because he knew there was no way his mother had forgotten about their earlier conversation. She would have used her time before work to continue to probe Nate about his sex life. He knew the questions would never stop but would continue until she got the answers she was looking for.

Nate went into his bedroom to lie down for a bit. Something was telling him that tonight would be a very long one and he needed to rest for it. Plus, he wanted to figure out a way to break away from Chico. First issue at hand was finding Chico some new runners. Nate had to have them ready and on stand-by, and they had to be someone he trusted or Chico never would. Nate was always thinking ahead. His mindset was, if you stayed stuck in the past or basked in the present you'd ultimately end up limiting your future.

The sound of his pager going off broke him out of his train of thought. Nate didn't recognize the number entered but saw O'Neal had put his code in. Something had to be up. Nate picked up the phone and dialed the number.

O'Neal didn't waste any time. "Meet me at your corner in ten minutes. This is urgent."

"Just come to the house, Moms broke camp for work early today."

"That's what's up!"

If Nate didn't understand the urgency of the situation by the tone of O'Neal's voice, he definitely did when he didn't waste any time getting to his house. He didn't even pull his '86 Dodge Aries all the way into the driveway. O'Neal jumped out of the car with the engine still running and came in the house.

The minute Nate and O'Neal hung up with each other, Nate had unlocked the front door. That way he could go ahead and get ready and not have to stop to answer the door.

"Aye, let's go. We need to be out of here ASAP! We have some real shit going on now!"

Nate noticed the Band-Aid over O'Neal's left eye.

"What the fuck happened to you?"

"I'll explain all that in the car. We need to be out. We still need to head around the way and get the fellas."

"Kill all that shit, O! Go turn the car off, come inside, and tell me what the fuck is going on. You are too hype right now."

"Nate, look, I'm not trying to hear all that. You aren't the one who was jumped by them bitch-ass Forest Heights niggas! They fucking jumped me!"

Nate was lost. He couldn't understand how that could've happened. They made sure to walk back to school together since they knew they'd have to pass Forest Heights. They didn't split up until they were well past the neighborhood and were close to the school. There was no way that any of the niggas around Forest Heights had the heart to come around the way and jump O'Neal. It wasn't like them to try to catch him back at the school because he was hardly ever there.

Nate decided to not even protest anymore. He knew the longer they were in the house, the less information O'Neal would give up. His only focus was to get back and as long as he was in the house, there was no talking or reasoning with him. They would argue about still being at the house. Nate locked up his house and they both headed for the car. The minute Nate sat down, O'Neal sped off.

"Okay, what the fuck happened?" Nate asked.

"That bitch set me up."

"Nigga, you are talking in circles. What bitch? Because none of this shit is making any sense right now, so do me a favor, slow it down. Start at A first before you take me to Z, shit!"

"The bitch from school, you know the one who we got into it with earlier. The same one we saw last night, that bitch. Well, before you came over and fucked the party up earlier, I had already given her my contact info so she could hit me up later.

"Well, Slim hit me up and I called back. I didn't recognize the number on my beeper. Anyway, once I find out who it is, you know I'm shocked like shit because I thought Slim would still be in her feelings. Instead she is giving me so much love.

Now you know I'm fucked up so I questioned everything, then she was like, she wasn't beefin' with me because you were the one who came at her wrong, not me. I'm talking Slim apologized for snapping at me and everything.

"That was all I needed to hear. The minute I saw an opening, you know I quickly slid back into mack mode. So ole girl started laying it on thick, talking about how bad she wanted to see me and how her folks wouldn't be home til late so I'm thinking, thank God, and I headed over there. Damn, I wish I hadn't. The greeting Forest Heights' finest gave me, I didn't have a chance."

"I swear I wonder about you sometimes. If you seen them niggas posted up, why the fuck did you even get out of the car? The minute you saw them posted up, you should have known something was up. You betta than that, come on!"

"I know I'm better than that. If I saw them, best believe my foot would have been on the gas. There was no one posted up out that bitch. Whoever planned this shit, made sure they caught me slipping. They were on top of their game. These niggas waited to catch me when I came inside the house. This bitch came to the front door in a robe and told me to come in. The second I saw flesh I relaxed and went on in. The next thing I knew everyone and their mother was throwing blows my way."

"I take it you left the burner in the car," Nate replied.

"Worse, I left the shit at home. Thinking I'm being smart about the situation, I wasn't trying to get caught driving out here with no license and a pistol. Go figure, the one time I do the smart thing it turns out to be the wrong thing for me because if I had my pistol, I would have laid all of them niggas down for real!"

Everything was moving too quickly. Forest Heights wasn't

known for its fire power but they had a couple of niggas with some heart. Nikki's brother, Kevin, was one of them. Nate knew he had to have been in on the ass-whipping part. He probably had the whole thing once Nikki had told him what had happened in school. Nate started to beat himself up a bit because he should have seen that coming.

Nate knew the situation had gotten worse. Kevin had ties to Chico. An ass whipping was one thing but shedding blood would take things to another level. There was a possibility that before they could do anything, everything would have to be approved by Chico. Nate needed to find out just how much Chico had moved up in the game. If his assumptions were right, Chico would now be out of the weed business. So that meant his business with Kevin had concluded and it wouldn't be as much a problem.

They pulled up on the corner of Alcoa Drive in Shadow High. O'Neal lived around the corner in Indian Head Manor but this was where everyone hung. As usual, the block was packed and everyone was outside getting high and talking shit.

Cheese didn't hesitate with the comments the minute he saw O'Neal's eye. Chico and O'Neal grew up together around the same neighborhood. "Who done gone and whipped your ass?"

"Them bitch-ass Forest Heights niggas jumped me," O'Neal replied.

Amusing, all the fellas started laughing. They knew O'Neal and knew it was no way he'd allow himself to get jumped by anyone let alone niggas from around Forest Heights.

"No really, what happened?" Cheese asked again. He turned and looked at me. "Nate, what happened to this fool? One of the bitches he deal with smack the shit out of his ass!"

"Naw, it's like he said. Niggas around Forest Heights caught the boy slipping over a bitch."

"Okay, what I am not understanding is where the fuck you were when all this shit was going down?" Cheese said to Nate.

"Cheese, I'm not sure if you are mixing me up with the bitches you surround yourself with. But you can pipe all that shit down. You aren't going to talk to me like you've lost you fucking mind or we can handle that shit now."

"Man, y'all niggas need to squash all that. Cheese, Nate didn't even know I was going to Slim house. I was by myself. This bitch is the one who set my ass up."

"Who jumped you?"

"How the hell would I know? They weren't wearing damn name tags or nothing and I damn sure didn't ask them their names either after they were done. Shit, what the fuck kind of question was that? "

"Nigga, I thought maybe you recognized them or something, shit," Cheese replied, getting defensive.

Nate jumped in. "Everything around there starts with Kevin, Black Will, and Big Lou. Everybody knows that. My guess is we start with Kevin since he is Nikki's older brother."

"Who the fuck is Nikki?" Cheese asked.

O'Neal jumped in quickly before Nate answered. "What! How do you know that is her brother?"

"Damn, you really don't pay attention to shit, do you? You mean nothing seemed familiar to you about her house?"

"Yeah, it did seem a little bit familiar but I didn't think nothing of it. Why, what's up?"

"Because ass, we've made a run there before for Chico. Shortie is the one who answered the door. I know they don't own the house together so what else could he be to her but her brother?"

"Fuck!" O'Neal yelled.

O'Neal realized getting at them fools wasn't as easy as going around there with guns blazing. Cheese had the slightest idea what either O'Neal or Nate was talking about and didn't care. Revenge was the only thing on his mind.

"So are we going to handle these niggas or what?" Cheese asked.

O'Neal was speechless. He turned to Nate as if he had the magical answer.

"Yeah, we are going to handle them niggas, best believe that. But our folks does business with Kevin so we gotta take care of that first. Let's hold off on everything until after we meet with Chico. When we talk to him, we'll just run everything by him then."

"Yeah, that sounds like the smart thing to do right there," O'Neal replied. He continued, "You think he is going to go for it?"

"Shit, I hope so because if not, then we are going to have bigger problems on our hands."

CHAPTER 5

T hinking about all that had happened was really starting to stress Nate out. He knew business was everything and money meant more. There was no way he could allow Kevin or his sister to come between either one. He also couldn't allow his personal feelings to affect his judgment, or Chico's or O'Neal's ego either. Everything would be so much easier if Chico was indeed not supplying Kevin any longer. Then, Chico shouldn't have any problem with Kevin or his crew being dealt with.

Once Nate's paper went off at 7:30 p.m. like clockwork, the waiting would soon be over. Whenever they did a pick-up or drop for Chico, he'd always hit them at the same time to let them know it was okay to meet up to get their cash. O'Neal and Nate headed to Glassmanor for the meet.

O'Neal didn't have much to say since he found out that it might actually be a problem getting back at Kevin. Though Nate hated to let it go, he knew it might be a possibility that they'd have to. How could they buck against the man putting money in their pockets? O'Neal was a different story. There was no way he'd let that go.

"Let me ask you something, homie. What's up with Chico tells us we have to give the boy a pass and let it ride. Are you going to be able to deal with that?" Nate asked, trying to see where O'Neal's head was.

"Fuck that! I'll be damned if I'm letting shit ride! How the fuck could you even ask me some shit like that? I'm not no bitch and I know you aren't. We let that shit ride, how the fuck does that make us look? Like some muthafuckin' bitches and you know it. These streets talk and you know that."

Nate realized O'Neal's point. If they didn't hit back, word would get around quick and then it would become open season on them fast. If Chico did decide to give them his old real estate, everyone would test them for sure on everything from price to robbing them. Nate wanted to please everyone and make the best out of the situation, but he wasn't going to do it at his own expense. The name of the game is making your own name and having it ring out. He wasn't going to have his ringing out he was a bitch.

"You right, son, but we need to do this like some diplomats and not off that run-at-the-mouth gangsta shit. Regardless what Chico say, don't open your mouth unless he ask you a direct question. Other than that, let me talk to this muthafucka and smooth things over to where he gotta give us the nod.

"First things first, we need to put the bug in his ear that we trying to take over his old real estate. I'm tried of brining in this chump change and I know you are too. If we are going to make some real money, now is the perfect time with him moving to the city. I'm not trying to be a fucking runner forever. Fuck that, we've paid our dues. It's time we start moving up, too, in this here game. Ya dig?"

"You don't have to tell me twice, you know I'm game. You handle the business side and I'll back your play either way. You know that! I'm telling you though, you never short no corners, do you. I mean kid, your mind is always fucking twirlin'. You always thinking about something."

"Come on, homie, I wouldn't have it any other way," Nate said with a grin on his face.

♣♦♥♠

They pulled up in front of Glassmanor Elementary School and parked on the opposite side of the lot from where Chico had parked. Nate was always cautious like that. Though he knew the feds probably wouldn't be following Chico, he didn't want to take a chance in case they actually were. That wasn't in him. He was the type to always be aware of his surroundings and to concentrate on anything that might seem out of place.

They walked around the side of the building and headed for the playground. Nate kept his eyes glued to everything around them to make sure nothing stood out. If so, they'd walk right past Chico as if they didn't know him and pick up their bread another day. Orlando, or as they called him "Big O," was standing next to Chico at the monkey bars.

Big O was Chico's right-hand man like O'Neal was Nate's. He was the muscle and a nigga you didn't want to fuck with. He had a very short fuse and an itchy trigger finger. He was the type of cat who would wear a *shoot first and ask questions later* T-shirt to advertise to the world not to fuck with him.

"What's up, Big O...Chico?" O'Neal said as they got close enough.

"Nothing, little homie. I hear you handled yourself well with those Southeast niggas. I must admit, I thought y'all would bitch up or fuck up the paper, but Chico said y'all little niggas were on y'all game. It's good to know y'all niggas are on the same page as us because we are about to make major moves and we don't forget who was there from jump."

"Come on, Big O, you should know by now we are about that paper. We had no choice but to make sure that deal went through like silk. Major moves, huh? So is it safe to assume that is going to be a permanent route for us?"

Paranoid, Chico looked around to make sure no one was listening.

"Yeah, we've moved on to better business. Of course, they'll be other stops in the city also so don't get stuck on just that one. We've moved on to new clientele and new customers."

"So who is sliding into your old spot and taking over that territory then?" Nate asked.

"What's up with all these questions?" Big O asked defensively.

"Shit, we all like advancement. It's as simple as that."

Chico started laughing.

"Lil' nigga, you must be kidding me. You aren't ready for a step like that."

"Chico, with all due respect, please do not insult me like that. I might be young but you know I handle shit better than most niggas twice my age who are in the game now. The bottom line is my ass is the one's who would be on the line if the paper doesn't add up. I'm the one who would need to make it do what it do. All I'm asking you to do is set up the meet with the man for the opportunity. After that, I'll handle the rest."

Frustrated, Chico started to rub his eyes. Nate had a reply for everything. It was obvious he wasn't trying to let Nate or O'Neal go. Thankfully for them, Big O became their saving grace.

"Chico, I really don't see the problem with setting up a meet for them. Shit, someone had to walk us in the door when we first started. Let Carlos decide if he wants them pushing that bud. We not even under that nigga no more, it's not on us," Big O said.

"Nigga, if they fuck them packages up we are the ones who referred them. It's always going to come back on us. We are branded with them, period, the minute we walk them all the way in the door."

In disgust, Nate started to laugh and cracked a fake smile.

"Am I missing something? What is so funny?" Chico asked Nate.

"Honestly, Chico, not a damn thing is funny. Personally, I think it's fucked up you think so little of us. O'Neal and I have been with you well over a year and never have we fucked up a run. Shit, today you were willing to allow me to take a bag from some niggas you don't even know for fourteen large and not even have me count the shit. I'm not calling you out or anything, only saying you out of all people should have the confidence in us to know that we can handle this shit. But it's cool though, champ, don't set up the meet. But make sure you find yourself two new runners also because we out. I'll be damned if I work for a nigga who think that little of me."

"Nigga, who the fuck do you think you are talking to? If I tell your ass to run these bags in them streets, that is exactly what you are going to do. You don't run shit here, I do."

"Yeah okay, maybe you need to ask around, Chico. I don't scare easy. So either you putting a bullet in me now or I'm sitting in my living watching TV tomorrow. Regardless I'm not running shit for your ass no more and you're still left fucked all over some bullshit. You lack that much confidence and think they'll pass the kid over, then it shouldn't be a problem. You let them tell me no and you've done your job. I can't do nothing but respect it then, but you let them tell me. Don't you be the one holding us back though."

"Fuck it, you want a meet, you've got it. Friday, I'll take you to talk to Carlos. I already know who he is going to slide into that spot anyway. That was the reason why I wasn't trying to set it up because it's pointless. But you think you can change the man's man and this pressed that you going to turn on me like this, you've got it.

"Y'all little niggas giving me a fucking headache. Here, take this bread so we get up out of here. I damn sure didn't plan on spending my night rappin' it up with y'all. It's two g's in there, a g apiece for ya."

"That's what's up, Chico, and good looking on the meet," Nate replied.

Chico turned to walk away. Big O was about to follow behind him.

"Big O, I need one last favor. I need to get another burner but I need to know how much it's going to cost me. I want a nine-milly."

"I'll have it for you tomorrow. It's on my little homie. I told you, I'm jive proud of y'all niggas and y'all initiative. Y'all did good."

"Thanks, Big O. I appreciate that," Nate replied before Big O walked off behind Chico.

♣♦♥♠

Nate and O'Neal waited until Chico and Big O were long gone before they started discussing anything. It didn't take much to know what O'Neal's mind was on.

"Nigga, you never brought up them Forest Heights niggas."

"I know, O, but that was for a reason. Now wasn't the right

time. Carlos is the key. Everything centers around the meeting. The shit didn't hit me until I started listening to Chico. Think about it, Chico always made his sales off niggas close to him which means Kevin ain't just a buying customer to him. The minute he found out what we want to do to this nigga, then he would have protested and there went everything.

"We get the territory and then we eliminate Chico. He has no control over how we run our shop. Carlos do and Carlos don't know this nigga Kevin from Adam. We approach him with the problem and he'll approve it because he knows the value of your name in these streets."

"That sounds good but what if we don't get the new territory? Then we back to running for Chico and them niggas get to skate? I'm not feeling that, son."

"I put this on everything I love, them cats not skating for shit. Kevin knows the hand he crossed when he went at you. He allowed something personal to affect business. That was his mistake. I'm no one's bitch and I know you aren't either. Them niggas will definitely get all that they have coming to them. I'm just trying to cover all angles before we have to resort to that last resort. No more, no less. Trust me on this one. Respect is everything and we'll both be in boxes quick if we don't respect the process."

Nate could tell that O'Neal's head was spinning. His was, too, but thinking and planning is what would take them to that place were they wanted to be. Going about things half ass would have them six feet under.

CHAPTER 6

Nate struggled the rest of that week trying to keep all the neighborhood fellas from attempting to pay back anyone in school who lived around Forest Heights. The minute Cheese found out what had happened to O'Neal and the others were full steam ahead and ready to start the beef. Nate didn't particularly care 'bout that. His concern was getting back to Kevin, Black Will, or Big Lou. He didn't want to tip his hand under no circumstance as to what was in the works. Even though he doubted any of them would have lost any sleep thinking either O'Neal or Nate were planning to come after them.

If anyone, they would have thought Big O was the one paying them a visit on behalf of Nate and O'Neal. If that happened, Chico would have been the next call Kevin made trying to smooth things over to prevent anything from happening. Then Nate's plan would go down the drain. Chico would feel as if he was led on and there went any possible meeting with Carlos and the paper was fucked.

O'Neal trusted Nate's judgment so he was on board with whatever Nate decided. He knew Nate was a man of his word and once he agreed, regardless the situation, they would be paying them cats a visit, and soon—Nate meant business. That was all the confirmation he needed. Until the word came down, he'd bide his time.

Luckily everything stayed pretty much low-key. There were

a couple of fights that almost happened at school but nothing major and no names being thrown out there to alarm anyone. What was a given was bringing Cheese into the fold on a permanent basis if things went the way they planned. At times he allowed his ego to get the best of him, but he knew Nate and O'Neal were connected. If they asked him to work for them, he'd be game regardless that he'd be taking orders from niggas younger than him. Lint in your pockets will do that to the best of men. Hard times always bring about desperate measures. If it seemed like a task, it was, but that was much farther down the line. First things were first and that was getting the real estate from Carlos.

Nate didn't bother to go to school Friday morning. Chico said he'd set things up in the morning so he didn't want to be in class when Chico paged him and possibly miss out. Instead, both he and O'Neal chilled at O'Neal's house playing video games to pass the time and relax. They were nervous wrecks. Neither of them knew exactly what to expect or how the meeting would go. Once Nate's pager went off, there was no controlling either of their nerves anymore.

The ride to the meeting spot was entirely silent. Nate tried to forecast how things would go down but kept drawing a blank. He had absolutely no clue and that scared him. Luckily, he was always quick on his feet with his responses. He thought them through instead of just replying. He'd have to rely on that instinct.

When they pulled up into the parking lot, they still did

things like normal. They parked on the other side of the lot from Chico even though the school was open. Nate made sure O'Neal parked in one of the visitor spots so they didn't come back to a towed car.

"Yo, leave the pistol in the car under the seat. Don't bring it with you," Nate said to O'Neal.

He didn't oppose. As he took it from his waist, Nate thought it probably would be better if O'Neal did have it.

"Better yet, bring it."

"What? They are going to pat me down when we get there. I'm not trying to have them thinking I'm on some setup shit," O'Neal replied.

"I know, just bring it with you. I got this. I'm going to use the pistol to our advantage."

Nate could tell O'Neal was worried about his plan. He was the one who would have the pistol so if Nate's plan backfired it was O'Neal's ass on the line, not Nate's. To put O'Neal's mind at ease, he lifted up his shirt to show him that he wasn't the only one carrying. Nate had on him the nine-millimeter that Big O had gotten for him as well. Though O'Neal was skeptical, he listened to Nate and kept his pistol.

Once they got into Chico's car, he immediately drove off. The tension in the car could be cut with a knife. Nate wondered what was on Chico's mind. His guess was the fact that Chico knew they were about to come up and there was no way he could stop it. That was fine by Nate. The possibility of bringing in close to ten grand a month surely sounded better than a thousand apiece per delivery, while Chico pocketed close to eight thousand.

They pulled into Anacostia Park. There was an all-black Chevy

Tahoe parked on the main strip. Chico drove past it and headed straight for the recreation center. Nate never would have thought this would be the meeting place of all places that crossed his mind. It became obvious to him, that he'd been watching too many old movies. All he pictured was some type of old abandoned warehouse or something.

Chico pulled up to the front door.

"This is as far as I go. Go up and ring the doorbell. Y'all on y'all own getting back but the subway isn't that far, so you'll be straight. Be easy!" Chico said.

They both got out of the car and headed straight for the door. An old lady in her mid-to-late forties answered the door. Nate was hoping she wouldn't ask them whom they were there to see. Since they were so young, he wasn't sure what the right answer would be. He knew who they were there to meet but yet wasn't sure if he needed to be using anyone's name.

Once they were inside she turned and started walking toward the offices in the back. She didn't even bother to ask any questions. It was automatically assumed exactly they were there to see Carlos. She led them into an empty office and they took a seat. Soon afterward, two Hispanic brothers who could both pass for light-skinned cats entered the room

One of them walked toward Nate.

"Stand up," he demanded.

Nate didn't decline. He proceeded to pat him down. O'Neal's eyes got big. He knew Nate was strapped and wasn't sure how everything would play out. As he continued to pat Nate down, he came across his pistol that was on his waist. He removed it and the loaded clip that was in it. He checked to make sure one wasn't in the chamber and then did the same to O'Neal. He took both their clips and then exited the room.

The other guy had sat down behind a desk.

"Hello, gentlemen. I'm Carlos. It's to my understanding that the two of you would like to work for me."

Nate quickly composed himself and got into form. "Actually, we'd like to buy from you, not work for you."

Nate's response caught Carlos off guard.

"What is the difference?"

Nate pulled out the four thousand dollars from his pocket and put it on the table. "We'd like to purchase eight pounds for five hundred dollars each. I requested the meeting to get your blessing to take over the real estate that was previously worked by Chico."

"Why would I do such a thing? There is no benefit in it for me."

"It might not be now, however, we do not intend in only supplying the real estate you extend to us. Within four months, we will branch out to other territories that are not under your control which increase our sales and your revenue since you'll be supplying us."

"A big thinker, I see. You both seem rather young to want to start your own shop. Your proposal sounds very reasonable but what is so special about Oxon Hill? It's not a cash cow now nor has it really ever been," Carlos replied.

"What can I say, it's home to us. Plus it hasn't been under the right management. We feel as though our worst month, we'll be better than any of the top months within the last year."

"Is that right? Well, my young friend, you do understand that with working at home come people wanting handouts and possible problems. To me, it makes more sense to keep my real estate and just have you work it with my people in place to make sure everything runs smoothly."

"This is true, however, by doing that you'd lose out on tapping the markets within the area we plan on hitting such as Suitland, Waldorf, Forestville, District Heights, Marlow Heights, and a lot of other areas."

Carlos started to smile. "We already have product in that area."

"I don't doubt that but I'm talking about centralizing everything. It makes for less people you have to pay from your revenue. You'd have it much easier. All you'd be doing is selling the product to us at wholesale while we take on the responsibility of making money, paying the runners, corner boys, muscle, and people in the stash house."

The light bulb flashed in Carlos's head and it was obvious. If he were a poker player, he'd be broke. There was no way he could bluff Nate any longer. At that very moment, Nate knew he was game for the plan and they were in.

"We have a deal but at eight hundred dollars a pound. You can sell a quarter for four hundred twenty five dollars on the street. I'm not stupid enough to give a pound away for only five hundred dollars," Carlos replied.

Nate wasn't satisfied and didn't feel as if he should settle for less than what he was offering. However, he knew it would probably be in his best interest to negotiate.

"With all due respect, that is a big jump from us purchasing eight pounds down to five. How about six pounds for the price of five?"

"Please don't mistake my kindness as weakness. I'm giving you something more important than product, so you say. I'm giving you territory. I think that is enough."

"For the price you are selling to us and the money I'll be bringing in as opposed to you, you aren't really giving us anything," Nate replied.

"How old are you?"

"I'm twenty-one by drug standards."

Carlos looked at Nate clueless to what he meant by that.

Nate decided not to keep Carlos in the dark and shed more light to his statement.

"Twenty-one is the legal age to drink, so by me saying I'm twenty-one I mean I'm of legal age to move product and make bread."

"I like you, my young friend. I'll give you the benefit of the doubt and ask you again, and please know that this will be the last time I ask. Do you really think you can pull this off?"

"Is money green? If so, then there is your answer."

"Not all money is green, little man."

"You are right about that but I'm not interested in anything other than dollar bills."

"I like the way you think. You have a deal, six pounds for four thousand dollars. Leave my secretary your number. Someone will call you to drop off the product. You are responsible for bagging it and distributing it. I'll expect to have another four thousand in two weeks. If not, I'll put my people in place to repossess my property. Consider this as rental property until I feel comfortable to sell. However, if you do as you say and I see that the orders are coming in every week, I promise it will be yours sooner than later."

That was music to Nate's ears.

"I have one other request. How I handle the territory is left up to me and my associate, no exceptions."

"This I can not agree to, my young friend. I need to be made aware of any and everything before it happens. Regardless of our agreement, it will be seen as Oxon Hill still belongs to us. Any heat on these streets ultimately costs us."

"I can respect that and I'll always keep you in the mix, but the final decision lies with us. If we see fit to handle something pertaining to our business, you'll be the first call. If it brings heat to the family, we'll pay the consequence or whatever tax deemed necessary."

"Your pockets aren't that deep yet, my young friend. You'll lose more men in consequences before you'll pay it out in taxes," Carlos replied.

"It will never come to that but your feelings are understood."

"Good, so please tell me what the fuck is going on? It's obvious something is on your mind with that request."

"Forest Heights needs to be taught a lesson," O'Neal replied.

Chico started to laugh. "So you can speak!"

Nate threw O'Neal a quick look of disappointment.

"You do understand this will cause problems internally. Chico has ties with a few people from Forest Heights. He'll definitely have a serious problem with you barking up that tree," Carlos said, back on business.

"If that is the case, then Chico becomes my problem," Nate replied.

"I'm not sure if I like your tone regarding this, so I'll make things a lot clearer. Chico is a part of this family. There will never come a time when he becomes your problem."

"I do not disagree, however, he does need to understand his place within the family. If you deem it fit for us to do what we need to do, he needs to accept that. His ties to that neighborhood have been cut. There is no product for him to deal there and we'll not be dealing with who currently is in place. I've told you, I'm about making money. This is a business decision and not anything personal."

Carlos started shaking his head.

"Good point, good point. We'll handle Chico, but whatever

you do, keep it quiet. Now if you excuse me, gentlemen, I have another meeting to attend. You can retrieve your clips at the front."

They stood up, shook Carlos's hand, then headed for the exit. Once they arrived at the front desk, the secretary already had their clips ready for them and a number where they could contact Carlos.

"Make sure you rip this number up. Do what you have to do to remember it but once you do, destroy it. You fellas have a good day."

Once they were outside, it finally started to hit them. They were on the verge of starting their own family. They had achieved something Chico had never dreamed up, which was freedom. Chico ran a shop. They were on the verge of starting their own family.

"Man, you worked that shit, son," O'Neal said.

"I know. I was nervous as shit but I wasn't going to let that ruin this. I had to close that deal."

"You did more then that, nigga. I'm still trying to figure out how the fuck you found a way to get our real estate."

"I told you, I had a plan and this is only the beginning. We have to take care of business with Kevin to a tee though because you know we are being watched closely on how we handle things."

As they walked past the Tahoe they first saw when they came into the park, they noticed two guys sharing a couple of laughs and beers. That is when it hit them, they were on the job and staking out Carlos. They made sure to continue their discussion about their promotion once they were long past the truck.

"Nate, what did you mean by we are being watched?" O'Neal asked.

"The way Carlos was pressing the situation; I can't see him not having eyes on us in some way. And I don't mean just the Forest Heights situation. I mean everything. He'll have someone probably watching everything from Forest Heights to sales, product, and the cash. He'll want to make sure everything is the way it's supposed to be before he releases total control to us. That is why we have to make sure everything is airtight from this point on. We don't need to give them any excuse to try to pull this shit. We need to show them we can handle this."

"So what's the plan?"

"That I don't know. Let's get something to eat first and then rap about it later on tonight."

"Okay. What about Chico, do you think he is going to come at us?"

"I know he will, but what concerns me is *how* he will," Nate replied.

"Damn!" O'Neal let out.

Nate felt the same way. Though they hardly hung with Francis, they still looked at him like family which made Chico family. They knew the minute he found out the penalties, his folks would pay because of them and he couldn't stop it, he'd buck. Losing his best runners was one thing, but to go from losing your runners to being behind them in power was a totally different monster to tackle.

"Shit!" Nate yelled.

"This shit is going to get ugly, isn't it?"

Nate didn't want to answer because deep down inside, he knew it was.

CHAPTER 7

The minute they made their way back to their side of town, they started to plan the hit. Nate knew Chico would try to find a way to warn Kevin what was being planned once he was advised of what was going to happen. Chico was dumb in a lot of aspects and mostly because of his loyalty. Though he knew he'd be crossing Carlos and the family by interfering, he wasn't going to allow something to happen to a friend without warning him. It wasn't hard to find a way to warn Kevin without having his name thrown in the mix for doing so.

Once Nate and O'Neal made their way back around the neighborhood Cheese was the first person they looked for. O'Neal knew he was in school so that's where they headed to. Cheese was the only cat they trusted who could get a burner. Also it was a perfect way to test him and see how far he was willing to go. Nate knew he could trust Cheese in a fight, but now he needed to know if he could trust him with his life. Nate's ultimate plan was taking territory around the city which meant they'd be going to war. It was nice to know if he had a soldier on his side.

By the time they reached school, it was close to letting out. O'Neal knew exactly where Cheese would be so he went inside to get him. They didn't have that much time. Nate wasn't sure when Carlos would talk to Chico. Now was the only time they could strike for sure and know that Kevin hadn't been warned.

This way, they'd be able to hit all four of their intended targets precisely.

O'Neal and Cheese came running out of the building and headed straight for the car.

"Cheese, do you have your burner on you?" Nate asked.

"I don't go anywhere without it. Why, what's up?"

Nate ignored Cheese's reply. "O'Neal, head around to the park so we can map this out. We can still see the buses from there so we'll know when they leave."

Cheese became annoyed with not knowing anything.

"Man, what is this all about? I have shit planned today."

"It's about paper. Last time I checked you were trying to make some, right?" Nate replied.

"I'm always game to add bread into my pockets. You know that, homie."

"That's what's up then. Well, today is your lucky day. We are going to hit those Forest Heights niggas today."

"That's what I'm talking about, baby! It's about time. I've been tweaking to get at them niggas all week! But that still doesn't answer how hitting their heads is going to add to the bread in my pockets."

"Simple, we now control Oxon Hill and we'd like to add you into the mix," Nate replied.

O'Neal looked at Nate like he was crazy. He knew Nate didn't trust Cheese for shit so he wasn't figuring out why he was offering a part of the business. More importantly, O'Neal wasn't feeling turning what were presently halves into thirds.

"We have it set up to where anyone who wants to get high will be buying the product from us directly."

Cheese wasn't buying it. Everyone knew Chico was the name

you needed to know if you wanted to get high, and he didn't even have power like that. If you bought anything from him, it was automatically assumed you were in Mario Cardoza territory.

"Bullshit!"

O'Neal pulled into the parking lot at Southlawn Park. The buses were forming and the school administrators were starting to come outside. Time was running short. Soon, students would be dismissed to go home and head for the buses.

"Look, we don't have time like that, are you in or out? We can go over the demographics later but pretty much you'll be the middle man. If they want to buy from us, they'll contact you. You'll handle the running until we find suitable runners to handle that. Once we do, then you'll handle the runners and make sure the paper adds up with the product. That also means if anything is short it will either come out of your ass or your pockets. And when I say if anything is short, meaning once and once only. Anything over once, isn't an accident but rather a habit. If you make it a habit, please *believe* there will not be two options the next time."

It was kind of scary to listen to Nate talk. He was giving commands and running the show as if he had been for years. Cheese didn't really like that if he agreed, he'd be taking orders from Nate. He could deal with O'Neal because they'd been friends since they were four. Cheese knew he could manipulate him but that wasn't happening with Nate. They always clashed because one of them was always on a power trip, mostly Cheese. Nate wasn't big on ego but he wasn't going to allow anyone to see fear in his eyes, either.

The way Nate saw things, ass whippings were a part of life so he wasn't afraid to receive one and wouldn't mind giving one. Nate refused to allow anyone to think they could talk to him any way they wanted to. If you did, he would definitely let you know about it. Cheese wasn't used to that, but either way Nate didn't care. If he couldn't deal with it, he'd be replaced with someone who could.

"You are a funny dude, Nate," Cheese said sarcastically.

"I wasn't trying to be. It's not about jokes, games, or pleasure. This is business! Now if you are in, cool. If not, then get the fuck out of the car."

Cheese swallowed his pride and said, "We good. What's the plan?"

"Okay, we all know those cats around Forest Heights are a bunch of bitches. That is no secret. The minute we handle Will, Kevin, and Lou, the rest of them will fold."

"True," O'Neal agreed.

"Now the only problem is Nikki. That is her family. Though she might be scared, she isn't going to betray her blood. She'll give up any information possible to the feds, then we stuck out here trying to beat a murder rap before we even get things started. That is not something I'm trying to deal with and won't."

The tension in the car grew. O'Neal was just trying to fuck her the other day and today her life was being discussed.

"Fuck them other niggas but I'm not too sure about icing this bitch too. That seem like some sucka shit to me in a way. Is it totally necessary to hit her head? I mean, it's one thing to be in the wrong place at the wrong time, but you talking about pinpointing the bitch," Cheese replied.

"Yeah, I'm with Cheese on that one. I'm saying, why not handle these niggas and then put someone on beating her ass or something to make sure she shut the fuck up. Killing the bitch, I'm sorry, that shit just don't feel right to me."

"Is that right? Do you think doing life in jail is better? How does that shit feel? If it's cool with you, then we can leave her breathing because trust me when I tell you, the minute she finds out something happened to her brother, that bitch is going to go straight to the feds and tell it all."

Neither O'Neal nor Cheese protested. No matter how much they were against killing her, their own freedom meant much more to them versus her life.

"Good, now Kevin always makes sure his little sister gets home from school every day. I put the buzz in Butter's ear a couple days ago and he gave me the scoop about the nigga," Nate replied.

"Shit, you told Butter! What the fuck for? You know that nigga can't keep his mouth shut," O'Neal said.

"Exactly and that's exactly what I want him to do is run his mouth. We going to run this shit so smooth and like clockwork, nothing else will even matter. I want everyone knowing who pulled this shit off. I want these streets buzzing about this shit here for a while. That is the buzz we need out here so niggas know exactly how serious we are. You fuck with us and your ass will be dealt with accordingly.

"We all know Butter isn't the type to go to the feds but he'll surely have these streets buzzing to all that happens. Then with Kevin and his folks gone, we slide who we want in Forest Heights to move our shit. We handpick who we want and have them move the product."

"I don't know about this, Nate. I mean it all sounds good but there is so much room for shit to go wrong. I don't trust Butter. Shit, I don't trust anyone but you," O'Neal replied.

Cheese didn't know how to take hearing that O'Neal didn't fully trust him.

"So you saying you don't trust me?"

O'Neal turned his attention to Cheese.

"I trust you but only to a certain extent. Look, this is not about me and you. This is about a nigga none of us trusts and the fact that he just about knows all that is going to go down."

"Well, it's too late to stop that now. There is nothing we can do about it. He knows and if we don't go through with this, then everyone will know we bitched up! So can we get on with the plan and handle this shit the way we suppose to."

"Fuck it, I guess we don't have a choice now, do we? What's the plan?" O'Neal replied.

That was the trick that was needed to move on to stage two. Time was running short. Students started to head out of the building and to their buses.

"Okay, Kevin always makes sure his sister gets in the house. As fine as her ass is, he makes sure dicks aren't going in and out of her. That is our window right there. We'll catch both of them before they get in the house. Big Lou will be at the playground. He doesn't leave from there, so we'll get him there. As for Will, we'll catch his black ass off the bus. We have to get to him before he gets either home or to the playground. He'll head to one place or the other. Now to pull this shit off, we need to handle it all at the same time, then break camp."

"What?" Cheese replied.

"You heard me. I'll take care of Kevin and Nikki since y'all both have problems with that. Cheese, you catch Will walking home from the bus, and O, you take care of Lou's ass at the playground. I mean the shots need to ring out back to back. Don't assume shit. Make sure they are down for the count and then head back to the car. The highway is up the street so we'll head across the bridge to Virginia and dump the car. Is everything clear? Are we all good?"

Cheese pulled his pistol out of his backpack and cocked it. "Let's do this."

Everything was set in motion and all knew what they had to do. The buses were almost full. They headed on their way so everyone could be in place by the time the bus pulled up. They parked the car at McDonald's on Livingston Road, then hiked up the hill into Forest Heights. Forest Heights had its own police station within the neighborhood so the minute the gunshots rang, they'd be Johnny on the scene. Kevin's house wasn't too far from Interstate 210. Nate could handle business and then head straight for the highway. He figured once the police heard gunshots, they'd go the scene to see exactly what happened first before they canvassed the area looking for suspects. That would be just enough time to get to the I-210 and walk back down to McDonald's with no problem.

Will lived near Flintstone Elementary School, and if he went home first, Nate told Cheese to make sure to let two loose in his head, then head for Oxon Hill Shopping Plaza. They'd pick him up at the Popeyes. Nate prayed Will would head home. It would make things easier. If he didn't, then there lay another problem. Cheese would be left out in the open and more than likely any neighbor who wanted to play inch-high private eye would get a good look at him. The chances of him getting out of the neighborhood without the police catching up with him would be slim.

O'Neal's escape route was probably the safest but also the riskiest of the bunch. The police would never expect anyone to come through the woods and to the station after they committed a crime. Nate hoped they'd continue to believe that. He told O'Neal to handle Big Lou and then head straight through the woods to the police station. He even told him to go inside the police station and let the clerk know that he had heard gunshots. Everything would be in such a panic they probably would not really pay him any attention, only ask brief questions hoping it would help them catch their perpetrator. Afterward he could walk out and head for the McDonald's. By then, Nate should have been there.

Nate waited outside Kevin's house for him to head down the street toward the bus stop. Once he was halfway, Nate ran across the street to Kevin's next-door neighbor's front yard. There was a broken-down car sitting on blocks in the driveway. He positioned himself behind it so he would have a good view of anyone coming up to their house while still keeping his position hidden.

Everything was going according to plan. Nate saw Nikki and her brother heading back to their house. They were laughing and having a good time. His nerves started to kick in knowing everything was about to go down. Though he'd seen people shot before, Nate had never killed anyone himself. A part of him couldn't believe he was actually about to go through with it. However, no matter what, he knew it was something that had to be done, a necessary evil. There was no way he was going to allow anything to come between him and his money. The only problem was, once the job was done, there was no more turning back. He was now in the lifestyle for good.

As Nikki got closer to the house, it became obvious that Kevin wasn't going to accompany her. His job was done and he more than likely was about to head to the playground to catch up with Big Lou and Will. Nate hoped Cheese was having better luck than him. Nate made his way from around the car with his pistol visible. Before anyone could realize what was about to happen, he let loose two shots at Kevin.

One pierced his shoulder while the other hit him in the chest. He went down to the ground once he was hit. Nikki didn't even turn to see who had fired the shots or why. She dropped all of her stuff and headed for her brother. Nate quickly walked over toward them. Everything was moving in slow motion. At that moment, he knew it was too late to turn back now. He'd taken the leap of faith that would surely lead him down the wrong path.

"Somebody help me! MY BROTHER HAS BEEN SHOT! PLEASE, SOMEBODY HELP ME!" Nikki cried out.

Before anyone could get to their window and see what was going on, two more shots were released from Nate's gun to the back of her head.

"NO! Nikki! Nikki!" Kevin cried out.

Nate stood over top of Kevin so he could see who was sending him to meet his maker so he'd know exactly why. The pain that filled his eyes after watching his sister's death sent shock waves through Nate's soul. With a squeeze of his index finger, he ended Kevin's suffering and sent him to see his sister.

Nate froze for a second, and then cut through Kevin's yard to jump the gate into the next yard that put him on the next street. As he came into view of the street, he saw police cars. He jumped back behind the van that was in the driveway as both cars sped past him. The minute they weren't in sight, he continued to head for the highway.

Gunshots sporadically filled the air. It sounded like total mayhem had hit Forest Heights and it was coming from all over. Once Nate reached the highway, he knew he was home free. There wouldn't be any police coming down the highway looking for anyone associated with the shooting. The only thing that he had to worry about was witnesses. Hopefully, no one was home or caught a glimpse of him or his getaway route.

However, witnesses usually found a way to make themselves scarce and unavailable in situations like these, especially for a double homicide. His heart was racing. It was funny how quickly things could change. When Nate woke up that morning, he was a runner for a small-time dealer but now had his own territory and was a cold-blooded murderer.

Once Nate made it to the car, he saw both Cheese and O'Neal waiting for him. He quickly jumped into the car. O'Neal turned on the ignition and they headed for the Woodrow Wilson Bridge to go into Virginia.

"Shit is fucked up, Nate! Shit is really fucked up," O'Neal said.

"What do you mean, 'shit is fucked up'? Both of those niggas are dead, aren't they?"

"Yeah, them niggas will be buried next week but they aren't the only ones."

"The fuck do you mean they aren't the 'only ones'? What is going on?" Nate asked.

"Man, I went to the playground like you said, and Big Lou was there waiting. I waited until I heard shots ring out and then I made my move, but then this nigga Will comes from nowhere. I wasn't sure if he saw me, so I let loose on his ass first, then Lou made a move for his pistol but luckily I got off the first shot."

Nate turned to Cheese. "Where the fuck was you?"

"Hold on, Nate, that ain't it. Chico was there," O'Neal injected.

"What?"

"Fucked me up too. I guess he was watching the park or waiting on Kevin, I don't know, but his ass was parked in the lot. I didn't even peep him. He got a shot off at me before Cheese plucked him off."

"What?" Nate said shocked.

"We had no choice. This nigga came at me. I'm best friends with his little brother. I've slept at his house and eaten at his table and this nigga comes at me over Big Lou. What the fuck? I'm not even mad. Ask me, the nigga got what he deserved," O'Neal replied.

"You don't get it, O! It's not that simple. Chico is untouchable until we get an okay from Carlos. Fuck!"

"So what was I supposed to do? Get killed, then wait for you to get the fucking okay. Plus, it's not like Cheese knew. He saw the man letting loose on me and plucked his ass off. We can't cry over spilled milk. What's done is done. What you need to do though is fix shit with Carlos so we not next."

"Please tell me Big O was there and he is dead too?" Nate asked.

"Naw, he wasn't out there."

"So let me get this straight. Not only did we kill Chico without an okay, but Big O is alive to avenge his man's death? Does that about sum it up? Fuck the okay, who the fuck is going to stop Big O from coming after us. I'm not trying to go toe to toe with that nigga!"

"I'm sorry, Nate. It's my fault. I should have gotten to Will before he made it to the park but this nigga was basically running and shit like he knew I was there waiting for him," Cheese said.

Everything made sense. Chico knew they were going to hit them and was there to warn them. Nate didn't expect him to get there that quickly though. That's why Kevin wasn't trying to follow his sister into the house and Will was breaking his neck to get to the playground. They were trying to catch up with Chico to find out what was what.

"You right, O, we just have to play with the hand we were dealt. Are you sure everyone is dead? I'm not trying to end up in no six-by-nine because one of y'all niggas can't shoot for shit!"

"There is no doubt in my mind, them niggas gone. Cheese walked over to where Will was laying and put one in his head and I did the same with Lou. Chico was hit so many times, there was no need to."

"Okay, we need to burn this car and get a new one. No one gets rid of their heat until I smooth things over with Big O and Carlos."

"Man, there ain't no smoothing shit over with Big O. You know that nigga is going to come at us with everything he can."

"Yeah, I know he'll want to, but as the Don would do, I'm going to make him an offer he can't refuse," Nate said, imitating Marlon Brando's character in *The Godfather*.

They started laughing.

"Seriously, I'll have to find a way to fix this. But in case I can't, I want everyone to be able to protect themselves if he does come knocking."

"Nate, I know I give you a lot of shit but do you think that is smart? I mean we all know about Big O and what he is capable of doing. We know his resume and the work he's put in. You've already made it clear you aren't trying to go up against that nigga and I know I'm not," Cheese said.

"Cheese, you have to trust me on this one. I'm not going to guarantee anything though. We need to move quickly on this. Shit is about to get real serious but we might be able to use this as a plus. We need to get a new car and then get to a phone fast."

Nate had the perfect idea.

CHAPTER 8

By the time Nate got Carlos on the phone, he already had heard the news of what had happened. He wanted to meet immediately. Nate should have known this would happen but a part of him was surprised at how fast. He'd only dealt with Carlos once so he didn't have a good read on him yet. An immediate meeting might not have been as bad a thing as he initially thought. Either way, they would find out soon enough.

Nate didn't want Cheese involved yet so he had O'Neal drop him off around the way. Things were extremely hot right now so he told Cheese to stay off the block and keep a low profile. The streets would surely be talking and his name would come up. It wouldn't be long before Big O knew everything that went down.

Nate thought about swinging past Francis's house to try to explain the situation but knew what the repercussions of that conversation would be. Instead, it was best if they cut their ties with Francis. Once Chico died, so did their relationship with Francis, regardless who was at fault.

They agreed to meet Carlos by the Navy Yard off Half Street in Southwest D.C. Once they arrived they were surprised to find that he wasn't alone. The situation couldn't be good. There were too many cars parked out front and a lot of bodies waiting on them. This was turning out to be more serious than either of them had ever anticipated.

Besides Carlos, there were three other men who stood out. Two of them were of Hispanic descent and the other was a brother. All of them were wearing tailor-made Italian suits. None of them looked like the ordinary run-of-the-mill cat from the street.

"Gentlemen, today you came to me with a business proposition that I was glad to accept. And at that meeting I made it very clear that Chico was not to be touched, did I not?" Carlos asked.

They both nodded their heads in agreement.

"Then please explain to me how Chico is dead."

"With all due respect, Carlos, it was also promised to us that Chico would be in agreement with what would take place today. Though he might have a problem with it, he'd accept that the decision was bigger than him and deal with it. This, however, wasn't the case. Instead of taking the instructions he was given, he decided to do his own thing and that alone is what led to his death; not our actions," Nate replied.

"How dare you show such disrespect? Do you know who you are talking to?" one of the unknown gentlemen said.

Nate knew no matter how he replied, it would be used against him. So instead of offering any explanation, he remained quiet.

The gentleman turned to another one of the unknown men.

"Mario, I lost a very good earner and worker to these two young punks. Regardless of his actions, his death was not their call. If he killed them all, then we would have seen fit how to deal with them. *We* would have set the punishment. Chico brought them into *our* family. He came to me and asked me for my blessing to meet with Carlos and this is how they repay him. For this to go unpunished would be a great injustice."

The seriousness of the situation was more evident than ever. Their lives were on the line and over something none of them even could have prevented.

"Mr. Cardoza, with all due respect, this was something that could not have been avoided," Nate said. "Before we made any moves we came to Carlos to get his blessing. He made it very clear that Chico was a problem the family would handle. That problem was not handled. I'm not trying to be disrespectful or say it in a disrespectful manor but Chico was there to warn them about what was going to take place. Unfortunately he was too late. Our plan was already put in motion and honestly that was the exact reason why we put it in place so soon. We feared he would defy the family and still try to warn them. We didn't want to put our lives at risk or jeopardize our business.

"Even with his defiance, once he realized he was too late, he could have easily got in his car and left. But instead, he tried to take out one of my guys. He left us with no choice. We didn't want this to happen. It's no secret Chico brought us into this family. We looked at Chico as family but this was business and if any of you here were put in the same position we were, I don't think any of you would have handled things any differently than we did."

Mario looked to Carlos for his opinion.

"Mario, I'm going to have to agree with Nate on this. It was explained to young Chico what was going to take place and this was something he needed to deal with. It was nothing personal but rather business. He chose his own way and that is what led to his death. This family has been successful for one reason and one reason only, because of our discipline. I liked Chico. I liked Chico a lot. If I didn't I never would have suggested we move him into Santana's operation, but he lacked discipline. He lacked self-control. He could never separate business from personal," Carlos said.

"That's easy for you to say, you didn't lose an earner. You still stand to make a good profit in Chico's death," Santana shot at him.

"Santana, I stood to gain a good profit if he was alive as well," Carlos replied.

"So how do we resolve this?" Mario asked.

"Mr. Cardoza, if I may?" Nate jumped in.

With his hand he gave Nate the floor.

"It's to my understanding the problem for Santana is the loss of an earner. What if his earner was replaced? It's my fault Chico isn't here. Though we might have a good reason for doing what we did and it was just, the fact of the matter is that he is no longer here due to us. I propose you allow us to step in his place. I'll run his territory until I stack enough paper to buy from Santana wholesale. We'll handle Prince George's County and all areas Chico was responsible. My only request would be to keep Big O, Chico's right-hand man, on to handle muscle for that area."

"You've got to be kidding me," Santana said with displeasure.

"What makes you think you can handle such a task? Marijuana is one thing but cocaine is a whole new ball game," Mario asked.

"I understand that but the game is the game whether it's cocaine, heroin, marijuana, or crack. There really isn't any difference. Either you know how to move the product or you don't."

"So you think you can handle it?"

"Is money green?"

Nate's comment awoke the last anonymous man. He wore a visible smile as if he was amused by Nate's comments. He waved for Mario to come toward him and he did. As they talked for a brief minute Nate started to feel very optimistic about their chances. O'Neal continued to remain silent praying Nate found a way to save their lives.

Nate knew that if they controlled the drug trade in Southeast, Big O would become his problem. He'd be an ally instead of an enemy. If he tried to buck, then it would be their call whether he lived or died and with the backing of the family they would have the power to complete such a task. But Big O would never betray the family. His loyalty ran deep, plus he knew he wouldn't last twenty minutes in the street if he did. Mario and the anonymous gentleman walked back toward them.

"You have a deal. If you need anything from now on, you deal with me directly. It doesn't make sense to deal with Carlos and Santana both. I'll take care of your accommodations. Chico's price was six per key, however, yours will be four for the first year to accommodate Santana for the loss of business. Santana, we've decided to move you into new territory and on to another new operation. We want you to handle Philadelphia."

"Philadelphia! Why? I'm not trying to leave my city," Santana protested.

"My friend, it's not an option. Carlos, since Money Green will take care of Prince George's County directly through me, we think it would be best to move you into Baltimore and Delaware. It's a substantial increase as I'm sure you'll know. You'll handle all products. Money Green, the metropolitan area is yours. You've gotten your wish, make damn sure the shoes you now wear fit or we'll have no problem burying you and your whole operation in them."

"Money Green?" Nate asked confused.

The anonymous man pointed at him and then it started to become clear, they were calling him Money Green. Nate started to smile. He liked it.

"Gracious!"

ONE MAN'S
TRIUMPH
ANOTHER'S
TRAGEDY

CHAPTER 9

LT's patience was starting to run thin. He had been waiting on Santana for damn near an hour. Something had to have been up. He didn't even know what he was doing here. All of a sudden Santana called a meeting out of the blue. Now he was late. Santana was always prompt. It wasn't like him to be late and definitely not an hour. He lived by the credo that time was money and money bought his time.

"Fuck it," LT spat as he started the ignition to his ride.

By the time LT put his car in drive, Santana was pulling up. LT turned the ignition back off and gathered himself. Santana was very cautious. He hated to speak outdoors where ears were available. LT got into the car with Santana and then he drove off.

"What's the deal, Santana? Why call off the late night?" LT asked.

"I wanted you to hear it from me, our business has concluded. I'll pass along your number to your new contact and he'll be in touch. I didn't want you to get suspicious about the change because I know I'd be very suspicious if I was approached incorrectly regarding it."

LT was dumbfounded.

"What's going on?" LT asked.

"That I am not at liberty to say."

Santana turned the car around at the next corner and headed back toward the waterfront. LT didn't know what to make of anything. Basically he was being left in the dark.

"I guess I don't have a choice but to take it now, do I? Do you have anything you can give me now? I'm running low," LT asked.

Santana ignored his question and continued to drive.

"I'm just saying, I'm not trying to run dry out here in these streets. If they aren't getting it from me, then they'll cop elsewhere. I can't have that."

"I don't know what to tell you. You'll have to wait for your contact to get in touch with you. Until then, you are on your own," Santana replied.

He wasn't leaving LT with many options. They pulled up to LT's car and he got out. Santana barely waited for him to close the door before he was off and in the wind. With his right hand, LT rubbed his eyes fearful that he might have blown his cover. If he had, he knew his life was in danger.

"SHIT!" LT yelled.

LT couldn't rest until he found out exactly what was going on. This was his life that could possibly be at stake. He rushed to his car and headed for the closest pay phone. The next call was going to Moe Betta who was Santana's muscle. LT had flipped him with a weapons charge in order to get to Santana. Moe Betta had walked him into the family. If something was being planned, LT knew Moe Betta would have the answers he needed.

"Who dis?" Moe Betta spat into the phone.

"Be at Federal Center Southwest in twenty minutes. We need to meet and we need to meet now," LT said, then hung up the phone before Moe Betta could reply.

LT was pissed and he refused to hide it.

A tap on the window of LT's car startled him. He turned toward the window and noticed it was Moe Betta. LT was so out of it he hadn't noticed him coming up the escalator from the train station. The stress of the situation had LT going out of his mind trying to figure what exactly was going on. LT reached over and unlocked the door.

"What was so important that you had to drag me out tonight?"

"Don't act like you don't know. What the fuck is going on? Tonight Santana calls a meeting only to tell me that he is passing along my info to a new contact. What the fuck is going on?"

"Things are changing around here and changing fast. There is a new playa on the scene and he is running the whole operation. The head man turned everything over to him."

"Huh? What do you mean there is a 'new playa' in town? Who?" LT asked puzzled.

"Fuck if I know. I can't tell you much about him, shit, no one really can. I don't even know what the boy's name is. What I can say is he is the one behind the hit in Forest Heights."

"What hit in Forest Heights?"

"Where the hell have you been? How can you be the feds and you haven't even heard about it yet? I see why people question the police department now. Well, this kid took out three small-time dealers, the man's sister, and one of Santana's boys. This muthafucka is no joke," Moe Betta replied.

"That doesn't make sense. How do you off one of Santana's lieutenants, then take over for the man himself?"

"Easy, I told you the call came from Mr. Cardoza personally. There was a meet on the Southside and everything was brought to light there."

"What! Mario removed Santana. Shit! So what's happening to Santana?"

"He is going to Philly and Carlos has been moved to Delaware or B-more, I'm not too sure on that one. Shit is real fucked up now. Niggas given choices either to move or get out 'cause who-ever this nigga is, he putting his own people in place."

This was what LT didn't need to hear. It had taken him near-ly two years to get close to Santana. There was no way he'd ever get close enough to Mario Cardoza now in order to make a case against him. There was no way LT wanted to start all over again with someone new. Especially if he was giving ulti-matums to either move your shop or don't have one at all.

"Shit!" LT yelled.

"After tonight, I can't see how I'll be any help to you. So does this squash our business?" Moe Betta asked.

"I take it that means you are heading to Philly?"

"Shit, I have no choice. I told you this man is bringing in his own people. When I say it's a new game, it's a new game in town. There are no points being given on a package. He is buying straight from the man and supplying the city himself. Mario has just about put himself in an untouchable position. It was bad enough he never came anywhere near a deal but now this man can't even be tied to the product. Your case is probably pretty much shot now!"

"Thanks," LT replied sarcastically

Moe Betta turned to get out the car. LT realized that every-thing had gone up into flames. Moe Betta was right. Once Mario sat back and collected a check, there was no way to tie him to the drugs. The straight money he was making now, overwhelm-ingly outweighed the dirty so he didn't have to hide it.

"Shit, shit, shit, SHIT!"

The only thing left to do was let Lieutenant Ross know the

bad news. LT got out of the car and went over to one of the many pay phones that were outside of the subway station. He picked up the phone, put in his quarter, and started to dial the number. Before anyone could answer the phone, he quickly hung up. LT knew the second he briefed Lt. Ross, that would be the end of the case. There was no way he was going to let all his hard work go up in flames. They had pretty good cases against Santana and even Carlos, but LT seriously doubted if either of them would ever turn against Mario. Without the head of the snake cut off, the body would reform and resurface with new people in place. LT wanted to figure things out first. There had to be another way.

CHAPTER 10

The loud knock at LT's front door woke him from his sleep. He still had a headache from the events the night before. He reached for his watch to see what time it was.

Who the fuck is knocking on my door at got damn six in the morning? LT thought.

He quickly got out of the bed and grabbed some shorts to slip on. The apartment the department had him staying in while he was undercover wasn't in one of the best neighborhoods. So the simple luxury of a peephole to see who was on the other side of his door wasn't afforded to him.

"Who is it?" LT asked.

There was no response.

"Who is it?" he repeated.

Again, no one answered. Against his better judgment LT opened the front door. It's funny how everyone has intuition but no one ever pays attention to it. This would be a day LT would have wished he had followed his. Awaiting him on the other side of the door was a forty-caliber Smith & Wesson pistol pointing directly at his head. Though he was staring down the barrel of the gun, LT tried to remain calm and play the situation cool.

"It's a little early for this shit, don't you think?" he said.

Silence awaited him. With his pistol the unknown man waved for LT to go inside the apartment. LT didn't protest. He turned around and walked back into the apartment. The walk to his living room gave him time to think of a way to make it to the bedroom to get his pistol. However, nothing came to mind. There was no excuse he could give to get there. The next thing LT felt was a smack to the back of his head and he was out like a light bulb.

When he woke, LT was tied up in a chair. He was still a little dizzy from being hit with the butt of the gun. He continued to squint his eyes trying to focus on anything until the cobwebs cleared.

"You up, son?" LT heard a voice ask.

His vision was still a little blurry so he couldn't really make out the two men who seemed more like kids in front of him. They were both dressed in black but neither looked as if they'd ever seen a razor. They couldn't have been no more than fourteen or fifteen years old. One of them was sitting in a metal folding chair LT kept in the closet in case he had company over.

"It's a little early for the bullshit, don't you think, fellas? Is there any way we can do this a little later on in the day once a nigga up and running?"

The two gentlemen found LT's statement amusing. They both broke into laughter.

"Can you believe this muthafucka? Here it is, we got him tied to a chair and he got the balls to ask if we mind coming back later on so he can catch a few extra Z's. Either you the dumbest muthafucka in the world or you are the craziest. I'll let you decide which one."

His man cut him off, "You forgot an option, son—or the boy is a cop and the talk is cheap."

At that very moment, LT knew exactly what the deal was. His cover had been blown but how he wasn't too sure. LT knew that his life now depended upon how quickly he could react and get out of the situation.

"Look, I had a very long night last night. How about you cut the shit and we sit down like some men and rap about whatever the fuck it is you want to get off your chest?" LT said.

"Detective Taylor, we can do this either the easy way or we can do this the hard way, the choice is yours. What I'm here for is information. The amount you provide truthfully will determine the amount of pain you'll experience. I can't make it any simpler than that."

LT was speechless. It was obvious bullshitting wasn't going to get him out of it. They knew exactly who he was and even his name. It wasn't Moe Betta because even he didn't know LT's government identity. All he knew him by was LT. These cats really did their homework.

"Damn, no smart remarks. We must have the boy's total attention now. It's crickets, crickets over there. Just in case we don't though, 8344 Tower Green Drive, Rockville, Maryland. Your wife's name is Denise Taylor, age twenty-six. She is a financial analyst for the electric company. I wonder if she can handle arrangements for me to make sure my lights stay on?" he said with a devilish smile on his face. He continued, "How about that precious little girl of yours? What is her name again, Alexis? How old is she, what four? Man, that is such a precious age but turning five is even better, don't you think? You now can control that. You can make sure she does turn five."

"Muthafucka, I put this on everything I love, if anything happens to my family, best believe you will have a better understanding of true pain than I ever will. I put that on everything I love. Your ass will fry already for killing a cop but you kill a cop's family and you'll have every cop within a two hundred-mile radius on your ass. If you're lucky, you'll only be beaten to a pulp."

He turned to his man. "Yo, I think this muthafucka has more heart than we took him for. Let's bounce and pick up Little Miss Alexis and see how much pain he really can stand. It's obvious he thinks we are a fucking joke or something and needs a reality check."

"Wait! Y'all obviously came here for something. Why don't you spit the shit out and get this over with," LT said.

LT was desperate. It wasn't as if his life didn't mean anything to him, it was that his families meant more. If this was the way his life was predetermined to end, it would end with saving the life of his own family.

"If there is one thing about me, it's the fact that I respect this game. I know that y'all boys job is to put us in that box, it's all a part of the chase. I get that, but what I don't get is the deception. Who is your snitch and how much has he shared with you on our family?"

"Nigga, I don't even know who the two of you are, let alone what family you are a part of. If you want answers out of me, then your ass is going to have to be a little more specific, shit!"

"Is that so? Okay, maybe I didn't word things clear enough, who the fuck walked you into the Cardoza family? That is the snitch right there. Before you answer, please remember your family doesn't mean shit to me. Make sure they mean more to you than this weak-ass nigga who is playing both sides of the fence."

Without hesitation LT replied, "Moe Betta."

"Yo, he is a part of Santana's camp. That's going to be a problem. We already done hit one of his captain's heads. If we go after someone else in his camp, you know it's only going to make matters worse. We need to..."

"Shut the fuck up! You talk too fucking much. As a matter of fact, go wait outside the door and make sure no one interrupts my business in here."

The guy looked embarrassed by his boy putting him down like that in front of their prey. It made things clear though as to who exactly was running this show. Scared of any confrontation, he turned around and headed for the front door, then walked out of the apartment. Once his partner was gone, he pulled out a pack of Newports from his pocket.

"Would you like a square, as you older cats say? I know this shit right here can be jive stressful. I'm saying, I can only imagine. I've never had my life in the balance but if I had, I'm sure the shit would be a little stressful for me to handle," he said, trying to be a smart ass.

"In a different situation or circumstance I'd probably welcome one, but right now I'm going to have to pass," LT replied unfazed.

"I can dig that. I need to quit these things myself but they help relax me," he said while putting the cigarette in his mouth and lighting it. Once he inhaled the nicotine from the cancer stick and blew out the smoke, he continued. "Well, back to the matter at hand. What exactly has Moe Betta told you about the organization, namely us?"

"My man, I don't know which way to put this for you. I don't know who the fuck you are. I don't know shit about you. You sitting in front of me talking like I should know who you are though, like you have some pull in this town. Your name isn't Mario Cardoza, we both know that. Now please, stop fronting and tell me what it is you really want."

"You seem like a very smart man to me, so I'm pretty sure you understand the difference between bravery, stupidity, and being crazy. Right now you are on the borderline of all three and that doesn't bear well for YOUR family. Please remember that when you want to go on your little fake-ass tirades. Don't let my young appearance fool you. What do you know about Santana and his operation?"

"There isn't much to know anymore, now is there. As I hear it, Santana is out and someone new has taken over. So why does it even matter what I do or don't know about Santana? I'm a D.C. police officer, not one in Philly or Delaware but D.C."

"Then next time, please don't sit here wasting my time acting like you don't know shit because it's obvious you do. What do you know about the new playa, as you say?" he said, making quotation marks with his fingers as he said the word "playa."

"I haven't met the nigga! Not much to really know except he is the one behind the hit in Forest Heights. I was told by Santana they'd get in contact with me. I'm guessing you are the message boy," LT replied.

"Well, your guess would be right with the exception of us doing business together. Unfortunately, we do not do business with cops in that fashion. My man, I'm not going to front like I believe everything you're telling me because I don't. But I don't think you are a stupid man and I'm sure you see it only took me a couple of hours to figure out who you are, where your family lives, and their normal routine. If I even think you are leaving anything out or bullshitting me about anything, I will be paying your wife and your daughter a visit very soon."

"I've told you everything I fucking know, now leave my family the fuck out of this. If you have beef with me, then take that shit up with me. My family has nothing to do with this."

"You sure you don't want a cig before I get out of here, my man?" he replied, ignoring LT's plea.

LT didn't respond. He had given him all he wanted. All he could do was pray the vibe he was getting from him indicated that his family's lives would be spared since his cooperation was genuine. The unknown man turned around and headed for the front door and as quickly as he entered, he left.

About three minutes passed and the front door opened again. This time it was the guy who was asked to leave the apartment earlier. He walked up to LT with a cold look in his eyes.

"Have you ever had smack before?" he asked.

"What?"

"I said have you ever had smack before? It's not a hard question."

"The fuck does that have to do with anything?"

"It was just a question. If you haven't, you won't be able to say that for long. Enjoy!"

It was then LT noticed the syringe in his captor's hand. LT tried his hardest to get out of his seat. He tried to build up enough energy to possibly break loose of his capture and whoop the young fella's ass for even thinking about injecting him with something. LT was happy a bullet wasn't being put in his head but he wasn't going to go out like that, either. All his efforts were for naught. LT couldn't move. He couldn't break free.

The man started to laugh as LT began to face reality and then gave up trying to get loose.

"Home boy, if it were up to me, I wouldn't even waste this good shit on your ass but it's not. So why not sit back and enjoy the ride. I hear you'll love every minute of it," he said before injecting LT in the arm.

CHAPTER 11

Everything was a blur. Nothing made sense or seemed right. The sunlight sneaking in through the cracks of the shade started to blind LT. A sudden rush of nausea rushed through his body. He leaned over and threw up on the floor. The way the apartment looked, it wasn't the first time either.

LT started to panic. He turned toward the door after he heard a loud bang. That's when he noticed he was strapped in the chair.

"Detective Taylor," LT heard a voice call from a distance.

He tried to muster up enough strength to respond but couldn't.

"LT, are you okay?" a man's voice said.

Then what seemed like reality became a faint dream. LT dozed back off into another deep slumber.

"Hey, baby," Denise said.

LT didn't recognize his surroundings. "Where am I?" he asked.

"You are at Washington Hospital Center."

"Huh…Washington Hospital Center, why?"

Before Denise could reply Lieutenant Ross walked into the room.

"Hey, Denise, how is he doing?"

She quickly disregarded LT's initial question.

"He just woke up," she replied.

"Would someone please tell me what is going on?" LT asked getting annoyed.

The more he tried to move, the more his body ached. He knew something was wrong and feared for the worst.

"That is what we are trying to find out. When we found you, you were strapped into a chair and had been pumped full of heroin," Lieutenant Ross replied.

"Heroin! This isn't making sense. How the hell did I have heroin in my system? Lou, you know me. I don't do drugs. I'm not a damn drug addict. Why the fuck would I have drugs in my system? How could I?"

"Baby, we know you aren't an addict, nobody is calling you one," Denise said, jumping to LT's defense.

LT tried to replay the previous events in his head but nothing was coming to mind.

"Lieutenant, I wish I knew. I really do. The only thing I remember is my cover being blown. I'm not sure how though. Hold on, hold on! There was a knock at the door and when I answered it, there were a couple of kids who had pistols pointed at me."

"Did you recognize them?" Lieutenant Ross asked.

"Lou, before then, I'd never seen them before. I mean, Lou, they were kids. They couldn't have been any more than fourteen or fifteen years old. They were practically babies, Lou."

"LT, are you sure? I mean, I can't see kids that young getting the drop on one of my best undercover agents. And I know Mario isn't going to send anyone that young for a job as big as killing a police officer."

"I know it sounds crazy, Lou, but I'm so serious. I don't know who they work for or who sent them but they were very organized. At least one of them was. He seemed like a pro. If I didn't know any better, I would have thought he was the man himself. That is how in control he was. That reminds me, I need you to have a car on the house. He let it be known that he knows where I live as well as they had information about my family."

"Excuse me, what do you mean they know where we live?" Denise asked.

"Baby, you have nothing to worry about. You aren't in any danger. If you were, they would have done something already to make their point. They wanted to show me that if they wanted to, they could get to you, so I'd tell them the information they wanted to know. It was never about my family, just to scare me with y'all," LT said, trying to calm Denise down.

"Denise, we'll take care of everything. LT is right; you have nothing to worry about," Lieutenant Ross reassured.

"That is easy for both of you to say. You don't have people following you. Look at what they did to my husband and he is a trained officer. How am I supposed to feel safe? I'm not trained. I think I have more than enough reasons to worry, so please don't sit here and tell me not to!"

LT could see things were starting to get to Denise. No matter what he said, he knew it wouldn't totally put her mind at ease. The only way was to try and take her mind off of things.

"Baby, can you ask the nurse to bring me some water? My mouth is extremely dry. Please!" LT asked.

LT wasn't fooling her. She knew exactly what he was trying to do. However, she didn't protest. She figured she'd fight the battle another day.

"LT, are you sure about the kids thing? I'm having a very hard time believing kids would be able to work you over like this.

Nothing about this says amateur hit; this has *professional* written all over it, if you ask me."

"Lou, I know it sounds wild. You are having a hard time believing it—how do you think I felt when I was going through it? No matter what I said or did, they had a comeback for everything. The worst part about it is, I don't even think Mario had anything to do with this. The whole thing isn't his style. How many times have you known him to leave a witness alive? I don't care if it's a cop or not. That isn't in his style. He leaves no traces. *If* this was at his orders, then why am I alive to talk about it and identify people?"

"Maybe because they are already dead or maybe they got cold feet, who knows? What we do know is he is the only sick bastard who has the mindset for something like this."

"I'm not sure about that, Lou," LT replied.

"Okay, well, if not Mario, then who?"

"What do you know about the hit that happened around Forest Heights?"

"Forest Heights! What does that have to do with this?" Lieutenant Ross asked puzzled.

"I'm not sure, but I think it's all connected somehow."

"Well, from what I hear, there isn't really much to know. There are no leads in the case. One of the DOAs was a young lieutenant of Santana's."

"Call me crazy, but I think I just met the culprit behind everything."

"If you are right about their ages, then you might have. From the tips Prince George's County police have been receiving, they seem to believe it's centered around a feud with a young girl who was killed and the others were caught up in it."

"Good. I'll make sure I give PG a call when I get out of here to see exactly what type of leads they have and work from there," LT said.

"No, you won't. You are off this case. I'm pulling you. You are too close to the situation right now. If you are right and the same kids who were behind the hit in Forest Heights are the ones who did this to you, there is no way I'm going to continue to allow you to work this case.

"Plus the first thing I need you to do when you get released is check yourself into a drug rehab program. Your health is priority number one. I'll assign someone else to the case to work with PG and we'll go from there."

"You can't pull me off this, Lou. This is personal now. They threatened my life, my family's life. I'll be damned if you pull me off of this. I think I've earned the right to make my own decision."

"I'm sorry, kid, but I'm not going to play around with your life. You are off!"

The doctor walked in interrupting them. "How are we feeling, Mr. Taylor?"

"I'll be a lot better when y'all let me up out of here. I know you are only doing your jobs but I'm feeling better. So when will I be able to check out of here?"

"Well, we have a few more tests to run to make sure we've gotten everything out of your system and then you'll be free to go. However, as we told your wife earlier, we think it would be best once you leave her, you check into a drug treatment center."

LT quickly became defensive. "I don't need to go to no rehab center. I'm not a drug addict. I'm getting sick of y'all saying that I am. I was drugged."

"Mr. Taylor, I completely understand. What I need you to understand though is you had very high quantities of heroin in your system which means you'll start to have withdrawal symptoms and they can last possibly as long as six months. The treatment center will help to prevent a problem from happening."

"That is okay, doctor, I'll be fine. I've never done drugs before and I won't start now. Trust me, I'll be just fine. I can handle it."

Denise walked into the room.

"See that pretty young thing right there, doc? That is all I need. The loving from that woman can cure a man of any illness," LT added.

The doctor started to smile.

"I definitely can understand that. There is nothing better than having a good support team around us. But sometimes, that isn't enough. I've seen it happen too many times, Mr. Taylor, where people think their will is stronger than the effects of those drugs and they have a relapse. There is nothing wrong with getting help. It doesn't make you any less of a man or person. It actually shows your strength. It shows you are strong enough to admit that you need help. The treatment facilities are there to help you deal with the after-effects of the drugs."

LT was too hard-headed to take heed to the warnings being bestowed on him and too pig-headed to seek help. This was a situation where he would simply agree to disagree and show them this was something he could indeed handle on his own.

"I understand, doc. Just make sure you give us some info on centers in the area and I'll check them out when I leave," LT replied, brushing him off.

"I'll be more than happy to. Just make sure you follow up with your end of the bargain. Please, make sure you do."

"Don't worry, Doctor Roberson, I'll make sure he does," Denise reiterated.

"And so will I," Lieutenant Ross added.

CHAPTER 12

L T was overjoyed the minute he came home from the hospital. It wasn't as if his safe house was bad but it wasn't his home. He was finally in his safe haven. There was something about sleeping in your own bed or being in your own surroundings that was surreal. It was an indescribable feeling.

Lieutenant Ross had given LT the next few weeks off from work. Though LT first wanted to protest, he eventually gave in. He knew it was only for his benefit. Instead, he used the time to spend with his daughter. Being undercover a lot, you missed out on so many precious moments with your family—moments he'd cherish.

There was one thing lacking: the entire time LT had been home he hadn't once visited a drug rehab program as he had promised. Denise continued to urge him to do so but those attempts always fell upon deaf ears. LT didn't feel the urge to get high. That wasn't a part of him or his makeup. Why even waste the time in a drug treatment program, he thought.

There was one thing that was eating away at LT. Who was the mystery man? He'd wracked his brain constantly trying to find out. At first he figured the best way would be through whoever had set him up. There was only one way they could have found everything they had about LT. It had to be someone on the inside. Even if Moe Betta had planted the seed that LT was an undercover, he didn't know anything about LT, not even his real name.

Trying to figure that out might prove to be harder. It didn't matter to LT. He was going to find out all that he needed until he was no longer breathing. He was determined.

LT decided to pay the Forest Heights police department a visit. They weren't too much help, however. All the previous witnesses they'd had either turned up missing or all of a sudden had selective memory. All they really got behind everything was a motive that centered on the young girl who was killed. However, all leads stopped at Oxon Hill High School. The investigation had reached a dead end.

The streets were buzzing about this new cat. The only thing he was able to come up with was a name—Money Green. But no one could put a face to the name. He, like Mario, stayed hidden in the shadows and this made things difficult. However, LT lived by the creed where if there is will, there is a way.

The stress of the situation was really getting to LT. He decided to call the afternoon quits and head to the closest bar possible. Though he knew he shouldn't be drinking, he needed something to ease the stress. It wasn't like him to have no answers. He was always able to figure out every situation or any problem. When one did arise, he tackled it head on and always found a solution. However, now, it wasn't as easy.

LT was never really big on alcohol. He'd only have a drink every now and then, mostly when he was undercover and in character. Outside of that he stayed away from it. Sitting at the bar throwing back drink after drink was starting to get to him. It was as if he were trying to compensate for something.

An urge had his name on it. It couldn't be what he thought. No, there was no way. He didn't have a problem. That wasn't a part of him.

It didn't matter what any doctor said, he could fight it on his own. He didn't have a problem. Sitting on that bar stool, LT tried to collect himself. No matter how many drinks he had, it wasn't quenching the urge that had built up inside him. That scared him, because the answer to what would subside that urge was frightening.

Maybe if I just had a small taste, that would help, LT thought. He knew it was a lie. That would only make matters worse. Soon, the urges would subside and he could go back to his normal life. Until then, alcohol would serve its purpose. If not, then maybe he'd actually go to one of the treatment centers for other ways to deal with it.

Work could be the trick. If LT kept his head buried in his work, there was no way the urges could surface to a dangerous point. That was the way. Plus, he had all the motive in the world to work trying to find out how his cover was blown in the beginning and to bring the culprits to justice.

Convincing Denise was another story. If she had her way, LT would have retired from the force and found another job. She didn't care how much her husband loved being a cop. Nothing mattered to her but his safety and there was no way he or anyone else could guarantee his safety while on the job. Getting her to agree or even be okay with him going back to work would be a task.

LT pulled up into his driveway and turned the ignition off. However, he didn't bother to open the door and get out of the car just yet. Instead he laid his head back on the seat and closed his eyes. Everything was still difficult to deal with. LT knew he had made his bones by bringing home the big cases. That's why he had been handpicked for the undercover detail in the first place. He had proven he could get the job done and do it efficiently. He was good at what he did and they knew it.

"Lionel, baby, is that you? Why are you sitting in the car? What's wrong?" Denise questioned.

He looked up and saw her standing in front of the car. He was so out of things, he didn't even hear the garage door going up. She was heading toward the trashcans when she noticed he was still sitting in the car. LT removed his keys and opened the door.

"Hey, baby. What are you doing?"

"Well, I was about to take this trash out but since you are home you can do it."

He didn't object. Instead he closed the car door and went to do as she had asked.

"Baby, you never answered my question. Is something wrong? Why were you sitting in the car?"

"Huh?"

"Baby, what's going on? I know you and you are acting funny. What is wrong? Matter of fact, why are you so late tonight?"

"Baby, everything is fine. I went to the bar to have a drink. I had a lot on my mind. I should have called you. I'm sorry."

"The bar! You know you shouldn't be drinking. Are you trying to kill yourself?"

LT knew not to answer her rhetorical question.

"Hello! I know I'm not talking to myself. I swear I don't know what I'm going to do with you. What is bothering you that bad that you had to go to a bar instead of coming home and talking to me or spending time with your daughter?"

"I was trying to figure out how to tell you that I'm…"

Denise quickly cut him off, "I know you are not about to sit here and tell me you are going back to work!"

"See, that is why I didn't come straight home. I knew it would be an argument. Yes, it's time for me to go back to work. I'm sorry, I'm a cop. That is what I am and what I'm going to do. Maybe I can't go back undercover but I'm not going to stop being a cop. I was in that hospital for a week and now have been home another two weeks. It's time I go back to work. I am going crazy!"

Denise calmed down. "You know what, baby, you are right and that is unfair for me to ask you. I apologize. I just don't want to lose you. How do you think it makes me feel to know that I could be a widow right now and our child could have lost her father? The only reason why you are here is because they left you alive. They could have easily killed you and that scares me, baby. It really does."

"I know it does. It scares me, too, but it's the reason why I have to go back. I can't let them dictate my life. I can't let them kill my spirit."

"I understand. Come on, let's get out of this cold and go inside the house. We can finish talking about it inside."

"Okay, baby. I'll be in," LT replied as he grabbed the trash-cans inside the garage and took them to the front curb. LT noticed himself looking up and down the street to make sure no one was watching him or his house. Usually it wasn't a big deal to be aware of your surroundings, but in this case it was out of fear. This wasn't a government house set up for his cover but rather his place of residence. His family lived here.

What the fuck is wrong with me, LT thought. He reached into his pocket, searching for his pack of cigarettes. The nicotine stick was exactly what this situation needed to lighten the mood and calm his nerves. He was too tense and close to the edge. Luck wasn't on his side though. Denise must have gotten to his secret stash of cigarettes earlier that morning. The box was empty.

"Fuck!" he yelled.

It was obvious this was one of those nights. At least there was one bright spot. He would be able to go back to work without having to fight his wife to do it.

CHAPTER 13

L T decided to hit the streets for a couple of days and try to unturn any and every stone possible for information. The only thing he had to go on was the name Money Green but that didn't mean anything. He needed a face with that name or maybe a connect who could paint that missing picture.

Everything depended on how much the streets knew. If word had been spread around about what had happened to him, then it wouldn't be hard at all. However, he wasn't having the best of luck trying to find any of his street informants. LT was down to his last straw and being tactful wasn't something he was going to be. He didn't care.

LT knew that whoever Money Green was, he had some type of ties to the Oxon Hill area. He had made a couple of deals while undercover in Glassmanor so he decided to hit up the area. The second he hit Deal Drive he saw his intended target. He pulled up to the corner.

"Bugg, get in," LT said.

Everyone standing there looked at him as if he was stupid. LT pulled his pistol and pointed it at the man.

"Get in the muthafuckin' car!" LT demanded.

Bugg knew that even though they were strapped, by the time anyone was able to pull their pistol, LT would have already emptied the clip. He valued his life so he did just as he was asked to do. LT sped off the second Bugg was securely in the car.

"How you been, Bugg?"

"Man, I don't have shit to say to you. The word is out on you in the streets. Your name doesn't mean shit anymore!"

LT pulled the car over behind in the parking lot of one of the apartment complexes in the area. He got out of the car, then walked around to Bugg's side and pulled him out.

"Let me tell you something, I don't give a shit what is going around about me in these streets. The minute my family comes into play, it's been taken to another level. So I'm going to give you two options, either you can tell me what you know or I'll bury your ass!"

He took his hands and started to go through Bugg's pockets. He pulled out six packets of heroin.

"Your dumb ass don't get it, do you? You've already killed me and don't even know it. I'm glad you got those packs up off me. Lock my ass up! I'll gladly take the three to five years. Shit, I won't even fight the charge. The minute them niggas find out you snatched me up off the corner, I'm gone! These niggas take no chances. I might not have said a word about anything and none of that will even matter to them. They aren't going to even take a chance that I possibly did."

"So why not do yourself a favor and let me protect you."

"You want to protect me? Then do me the favor of locking my ass up. That is all the protection I need. Hopefully they'll think I didn't turn since you still put me in the box. I take it you going to protect me like you did your man Moe Betta!"

"What are you talking about?" LT asked puzzled.

"You cops are always a day late and a dollar short when it comes to a nigga in the 'hood life. Y'all so concentrated on the big fish, y'all don't give a shit about the others in the pond. They found that nigga was snitching and they cut his tongue out and mailed it to Santana! That is how these new cats are going. They don't care and the order came from Mr. Cardoza himself. You can't protect me from that."

"What choice do you have? I'll kindly drop you right back off around the block and say thanks for the information. Let them do what they want with you and try another way to get these niggas. I don't care about your life. How many times do I have to say that? The only thing I care about is the one they call Money Green."

"I should have known. That's the nigga who worked your ass over. Yeah, I heard about that. Well, I hope you caught a glimpse of his license or something because he deals with no one. If you want to buy from him, he has people in place who you contact. From what I hear, the man doesn't come anywhere near the product or even the cash at that. Good luck with that one, champ. He isn't the man's protégé for nothing."

"He has to be getting paid somehow."

"Yeah, you are probably right, but I don't ask questions and damn sure don't want to know. That is for you to do your homework on, DETECTIVE!" Bugg started laughing.

"If I wanted to cop weight, who would the connect be?"

"Your mother would be! I told you, I'm not giving you shit! I've said all that I'm going to say. You work with that and find a way to fill in the rest of the holes yourself," Bugg replied.

LT could see no matter how much pressure he put on him, nothing was going to work. He knew he couldn't arrest him because then he'd have to explain the charge in the arresting document. He wasn't supposed to be anywhere near this case or even back on street work. Lieutenant Ross had agreed to allow him back to work but only at a desk.

LT did the only thing he could do. He turned to get back in the car. "You be easy, Bugg."

By the time he had put his car in "drive," Bugg had pulled out his pistol and shot himself in the head. He knew it would only be a matter of time before the word got back to either Money Green or someone else within their inner circle that he had talked to LT. The sound of the gunshot startled LT. He wasn't sure at first if Bugg was firing at him. Once he stopped the car and turned around to see, he then knew exactly what had taken place.

It was at that point he realized the severity of the situation. Fear went a long way in the streets. People wouldn't dare cross you and risk their life. Bugg feared for his so much on the street he decided to end his own life. Even the thought of Moe Betta bothered LT. He was an untouched man. If Santana, a loyal and respected lieutenant within the Cardoza organization, couldn't stop the fate of one of his trusted soldiers, it said how much power the new face of the city had.

LT dug through his pockets looking for a number and came across the six packets he had taken off Bugg. The urge started to come back over him again to quench his needed thirst. Now, he had the supplies to do so. LT couldn't help but think of what harm it would do. No one would know. He needed something to ease his mind. The stress of the situation of trying to find Money Green was getting to him. He'd only try it once.

LT's mind was made. He drove to a back alley, fired up one of the packets and pushed it into his veins. As the drug traveled though his veins, he felt a soothing cool and calm come over his body. It was exactly what he needed and craved. However, it would only be a one-time thing. He would only do it this once and that was that. He wasn't an addict and didn't have a problem. Those were all the thoughts that were going through LT's head. And then he fired up the next packet.

CHAPTER 14

The ringing of the telephone awoke LT from his deep slumber. He struggled trying to move to answer the phone. He was extremely tired from a long night and needed a few more hours of sleep to compensate for it. He decided to roll back over and ignore the phone. Only problem was it wouldn't stop ringing. Whoever was calling must have had something very important on their mind because they were persistent. LT figured the only way he'd be able to go back to sleep was to answer the phone.

"Hello," he said into the receiver.

"Please explain to me why YOUR ASS ISN'T AT WORK! You should have been in over three hours ago. What the hell is going on?" Lieutenant Ross yelled.

LT turned toward the alarm clock and noticed it was close to eleven a.m. He didn't remember it ever going off. He was past late for work. He was supposed to have been in for role call at seven a.m.

"Shit! Lou, I'm so sorry. I overslept. I swear my alarm clock didn't go off. Let me take a quick shower and I'll be right in."

"A quick shower, have you lost your fucking mind? I have to take a piss, by the time I finish shaking my dick and washing my hands, I better walk past your desk and see your tired ass sitting there doing paperwork. Is that understood?" Lieutenant Ross replied.

"Yes, sir, I understand completely."

By the time LT said the first word, he had already hung up the phone.

"Shit!" he yelled.

LT knew he was messing up and fucking up bad at that. His mind was far from clear. He started to feel queasy and ran to the bathroom. No matter what he did or ate, he couldn't stop throwing up. He stood over the toilet bowl sweating profusely as the vomit escaped his mouth.

As much as he was in denial, it was evident the call of that monkey on his back was strong and hard to ignore. He didn't know how, but there had to be a way to block it out. Unsuccessfully he'd already tried everything. LT picked his head up from the toilet and rinsed his mouth out. Maybe a shower would be exactly what he needed in order to remove those feelings.

He turned on the water and escaped his clothes. He felt dirty and grimy and needed to rinse himself clean from his filth. The more he washed, the dirtier his body felt. He continued to scrub and scrub, harder and harder, but the feeling would not subside. The urges he was feeling wouldn't leave but continued to only grow stronger second after second.

The tears started to flow from his eyes down his face. He knew he was helpless from the call. He just didn't want to admit it. By doing so meant he indeed was a failure. LT turned off the water and jumped out of the shower. There was no more denying what he needed. He knew exactly who he was and what he had become. The thing he couldn't explain was when it happened and how it got to the point of being too far. He had long passed the point of no return and never even knew it.

Style wasn't an issue. LT quickly grabbed the first thing he saw and got dressed, picked up his car keys and headed out the door to his destination. In no time he was at the candy store. He pulled up to the corner and rolled down the window.

"What you need?" the distant voice asked.

"Let me get two," LT replied.

He patiently waited for LT to provide him with the key to successfully complete the transaction. LT reached into his pocket and took out his last forty dollars. The corner boy motioned for one of his counterparts to serve LT and then he was on his way.

He rushed back home like a kid would into the living room on Christmas morning. He grabbed the aluminum foil from the pantry and wrapped it around a spoon. Then he poured one of his packets into it, added water, and then heated it up until it turned into a milky-like liquid. Once that was complete, he took a cotton ball and placed it on top of the liquid. Next he took his syringe and filled it. His eyes bulged with excitement. He wrapped his belt around his arm and tightened it to get a good vein.

Within seconds an instant rush raced throughout his body finally relaxing any and everything. That quickly, he was sent into a deep metaphoric state. Only this time, the high that would usually last for hours started to fade as fast as it came. LT opened the next packet and repeated the process. Finally he was brought back to his reality. His body started to feel as if it was normal. It felt as if this was how it was supposed to feel. Instead, it had now grown dependent upon that extra punch to get it there.

His sense of normalcy was lost. The revelation LT had in

the shower was one that added clarity but not sanity. Insane was now his state of mind and dependency was now his way of life. He searched through his pockets for more money yet felt nothing but the thin lining between his hand and his leg.

LT picked up the phone and called his bank to see how much he had in his account. To his surprise, his account balance was overdrawn by seventeen dollars. Even knowing he was dead broke wasn't going to deter him. He couldn't allow it to. He wasn't sure how long he had until he'd start to feel sick again, but knew he needed to do whatever it took to avoid that from happening.

He scavenged throughout the house, trying to find any loose change. It didn't matter how much he found or how he found it as long as it added up to twenty dollars. That would be enough to hold him off until he could come up with some real money. LT searched high and low but still found himself short of his desired goal. That was when he noticed the digital camera he'd gotten Denise for Christmas the previous year. He remembered he had paid close to three-hundred for it. That was just the thing he needed. He figured he could borrow the camera, pawn it, and then get it back out on pay day. Denise would never know it was missing. Pay day was a couple days away. She rarely used the camera anyway.

He could even do one better: get her a brand-new one and make it all a part of his excuse about why it was missing, if she were suspicious. Once LT had the plan totally worked out, there would be nothing in his way to stop him.

LT knew he still needed to get to work so he rushed to the closest pawn shop which was about fifteen minutes away. The way he was driving seemed like it only took him five to get there.

"How much can I get for this?" LT said as he placed the camera on the table.

"Where did you get this from?" the salesman inquired with his thick Arabian accent.

"My damn house, now how much?" LT snapped.

He could tell he was skeptical to do business with him. LT didn't care.

"I bought it from Best Buy last Christmas for my wife. However, she won a contest at her job and they gave her a new camera for a prize. It actually is better than this one, so I decided to try to get some money for it. I'll get her something else with that," he explained, hoping to ease him.

"If that is the case, why not take it back to the store and try to get the full amount you paid for it back?"

"What is this, twenty-twenty or something? Shit! I said I got it for her last Christmas. Now can you please tell me how much you'll give me for the fucking camera?" LT said seriously agitated.

"I'll give you one-eighty for it," he said reluctantly.

"ONE EIGHTY! This is a three hundred-dollar camera. You must be out of your fucking mind."

"Do you have a receipt? If so, you can take it back to Best Buy, my friend, and get a refund. If you don't, then I'll give you one-eighty and that is it."

"Come on, you can at least give me two hundred and fifty for it," LT pleaded.

"One-fifty!"

"You just said one-eighty. How are you going to go down?"

LT started to scratch his neck. He could feel himself starting to feel sick. He knew it wouldn't be long now. LT was left with his last option. He pulled out his badge.

"I should lock your fucking ass up. Do you know who I am? I can have your ass sent back overseas to your fucked up-ass Third World country and there wouldn't be shit you could do about it. I'm not some sucka from off the street. This camera cost me three hundred dollars and that is exactly what I fucking want for it. I don't want no one-eighty, no two-fifty, or even two hundred and ninety-nine dollars and ninety-nine cents. I want three hundred. Do you fucking hear me?" LT demanded.

Though in reality the store clerk was in control and actually had LT by the balls, the power still shifted. The seriousness in LT's eyes told the clerk that he was desperate and meant every word he uttered. He didn't want to chance being wrong and call his bluff. There was no telling how far LT was willing to take things.

"Okay, okay, I will give you three hundred for it. I don't want any trouble," he replied as he opened the register.

Before he could count out the money, LT had already taken it out of his hand and was on his way out the door. It was obvious he was way past gone. Any person in their right mind would have waited until every single dime was counted out and verified.

LT rushed to his pharmacy for his new-found medicine.

"What you need?" the dealer asked.

"Yeah, let me get two."

"Yo, I've seen your ass before. I'm not sure where but I know I've seen you somewhere before."

"Yeah, you saw me here earlier today. Now can you cut the small talk and come up off the packages. Shit!"

"Nigga, the fuck you talking to?" the dealer asked squaring up.

"Look, I'm just trying to get my two and be on my way. Okay, boss!"

Before he could even reply, they both were surrounded by four unmarked police cars.

"Jump-outs!" one of the corner boys yelled from a distance.

The dealer tried to turn and run but it was too late. He already had three officers with the guns drawn and pointed at him.

"Get down on the ground NOW!" one of the officers yelled.

This was the last thing LT needed. He tried to collect himself and get his self together. There was no way he could lose his job over this.

"Driver, place your left hand on the steering wheel!" The officer paused. "With your right hand, turn off the car and then place it on the steering wheel of the car where I can see it."

LT knew the drill like clockwork. One wrong move and his car would be filled with bullets. This was not an option. He had no choice but to do as he was asked.

"Now, with your right hand, slowly open the door and get out of the car."

LT continued to follow the instructions given to him.

"Turn around, then slowly fold both hands over your head and get on your knees," the officer demanded.

The minute LT was down two officers rushed him to place him into custody.

"Easy boys, easy…I'm one of you," LT said.

"Shut up," one officer said as he placed his arms behind his back so he could cuff him.

"Check my pocket. I have my badge in there. My name is Detective Taylor and I'm with the fourth district," LT reiterated.

The officer reached into his pocket to confirm LT was indeed telling him the truth. Once he had his badge out, the sign of egg was written all over his face.

"I apologize. You can never be too safe these days," he quickly said.

"That is okay. Look, he is one of my informants. I've been working undercover for the past two years now. I was just meeting with him getting information on a pending case."

"Say no more, again I apologize. We've been doing surveillance building cases the past three days on this corner. We had no idea he was a friendly though."

"I'd really appreciate it if you'd cut me a break. You know what I mean? I really need him on the streets. He has ties to the whole Cardoza family."

"Don't worry about it," the officer replied. He turned to his partner. "Take the cuffs off of him. He is free to go."

"Thanks, I really appreciate it," LT replied.

"Say no more. You be safe," the officer said.

"You do the same."

They both waited until the scene was clear and police free before either of them said a word. It was obvious the dealer didn't know what was going on or why he was free but knew he had LT to thank.

"Yo, what's the catch?" he asked nervously. "What, your boys gone around back or something waiting so they can whip my ass?" he continued.

"No, it's nothing like that. I have more to lose with you going to jail than you do. Plus I figured we could help each other out from time to time. As I'm sure you know now, I'm a cop. I have ways of being a help to you."

"What's the catch? What, you want some of the action or something? You starting too low on the chain, don't you think? I'm no heavy hitter or nothing," the dealer said.

"No, I just need you to look out for me from time to time, if you know what I mean," LT replied.

It was then when the dealer remembered why LT was actually there. It wasn't to catch him in the act of dealing but to feed his own habit and cop a fix.

"I can live with that. So what you need?"

"What you got?"

"As you can see, your boys done ran off most of my workers so not much. I have four loose ones on me but I can catch up with you in an hour and give you a pretty good fix for a wholesale price."

"I'm not trying to deal the shit. I just need it."

"Okay, I'll look out for you and have my runners find you to give you what you need at a more secure location. That way, you in the clear and so am I. Just make sure you look out for any news I might need to know, cool?" the dealer suggested.

"Perfect!"

"Okay, here is a number you can use to get in contact with one of my runners. He'll know your prices. Keep in mind these aren't family discounts or no shit like that, so make sure you don't go running your fucking mouth. I'll give you one for ten, six for fifty, and ten for eighty."

"What about that four you have on you? Can I get that now until you catch up with your people?" LT asked.

"Damn, boss, I almost forgot! Sure, no problem. I'll even give you these on me."

He handed LT the packets and the number. Both of them went their separate ways.

CHAPTER 15

As much as Denise tried to deny the facts, she knew her husband had fallen off and gone to drugs. There were too many symptoms for her even to try to ignore. Money was missing, items around the house, and he was always broke— not to mention his late-night hours and his demeanor when he came home.

LT wasn't the same man she married. She knew it was only a matter of time before things escalated and got worse. LT recently had become unpredictable. At times she even feared for her own safety. The only thing that kept her sane was their child. She knew how much LT cherished her and would never do anything in front of her.

She figured the best thing to do was call Lieutenant Ross and see if he could help in some way. She didn't care. Anything was better than what she was getting at home. They didn't make love any more nor spend time together. He slept in most mornings and came home late every night. The married, loving couple they once were turned into roommates occupying the same space.

Though Denise tried to act as if maybe the stress of the job and not being on the street was getting to LT, Lieutenant Ross knew what was what. He was a highly decorated officer trained to notice habits and people. He, too, knew the turn LT had made but tried to give him enough rope to either correct the situation or hang himself. He knew that there wasn't much he could do because LT would continue to hurt himself and ultimately his family if he continued to ignore the situation. He assured Denise that he'd talk with him and straighten everything out. What he didn't say was how exactly he'd do that.

The minute LT walked into the house, Denise knew it wouldn't be long before she found out.

"Hey, baby," she said, hoping to lighten the mood.

"You couldn't leave well enough alone, could you?" LT replied.

"Baby, what are you talking about?"

"Don't act like you don't know what the fuck I'm talking about. I know you talked with Lou and filled his head with a bunch of bullshit. Well, guess what, I've been suspended pending a fucking drug test."

LT walked off and went in their daughter's room to check and see if she was in the house. He didn't want to discuss it with Denise anymore. He knew that the minute he took the drug test, he would come back positive and then everything would be ruined. Denise was right on his heels.

"First of all, I didn't say anything to Lieutenant Ross like that. I told him that I believe something at work had you stressed out. You never talk or open up to me anymore. I asked if he could talk to you hoping you would open up to him and not continue to take the shit out on us. Second, I don't understand what the big problem about taking a drug test is. You don't do drugs. Take the test, prove him or them wrong, and keep it moving. What is the issue?"

LT knew it wasn't that simple. He ignored the question. Once he saw his daughter wasn't in her room, he turned to head for his bedroom to see if she was there.

"There you go again ignoring me. Can you stop and talk to me?" Denise pleaded.

"Where is my child?" LT asked.

"Alexis isn't here. My mother picked her up from daycare and took her out shopping. She'll be back later on tonight."

"Shit!" LT yelled.

The walls were starting to crumble in and his habit was calling him. The only thing that came close to subsiding it was spending time with his daughter. She could turn the worst days into the best with one smile.

"Baby, please, talk to me. That is all I ask. What is going on?"

"I can't take that test. If I do, then I'll fail. Your husband is a fucking addict. Are you happy now? Now you know, so deal with that."

Denise was stuck. She always suspected the worst but still figured there was a chance she could be wrong. Knowing that she wasn't changed everything.

"Yeah, now your ass don't have shit to say. That is what the fuck I thought," LT replied.

"Baby, please, calm down and let's talk like adults. I've always told you, together we can get through anything. This is no different. Yeah, it might be hard, it might even be a struggle, but we can push through."

"That is easy for you to say, you aren't the one going through this. I am. I'm the one losing his mind. I'm the one who will lose his job. I'm losing everything but we going to get through this, huh? I need a fucking hit!"

Denise couldn't believe her ears. After all that was going on, he would say something like that to her.

"You need what? You think this is only affecting you? My mother has Alexis because I don't want her to see her dad like this. Do you see what you are doing to this family? And then your selfish ass is going to say something like that to me."

"Whatever! You keep my daughter away from me if you want to, and we'll have more than just this as a problem," LT said, dismissing her plea.

"You can threaten me all you want to. I'm not scared of you," Denise lied. She continued, "What happened to my camera? How about the money for the gas bill? Where did all of that go?"

"What are you talking about?"

"You know exactly what I'm talking about. I have to hide money from you. I know you go through my purse. I have to hide money from my own damn husband. And you think your habit doesn't affect us. I shouldn't have to. I should be able to trust you. I should be able to trust you around our child, around me. But I don't. I don't trust you at all."

LT became defensive. He could see the walls of his life starting to crumble. He loved his family more than anything but nothing outside of his addiction or his daughter seemed to matter. He didn't want to have to choose between the two. However, he knew that choice needed to be made. LT felt as if a noose was tightening around his neck.

"So what are you are going to do, leave? Fuck it, leave then! Shit, I'm losing everything else but Alexis is staying with me."

Denise started to laugh.

"First of all, I'm not going anywhere. This is my house as much as yours so if anyone is leaving, it will be you. Second, you will never get my child. You can forget that!"

LT because furious. He lunged at her. Before he knew what he was doing, he'd smacked her in the face and knocked her to the ground. He began to choke her.

"You take my child from me I swear to fucking God, I'll kill you. I will kill you, I swear. She is the only positive thing in my life. I'll be damned if you take my baby girl."

Denise put up no resistance. A part of her couldn't. She lay there with his hands around her throat gasping for air. LT snapped out of his mental insanity and realized what he was doing. He quickly stopped choking her and got up off her. He grabbed his car keys and headed straight for the door. He knew the minute his hand touched her in that way, there was no turning back. There was no way he would ever be able to right that wrong.

He continued to drive. He didn't have a destination in mind but knew he needed to drive. It was obvious the place he called home wasn't home to him anymore.

NINE YEARS LATER

REDEDICATION TO LIFE

CHAPTER 16

There was a knock on the door, and Money got up to answer it. No one knew where he laid his head at night, so he wasn't too concerned. It couldn't have been but only one of two people, either O'Neal or Cheese. This time it happened to be both of them.

"What's going on?" Money said once he opened the door.

"Shit, homie!" O'Neal replied.

"You have anything to eat?" Cheese added.

"Nigga, is that all you think about is food. We just ate about an hour ago," O'Neal shot back.

"Fuck y'all skinny-ass chumps. I eat, that's what I do. Stop acting like you don't know."

"No, that's not what you do. That is *all* your fat ass does!" O'Neal replied and started laughing.

Money couldn't help but laugh too. The two of them were so comical Money didn't even notice the extra houseguest walk in behind the two of them at first. Once he spotted him, he looked at O'Neal.

"Who is little man?"

"That's BC's little brother."

BC was one of the most feared soldiers in the game. His real name was Neptune but everyone stopped calling him that long time ago. In this game, you always ran across a youngster who thought he was smarter than you. The young fellas these days didn't really have a true respect for code of the game like Money and O'Neal did back in the day when they were coming up. And in situations like these, the "Bill Collector" was the one who came to pay you a visit and when he did he took the payment out on your ass. By O'Neal being in charge of the muscle for the family, BC was his top lieutenant, right-hand man and considered by him as family.

"Where is he?" Money asked.

"Who, BC? Yeah, that's why we over here. He's on a possible situation we might be having right now."

"I should have known this wasn't a pleasure visit. What's the deal?"

"Well, we got a couple of…"

"Hold up," Money cut him off. "Lil' Nep, do me a favor, champ. Why don't you head down to the basement and chill out for a few ticks while we handle some business."

"It's okay, Money, he cool," O'Neal said, coming to Lil' Nep's defense.

None of that mattered to Money; he quickly dismissed O'Neal's comments.

"There's a fridge down there with sodas and shit in it. Go ahead and help yourself to anything you want while you are down there."

Sensing he wasn't getting anywhere with Money, O'Neal motioned for Lil' Nep to go downstairs.

"Keep it tight and we'll never get caught slippin', right?" Money said to O'Neal.

"What the fuck is that supposed to mean?" O'Neal shot back.

"There is a reason why only two people in this world know where I lay my head at night. Those are the only two people in this business I trust. But yet, I have a little nigga in my house walking around that I barely know. And the two who know me better than anyone are the ones who brought his ass here. Now tell me how that shit happened?"

"Nigga, I didn't think it was that serious. He was with BC when we met up with him earlier. I needed BC to jump this situation ASAP so I wasn't going to leave the little nigga stranded. I didn't think it would be a thing if we brought him with us. It's not like he new to this. Shit, this is BC we talking about. He is as real as they come. You know that."

Money didn't want to hear it. "Cheese, get your boy. I don't know what the fuck I'm going to do with him. It's like he hears me, but yet the shit doesn't click."

"Don't put me in that shit. I'm not the one who brought the little nigga over here. I told O to make his ass walk home or something. Shit, he damn near sixteen. We were walking and then some back then. Shit, the more I think about it, we had whips and our own block by then."

"I'm jive insulted. BC is my family, so that makes Lil' Nep family. I don't do family like that so y'all can kill all that. Y'all niggas really kill me. If it was one of y'all, I wouldn't leave either of you high and dry, but I'm supposed to leave my little man like that. If it's that serious, I'll talk to the lil' one when we leave to make sure he knows the deal. You have my word shit won't leave his mouth at all."

"Yeah, okay, remember, that's your family, O, YOUR family!" Money replied.

"Really? That is how you are going to sit there and go on your man like that? You are going to shit on our truest soldier, a nigga who would ride or die for any of us?"

"Man, pull up your skirt and stop crying. I don't know why you trying to act like you don't know how sensitive Money gets. Both of y'all niggas some old soft-ass buttercups with this back-and-forth shit!" Cheese replied, looking at both of them.

And with that comment, the mild tension was gone and everything quickly went back to normal.

"Shut your fat ass up," O'Neal and Money both said in unison.

They all started laughing.

"Naw, seriously though, that's my bad, Money. If it make you feel any better, the little nigga was sleep most of the way up here, so he don't really know where you truly rest your head up, at least not the way to get here. I guess BC had him out late last night working. When we met up with them, they were just crossing the bridge."

"Fuck it, what's done is done. It is what it is. Now, what is this situation you keep bringing up?" Money asked.

"Word is some cat from up top trying to get a couple of packages. He sent a couple of NY boys down here to broker the deal. Usually I wouldn't think nothing about nothing except these cats throwin' out names and everything. They aren't being discreet about trying to cop or nothing and the only name that keep coming out their mouth is yours."

Money's alarm instantly started to go off. This possibly was a troublesome situation. The initial scent said feds setting traps but it also could be a possible setup for a caper. Either way, Money's antennas were up and eyes were wide open.

"Put someone on background intel on them first. They want to make a deal, cool, but we don't do shit until they are checked out and verified."

"I'm all ready on that. That's actually what I have BC doing.

He uptown doing a surveillance to see what is what with them. You know I needed faces for these cats like yesterday. Plus I wanted to find exactly who is going in and out, who they are associating with, and anything else they doing out in the open. I'm not trying to take any chances with them. Though this seems like a small situation, everything isn't always what it seems and it could turn out to be so much more."

"Good, I'm glad to see your ass is finally starting to learn how to conduct business. Glad to see all these years I've been teaching your ass didn't go in vain. Let's just keep a close eye on them for a while to make sure. If they turn out to not be who they say or their intentions are fraudulent, we'll already have our people in place to deal with them and handle the situation. As a matter of fact, Cheese, go on ahead and send someone up there to set up a meet. Let's really test them and see how serious these cats really are. Does anyone have a name on the nigga?"

"Not yet, they kept that jive close. Only thing they are really putting out there is new folks in town trying to catch up with you. And they know exactly where to go to spread the word to make sure that it would get back to us. They can't be that smart. That's what has me worried the most," O'Neal said.

Money looked at Cheese.

"I haven't heard anything, either. I'll make sure to get it though when I set up the meet. I'll handle that personally to make sure everything goes smoothly."

"Naw, don't do that. Right now too much is at risk for personal attention. Send someone to make the deal. Plus, I want you to finish up the arrangements for the new shipment from MIA. Without that, we can't deal with anyone. Just make sure whoever you send to make the deal you stay in constant contact with them to make sure everything went smoothly."

"What's there to handle with the shipment? It's a regular shipment, nothing special. We've never had a problem before with one."

"I know and I want to keep it that way. I don't have the best of feelings with the timing. If these boys are feds, then that might be why they are trying to get close to us. Someone might have flipped and tipped them off about the shipment. Just make sure you keep an extra eye on this one. As a matter of fact, make the call to switch everything up. Move the checkpoint up to South Carolina and make it two days earlier than what we are originally scheduled for. If that is a problem, tell them to contact me and I'll squash it, but I don't want this to become a serious situation. Also get in contact with Mario and make sure he makes and takes the same precautions on his end as well."

"Damn, Money, do you really think this is that serious?"

"I'm not trying to take the chance that it isn't, especially without things being settled with these cats uptown. We are going to play this one safe and keep in very close. These niggas namedropping and calling me out. Who the fuck you know is that bold? You keep knocking on the devil's door and sooner or later he will answer it. They wanted to get our attention, well, guess what? They have my undivided attention now. My eyes are wide the fuck open on this one, homie."

"I feel ya. I'll make sure the shipment goes smooth and I'll send Lenny up to set up the meet."

"Lenny! Are you kidding me? What about Mel?" O'Neal said, displeased with the choice.

"Mel is on lend to Los in B-more. He is brokering a deal for him. One that we are getting thirty percent of when it's completed, let's not forget."

"Who gives a fuck? This is some serious shit, pull Mel's ass off of that shit and send Lenny to Los. Our shit is more pressing and comes first. Fuck, Los has workers like we do, damn it. How the fuck does that look, he has one of our best to broker a deal for him and we caught with our dicks between our legs with sucka-ass Lenny?" O'Neal replied.

"Naw, we can't do that," Money chimed in. "Lenny is cool. I actually love son's mindset when it comes to the paper. Make sure BC is with him because we all know he don't have the stomach for the violent aspect of this game. He'll fold the minute he senses a pressure-type situation."

"Yeah, and if them boys really are feds, then he will give everything up to them, including my best soldier. If you are sending Lenny, I'm pulling BC now, and that nigga on his own. I can't leave my man out to dry like that."

Money knew O'Neal had a point.

"True! What's up with Joey then?" Money asked.

"I didn't even think about Joe, he'd be perfect," Cheese replied.

Money turned to O'Neal. "Joey good with you? You know he one hundred percent bona-fide soldier, true and through."

"I can deal with that. Joey straight," O'Neal replied.

"Good then, there it is."

"I'm on it," Cheese replied.

O'Neal changed the subject briefly to a more pressing matter. "Are we still on for tonight?"

"What's tonight?" Money replied confused.

"Cheese, I told you this fool would forget about the party."

"Shit! You are right. My bad, I totally forgot. I'm not even going to lie."

"Man, I know you, Money. You aren't going to wiggle your way out of this one. You are going. There aren't any ifs, ands, or buts about it. Your ass is going to be in the place if I have to drag you out of this house my damn self. Your ass never parties with us anymore. You act like we fucking fifty-five years old instead of twenty-five."

"I have to act that way. There aren't too many twenty-five-year-old CEOs either. I can't afford to relax and party. I'm running a multimillion dollar enterprise, in case you forgot."

"How can I, we all are running it, but it's okay to get your ass out of the house and have a little fun every now and then. Shit, you going to spend your time bottled up, you'll miss out or a lot that life is offering us. The world is ours right now. We are both young viral men who need to enjoy life and all that it brings. I know I'm going to enjoy exploring some nice young or old pussy later and your ass will be fucking joining me. I can't even remember the last bitch you were with. Shit, I'm starting to wonder about you."

"Keep fucking around there and that pussy is going to be the death of you. Hear me when I tell you. Your ass is always chasing those skirts. One day your ass is going to learn. There is a time and place for everything. Most of these chicks looking for a quick come up and that is all you are to them."

"I'm not tripping because all I'm looking for is something to quickly come in… Their mouth, that is." O'Neal laughed.

"I take it you going to keep pressing me to go tonight until I actually agree to?"

"You know it," O'Neal replied.

"Fuck it! I'll be there. I'm telling you now so don't say I didn't warn you, I'm not staying that long though. You know that isn't my type scene anymore. Now, can we get back to some real shit? Cheese, go make them calls and get that out of the way now. No need to let that shit just simmer."

"Damn, nigga, can't even take a break for five fucking minutes, huh? Shit! We bringing in more paper then we ever imagined. When are you going to enjoy that? Shit, enjoy life. We going to handle things with them NY niggas. Don't worry, just chill."

Cheese got up and went outside to make the call. He knew regardless how much O'Neal pleaded or what he said, Money would still want him to follow through on what he'd asked. Anyone who knew Money or of him, knew well enough to know, when it was business, he was business. Time was everything and to him, money bought time.

"Y'all niggas, I swear," O'Neal mumbled in disbelief. He yelled downstairs, "Yo, Lil' Nep, we 'bout to be out! Let's go!" He turned back toward Money. "I'll see you tonight."

"Bet!"

CHAPTER 17

L T closely watched the front door waiting for his next victim to leave their home. He was in desperate need of cash and would do anything to accomplish getting it. He had already stolen from his family and had lost his dignity, so nothing else mattered to him anymore. Heroin was his family now. She was his mother, his daughter, his wife, and best friend.

As LT watched the front door, finally it opened and the elderly white couple exited their home. He patiently waited for them to get in their car and make their way down the street. Once the coast was clear, he made his way around to the back of the house. He moved quickly to get in the back door. The minute it opened, the alarm started to go off.

LT had breaking and entering down to a science. He knew there was not even a need to try to figure out the alarm code or defuse it. He had two minutes to be out of there before the police arrived in five. Being an ex-police officer, he knew burglary wasn't a high priority in the city. Especially one where the murder rate seemed more like the population of a small town. D.C. definitely lived up to its name of the murder capital.

LT didn't bother around with the small stuff within the house. He headed straight for the bedroom. In a span of a minute and a half the bedroom was stripped of any jewelry and for good measure, two high-priced paintings were also taken. Within a blur, he was out of the house and in the wind.

LT unloaded all his stolen goods and received a nice pay for them. The first thing he did afterward was head to his dealer so he could shoot up his profits. Food didn't matter to him nor did a stable home. Now, the only thing he lived for was getting high. He worked only to feed his habit.

LT entered the sky dome, an abandoned apartment building where addicts went to shoot up. Crack, heroin, PCP, it didn't matter the drug. If you were in the sky dome, you found someone there using whatever you needed. There was no talking or any conversations, only addicts getting high. He opened packet after packet and continually pushed it into his veins. Finally, he reached his state of ecstasy and calm.

"Police, everybody, get down on the ground NOW! Move, move... Get down!" LT heard as he lay on the urine-stained mattress.

He was powerless due to the effects of the drug. He knew he needed to try to make a run for it but his body wouldn't allow it. Helpless, he lay there and didn't even try to fight it. The officers swiftly moved throughout the house, rounding up as many addicts as possible.

One finally approached him. "Please place your hands behind your back," the officer said.

LT didn't move, respond back, or anything. He did nothing. He lay there staring lost into the air.

"Please, turn around and place your hands behind your back," the officer repeated with his hands on his gun holster.

LT still didn't acknowledge the officer. The other officers

noticed LT's non-compliance and started to make their way over to aid their fellow officers in case things got out of hand.

"Lionel, is that you?" an officer asked.

He didn't reply. The officer moved in closer to get a better look.

"Shit, LT that is you." He turned to another officer. "Look, take him in a squad car separately. I don't want him going in the wagon. When you get to the station, hurry up and get him booked, processed, and then put him in a separate holding cell. Make sure he isn't put in the bullpen with the rest of them. Okay?"

The officer didn't offer any resistance to his request. He replied, "No problem, Sarg, I'll take care of everything."

The officer picked LT up, cuffed him, and then escorted him out of the sky dome.

Once things were settled down at the police station, LT's old friend and former colleague made his way down to his cell to check up on him. So much time had elapsed that LT was down from his high and craving another fix.

"How are you doing? Are you feeling better?" the officer asked LT.

LT barely looked at him and if he did couldn't even make out who was talking to him. He was that far from reality the memories from his past had slowly faded away.

"I'll be better when y'all let me the hell up out of here," LT replied back coldly.

"That won't be happening any time soon. The earliest it will be is in the morning. But I am trying to pull as many strings as possible to get you out of here and into some type of rehab center. I know you won't get straight release."

LT started laughing. "Don't do me any favors! I don't need rehab. All I need is to get the fuck out of here!" he said, getting louder.

LT's response caught the officer off guard. "Excuse me?" he replied.

"Damn, what, all the donuts affecting your hearing? I said get me the fuck out of here!"

The officer couldn't believe what his old friend had to say. Instead of getting upset, he laughed it off.

"Still the same old LT, never know what to say out of his mouth and always cocky as hell, even when your back is up against the wall."

"Nigga, stop talking to me like you know me! Can I get my damn lawyer or something? Shit, anything besides sitting here rapping to you, because you can't seem to understand that I need to get the hell out of here. You want to talk the damn time away. Get me my lawyer."

"Let me calm myself down because it's obvious that you are on that shit harder than what I first thought. You have absolutely no sense of reality. If you did, you'd realize the situation you are in and the fact that I WAS offering you a helping hand. Do you even know who you are talking to? Do you even know who I am? Do yourself a favor and take a good look at me."

LT ignored his request.

"LOOK AT ME!" the officer yelled.

LT jumped. Nervous, he turned toward him to get a good look.

The officer continued, "You see this badge? You used to have one on your chest. You used to wear it proudly and when you did, I was one of your biggest fans. Now, you are a disgrace. Even when someone tries to go that extra mile for your ass, you shit on it the same way you've done your life. No wonder Denise left your sorry ass!"

The mention of his wife's name triggered memories of a past filled with pain caused by him. LT jumped up.

"Open your mouth about my wife again and I promise you, I'll do life in this bitch!"

The officer broke into nonstop laughter.

"Denise! Denise! I need you. Please come back to me, Denise," he mocked as if he was LT. "Yeah, you need to watch what you say out your mouth when you are comatose, playa. You've been mumbling the shit for the past two hours. I guess it don't pay to be high on that white horse all the time. Never know what you'll say or who is listening," he said still amused. He continued, "Look at you, why on earth would she want you? You've got to be kidding me. Denise is gone. Why would she want to be with a washed-up drug addict? That is so funny! You need to face facts. Denise has her a real man now. One who has a real job and who is probably hitting that real nice *fine* ASS!" He broke into laughter again.

"You muthafucka! I'll kill you. I swear to God, I'll fucking kill you!" LT could feel the room starting to spin. His temperature was at a boil. All of a sudden a sudden rush hit him. By the time he realized it was nausea, he had already thrown up all over the floor.

"Like I thought, you are nothing but a joke," the officer added.

"That's enough," a voice in the distance said.

The officer turned to see who it was. Once he saw it was his commanding officer in front of him, he left matters alone, but not before getting in one last parting shot.

"Thanks for the laughs!" he said as he walked away.

LT ignored the asshole's last comments and focused on a voice he knew, a voice he'd never forget.

"Lou, Lou, is that you?"

Lieutenant Ross appeared in front of LT. He didn't say a word. He looked him up and then down again, disgusted by the sight he saw before him. The man in front of him nowhere near resembled the young wide-eyed rookie he had taken under his wing years ago. In front of him, was a thirty-year-old man who had aged way beyond his years. The pain cried through his eyes. It hurt him to see LT this way.

The last time he had seen LT he was close to two hundred and thirty pounds. Now he stood in front of him barely one-third of that, probably not even one hundred and fifty soaking wet. If there was ever a poster boy for how drugs could ruin a life, the picture was being portrayed in front of Lieutenant Ross that day. With everything in him, Lieutenant Ross tried his hardest to act as if he was unaffected. He turned to the guard.

"This isn't the Comfort Inn and we don't make special requests. We treat all prisoners here alike. Transfer him back to the bullpen with everyone else waiting to go before the judge."

"Lou, you can't even look at me?" LT asked.

With his back turned to him, Lieutenant Ross said, "I don't know the person I see. You have five minutes to get yourself together."

"I get it. It's business as usual, huh, Lou? I lost my life because of the job but fuck that, huh, Lou! To you, I'm nothing but trash."

"No, trash is what is all over my cell floor and on your clothes. Trash is what caused you to lose your job. You are the man who chose the trash!" Lieutenant Ross said and then walked away.

LT stood at a loss for words. What Lieutenant Ross had said found a way through LT's dead exterior and cut straight to his heart. He knew Lieutenant Ross was right.

CHAPTER 18

Club Mystic was jumping. The club was packed from wall to wall. O'Neal was eating it up and living the high life. It was as if he had to let it be known to everyone that he was in the building. Though the streets knew exactly what role he played in society, no one truly understood the full extent. He was only known as a ruthless killer for the family. No one knew he was a head man.

Money had instilled in him the less the streets talked about you, the less the feds would inquire. The minute that target was on your chest, it would only be a matter of time before you were brought down. To Money, the only thing that mattered was the family name ringing out. If the streets respected the name, no one would dare to cross it because they knew what fate would be awaiting them. The face of family wouldn't matter.

O'Neal, however, didn't share the same sentiment. He hated that the only time people truly understood his true power was if it was time for them to meet their maker. That actually was how he made his bones in the street; his name rang out loud because of it. Everyone knew how twisted O'Neal could be in the murder game. The only problem was no one could ever put a face to the name. All that was known was if you were meeting him that would be the last person you were meeting.

O'Neal always felt as if he was being restricted. He wanted his name to ring out in the streets. He wanted to be feared and people to know exactly who they were fearing. He felt like he was young, and making money, so why not enjoy it. That was one of the major reasons why whenever he went out he made sure to have his cake and eat it too. It didn't matter the cost, he spent it. And no matter how much Money didn't want it to happen, people were starting to take notice.

Once Money made his way into the club, he headed straight to the bar. He wanted to get a good look and survey everything. Flash wasn't his style. He was more the observant type, a true student of the game and evaluator of people. Achieving cash was Money's high, but his ultimate goal was being able to enjoy the money he made later on in life. Money decided to get the night over with and make his way over to O'Neal's table. He knew it wouldn't have been too long before O'Neal started to call him to check and see exactly where he was anyway.

"Here he is. Nigga, it's about time your ass showed up," O'Neal said to Money.

"I told y'all I'd come through and I'm a man of my word," Money replied.

"My nigga! Come on and cop a squat. It's time to get this party started. What are you drinking on?"

"Don't trip, I'm cool. I already had a few at the bar."

"Nigga, please! You are drinking tonight. It's not like you party with us all the time. We are getting your ass blasted tonight!"

Money didn't even try to fight it. He didn't want to deal with the headache. He sat back and watched as O'Neal ordered up the bar. Money wasn't the only one watching O'Neal's actions. The minute the first bottle of champagne arrived, so did the ladies. O'Neal, being the ladies' man he was, was more than happy to oblige each of them.

"Damn, can you please save some for us? You all over here ordering up the whole bar; we are trying to drink too," one of them said with a little sass.

O'Neal laughed it off. It was something about a woman with a little attitude that turned him on. He hated for his woman to be all prissy. He lived the streets so it was only fitting that his woman had a little street in her too. Her attitude was perfect. Plus he had a thing for light-skinned women. She was slim but with ample body. She reminded you of Meagan Good, only with more attitude.

"Is that right, Miss? Well, I have the perfect solution to your problem then. Why don't you and your friends join us, that way you can drink with us?"

"With you, huh, why would we do that? We don't even know you," she replied.

"Smart lady! I can't really argue with that. Well, I'm O'Neal, and you are?"

"Starr."

"Yes, indeed you are. Well, it's nice to meet you, Starr. Well, now that you know me, how about you and your friends join us for drinks?"

She started laughing.

"All I know is your name, that doesn't classify as me knowing you."

"The longer you stand up, the harder that will be. How about you sit your ass down, then maybe we can work on changing that classification. What's the matter, your man going to get upset or something? I should have known. That's so cute. I like that. I like loyalty in a woman. Too bad for your man that I don't like to share my women."

"Who said I was yours?" she asked.

"You aren't yet, but I always get what I want," O'Neal replied.

"Is that right?"

"It came out the way it was supposed to so it must be. Look at me, being rude and shit," he said, dismissing Starr. "And your names are?"

"None of your damn business," Starr replied for them.

"My name is Mocha," one said with a smile.

"And mine is Nikki," the other jumped in.

"Well, it's nice to meet both of you. This is my man Nate and that's my man Cheese."

Cheese waved at them. Money acted as if he hadn't been introduced. He continued to sip his drink and count the minutes until it was time for him to exit the club. That was the only thing he was truly interested in. The ladies, on the other hand, had no clue of this. To them, it seemed as if their presence wasn't wanted at the table by him.

"Humph, whatever!" Nikki replied.

"Don't be like that, sweetie. You got to get to know him first to truly understand him. Sit, you never know, you could actually be the one to help him get that stick out of his ass," O'Neal said, trying to break the tension.

Everyone started laughing at the table except Money. Money turned to Cheese and he quickly stopped laughing too.

Quickly trying to change the subject, O'Neal said, "So, are y'all going to sit down or what? It's obvious your man isn't here if you have one because he damn sure isn't doing his job if he is. I'd be damned if I'd allow my woman to be all up in another nigga's face."

"First of all, no one allows me to do shit. I'm my own woman.

Second, I'm far from being up in your face and you know it. That's why you are trying so hard as hell to get me to sit down."

"Boo, we can go back and forth all night long. You know damn well you want to join us; I don't even know why you are faking. If you didn't, you wouldn't have gone out of your way to stop past our table and make your little comment. That was your way of opening the door to get an invitation. Come on, boo, don't let your ice breaker go to waste because you want to play too hard to get. It's just a couple of drinks. Besides, dinner will be tomorrow night."

Starr sat back and thought about it, acting as if she didn't hear the dinner comment. Mocha wasn't as patient. She moved Cheese over and sat down next to him. Starr couldn't help but look at her as if she was being betrayed.

"Shit, girl, my damn feet hurt. Y'all can continue to flirt but until one of you give up, I'm going to sit my fat ass down." She turned to Cheese "What are you drinking on? I need me something quick the way these two are going back and forth."

Cheese waved to the bartender to send over their waitress. She wasn't really trying to wait though. She picked up his drink as if she was about to take care of it for him.

"Whoa, slow down there, ma. This is a rum and Coke with Bacardi Select. That might be a little too much for you."

"Humph, nigga, please, you can keep that! I need me a real drink."

Right on cue, the waitress made her way to the table.

"Yeah, let me get a Blue Goose. That's Hpnotiq and Grey Goose and can you make sure they put a little bit of lime in it, too, please."

Nikki decided to put in her order as well. "Me too."

The waiter looked at Starr to see if she wanted something too.

"Fuck it. Let me get a Mimosa and I want a White Star. I don't want that cheap-ass Korbel or nothing."

O'Neal couldn't help but laugh. "Damn, a nigga had to go through all that to get you to sit down?"

"Forgive her; she can be like that at times. In time, you'll learn not to pay her any mind. We don't. That is just the diva in her. That is how we divas are. We crave attention," Nikki said.

"It's too late! I already have his full attention and you bitches are just jealous," Starr replied.

"Bitch, please! He is not my type!" Nikki snapped back. She quickly turned to O'Neal. "Please don't take that the wrong way, either."

"It's all good, sweetie. I can't be everyone's type."

"So what do y'all do? I don't just associate with anyone," Mocha asked, getting straight to the point.

"We work, sweetheart, that's all that matters," Money responded coldly.

"Okay, doesn't everyone? And that's not what I asked anyway; I asked what do you do?"

"We run shit, that's what we..."

"Nigga, have you lost your fucking mind?" Money quickly snapped at Cheese before he could finish speaking. "What have I told you about your mouth? Got damn!" Money took out a couple hundreds and threw them on the table. "Y'all have y'all a good night. O, we need to meet in the a.m."

"Nigga, I know you aren't rolling. You promised you were going to party with us tonight. It's still early as shit."

"I know but you know this isn't my scene. Plus y'all good, y'all got company now. I would only kill the mood. Just get up with me in the a.m. so we can rap."

O'Neal decided to leave matters alone. He knew Money wasn't going to change his mind. Plus, he had a new agenda for the night now.

"No problem, homie. I should have the report for you, too, so we'll know how to play everything. I'm sure it went smooth though so I wouldn't worry too much about it tonight. I know how you are."

Money started shaking his head. It was as if neither O'Neal nor Cheese got it. The first thumb of business was to never discuss it in front of any outsiders. No one is who they seem to be and everyone is out to replace you. That is the only way to think if you wanted to survive.

CHAPTER 19

BC sat back and observed the whole scene that played out in front of him. The streets definitely weren't wrong about this one. As first reported, there were new players in town. They weren't what BC was expecting, however. By the looks of them, they were fairly young cats to be trying to set up a deal. This alarmed BC that it was definitely something more than what was being shown. Though Money and O'Neal proved age wasn't but a number in this game, they weren't the norm, either. Young cats were coming up and not that fast.

The five of them stood on the corner of Kansas Avenue and Thirteenth Street in Northwest Washington, D.C. By their positioning it was easy to pick out the muscle from the brains. One nigga never moved from the stoop. Two of them were on the street overlooking everything. Then there were another two who must have been the ones putting the word out in the street that they were trying to get in touch with Money. There wasn't too much outside of that going on.

As BC was about to pick up his cell and call in his report, there was a knock on his window that startled him. He turned briskly toward the passenger side of his car with his pistol firmly aimed for the target. It was then he realized the foe before him was Joey. He lowered his weapon and unlocked the door.

"Nigga, do you value your life? You must don't, any time you knock on my damn window unannounced. Don't ever walk up on me like that again. You lucky I didn't start squeezing first."

"I thought O or Cheese would have got in contact with you to let you know the deal. They sent me up here to set up the meet with these niggas."

"Well, you thought wrong. I haven't talked to O since early this morning. So I take it Money game to do business with these cats," BC replied.

"That is the way it looks. So, what's the deal with these niggas? Do you think it's going to be a problem or smooth sailing?"

"It's jive hard to say. On the outside it doesn't really look like much of shit. They definitely don't seem like a threat but that is just the appearance. We don't have the slightest idea who the fuck they working for nor that person's capability. It's too much uncertainty for me."

"How do you know they aren't running shit and trying to cop to set up a shop up north?"

BC pointed them out.

"Look at them. They are a couple of little youngins, really. They aren't running shit. Someone is pulling the strings and even with that, I can't see anyone sending them down here to set everything up by themselves, either. Whoever is pulling the strings to their operations has to be close by."

"Well, for our sake, I hope you are wrong because Money damn sure is not waiting around for whoever to show himself."

BC started to grin.

"Boy, I tell ya, that nigga Money is all about that cash, ain't he? It don't matter how many bodies might drop because of this shit right here. As long as we getting that paper everything is alright in his book, huh, man?"

"Why are you sitting over there like you don't already know the answer to that?" Joey asked.

BC shook his head. "I want this shit on the record that I said it, I don't trust it. It's something about these cats I don't trust. Look at them, it's like they not even trying to hide. They all out in the open with their shit, who does that? Who comes to another man's house and shits on his sofa? It's like they are purposely trying to be disrespectful. I don't know many folks out here who are like that and not have a hidden agenda.

"Shit, I know the Cardoza family name still ringing from D.C. to New York all the way to Cali. It's like they straight on some disrespect-type shit, not even giving a fuck. Heart or no heart, it don't even matter. They calling us out and niggas don't do that. They might send word down the pipeline that they interested but no, they want everyone to know that they looking for us. They are straight broadcasting the shit. Watch what I tell you, it's more to this whole situation than what we know right now. This shit going to fuck around and blow up in our face if we not careful about how we handle things. Watch what I tell you!"

"I'm with you but there ain't shit I can do about it. Ain't shit you can do about it, either! If the man wants me to set up the business connect with them, then that's exactly what he is going to get. If he wants you to get them the fuck out of town, then that's exactly what you'll do. We all have our role to play and I'm here to play my position," Joey replied.

"Yeah, I guess. Honestly, I'm not even trying to hear that shit. Let's get this shit out of the way. The more I start to think about it the more my fucking stomach starts to turn," BC said.

Both of them exited the car and headed for what seemed to be the head man. They didn't want to be too obvious and bring any attention to themselves. Once they were close enough, they swiftly approached him.

"Yo, son, can I help you?" one of the guys, supposedly the

muscle, quickly said once he noticed who they were trying to approach.

Before anyone could react or knew what had happened, BC had already taken action. He released two shots in the air with each of them hitting their designated targets. Then with his other hand, he aimed his other nickel-plated nine squarely at the head man's head. In a span of two seconds, BC had crippled their security, and had his sights on the head man and the two youngins who they had putting the word out on the street.

"Do I have your attention now?" BC said.

The head one shook his head in acknowledgment.

"Good, now word on the street is that y'all going all around town looking for someone. How can we help you?"

"I take it one of y'all niggas must be the kid they call Money."

Joey quickly replied, "No, neither of us is. But if you don't tell us what it is the fuck you want, you don't have to worry about who the fuck Money is because you'll never meet him."

"To cut the small talk, my boss would like to do business with him. We have a mutual friend who suggested that he'd be able to help us out with a little situation. Due to unfortunate circumstances; we are in the market for product. The word on the street is Money is one of few who can handle the type of order we'd need."

"How much are we talking?" Joey asked.

"I'm not at liberty to say," the head man replied.

"Then what the fuck am I talking to you for then. Who is at liberty to say?"

"Patience, my friend, how much product we are interested in all depends upon the quality of the product you supplying We'd need to test the market with it first to see if this is something we really want to explore further or if we need to go another route. If it's what we hear, then we'd be ready to explore a permanent shipment up north."

"What you hear, huh? Who are you getting your information from?"

"I'm not at liberty to say."

"It doesn't seem like you are at liberty to say shit. I wonder if that is by design," BC replied.

"It doesn't even matter. That's neither here nor there. Bottom line, fellas, we don't do business with strangers. If your boss wants to do business with us, then he'll need to do it in person," Joey added.

"We can respect that but there is a time and place for everything. I'm prepared to get a key now and take back up top. As I said before, if it's what we hear, then we'll be calling."

"If it's not your boss calling, then don't even bother to pick up the fucking phone."

The head man nodded in agreement. "So how do we do this?"

"Easy, give me a number and we'll be in contact with you. Once we contact you, we'll let you know where you can pick up the product."

He gave Joey a contact number to seal the deal. Joey then tore a dollar bill in half and handed it to him.

"You are going to need this. Once we call, you'll need to give the serial number as soon as you answer that phone. I don't care if you miss it by one number, you do and the call ends. Once you verify the number, we'll give you a time to meet for later that day so you can pick up your package. Inside it will be the product and a number for you to call if you want to re-up. It's a pager. All you'll need to do is enter the last four digits of your serial number and a number to reach you. Someone will get back to you at that time and set up the meet with your boss. I hope you got all that because I'm not repeating myself."

"How much?" the head man asked.

"Fourteen per so that's fifty-six."

"I said one key, not four," he quickly replied.

"I'm glad to see you can add. One key isn't going to do shit. You want to test the quality of our product on the streets—fine, then test it. Now, what are you going to do? Your boys over there look like they need some medical attention as soon as possible."

The head man nodded in agreement.

"Good, we need one-fourth up front and then bring the rest to the deal."

"You aren't getting any of our money until we have the product. We might be young but business never changes, no matter how old you are."

"I'm not out here for my health, nor a history lesson. You can do either one of two things, come up with fourteen K up front or we walking the fuck off and you can try to cop elsewhere," Joey replied.

The head man didn't want to call Joey's bluff. He motioned for one of his runners to get the cash from their stash. He turned and went inside the building. He returned with a gym bag and handed it to Joey.

"I hope the lil' nigga can count. If this is anything less than fourteen, we'll be back and it won't be a pleasure visit. Now if you don't mind, kindly slide your pistols over this way so we can be out. I have a problem about turning my back toward lil' niggas I don't know. It doesn't sit too well with me."

The head man lifted up his shirt to show that he was bare. The runners followed suit and did the same. Joey shook his head in disbelief.

"I'm going to need you to get it together. Who the fuck travels bare? I thought y'all New York cats knew how to properly conduct business."

Joey turned to head toward the car.

"Have a good night," BC said, then turned and walked away too.

CHAPTER 20

Money left the club clueless as to what he was going to do. It was obvious that O'Neal craved the spotlight and needed for everyone to know what role he played in society. That frustrated Money so much. He could never understand why it was so hard for O'Neal to fall back and enjoy the money they were bringing in. It was like he didn't understand, attention attracted police.

Police attracted the DEA and once the DEA had your photo on their bulletin board, it was only a matter of time before you and your entire organization were spending the rest of your life in a four-by-six box. That was not the life Money was trying to lead. If there was one thing you could take to learn from Mario, it was that you could retire from the game. Though a very slim one, it was actually a possibility.

Money knew that Mario was a special breed. A lot of the things he accomplished would be by no other. But Money was more a student of the game versus anything else. He saw how Mario had a very small inner circle. There were only two people he'd deal with until his trust built up in Money. If you weren't one of those two people, you weren't talking to him and you damn sure weren't in his presence. He never attended any deals or ever discussed any prices. He was like a myth in the streets. His name rang out loud and clear throughout the streets, but you couldn't find anyone who could ever match his face with the name.

Mario wasn't flashy and didn't flaunt his wealth. Though he was worth millions, he looked like your average hardworking person. He could stand next to an employee from Home Depot and you probably wouldn't be able to tell the difference between the two of them. His appearance clearly disguised the cold-blooded killer he actually was.

The police had tried for years to try to infiltrate Mario's organization and each time they were unsuccessful. It didn't matter how many cases they'd built on low-level dealers or clientele, the trail always stopped with someone and that person was nowhere near important. Once they took the rap and did the years, someone else was quickly slid into their position. There was truly no way to flip anyone against Mario.

The streets couldn't dethrone him, either because no one knew enough to get to him. It's hard to cut the head off of the snake if you don't even know what the snake looks like or where it is. That is what made Mario one in a million. In this game, there were only two guaranteed ways out and Mario found a third.

Money couldn't help but to think if maybe it was time to step aside and get out of the game while he still had the option. He could cut his losses and turn everything over to O'Neal. Things probably would be better that way. He wouldn't have to worry about what either O'Neal or Cheese were saying and who they were saying it around. If they wanted to be out in the open, it was fine because nothing would come back to him. He had enough money saved up to start a new gig. A hustle was a hustle to Money. It didn't matter if you were selling CDs, crack, or shoes. The only problem was he never really pondered life outside the game. There was nothing set up for him to do. That was the only thing he didn't truly plan and plan thoroughly for a smooth transition.

Money pulled his SUV over to the side of the road and sat back and thought. The sound of his cell phone ringing broke him out of his temporary daze.

"What's up?"

"Everything is done uptown," Cheese said

"Where are you? I know you aren't in the club because I don't hear any music."

"Naw, I stepped outside for a few. I'm in my car. My son texted me while I was in the club and you know family take precedence. I came out there to talk to him and make sure everything was alright."

"Yeah, I can dig that. So is everything straight? What's up with the letter of intent? Did he decide where he is going to sign?"

"Yeah, he decided. He's going to go ahead and sign with G-Town and play at home. For a minute I thought we were going to lose him to Boston College but everything is all good now," Cheese replied.

Money made sure no one ever talked straight business over the phone. If it was something that couldn't wait, like this, then they talked in code using sports analogies. Signing with George-town instead of Boston College meant the N.Y. boys decided to take the offer instead of BC having to get rid of them. Money never knew who was listening to their calls so if someone was, they'd have to work to figure out what was being said.

"That's music to my ears. You know how BC can ruin a good player."

"That I do," Cheese replied.

The bright red and blue police lights behind Money's truck diverted his attention.

"Look here, I have Christmas lights. I'll get up with you tomorrow sometime after I head up to T-Mobile."

"That's a bet."

Money hung up the phone. Usually he wouldn't have tripped because his truck was legally registered. However, he rarely traveled without a pistol nowadays. You could never be too cautious was his motto. If this turned into more than a regular traffic stop, he knew he was up shit's creek.

Money made sure to make reference to Cheese regarding going to the T-Mobile store. The he'd know that everyone needed to dump their Nextel cell phones and switch to the T-Mobiles. None of them ever programmed key numbers into their phone books under a specific name. Instead, they programmed numbers they didn't know under fictitious names and memorized one another's numbers.

Money saw fit to always have a backup plan for his backup plans. That's why it was so frustrating to him that he didn't have a backup plan for when he decided enough was enough and get out of the game. That should have been the first thing he started preparing for once they started making major money. But that soon would be a mistake that would be taken care of as well.

The officer took his time approaching the car. Money didn't panic. He figured the officer was running his plates to make sure the truck wasn't stolen. Then he noticed another police car pulling up. That was a sign that things weren't that good. The first officer shined his car spotlight into Money's truck. He then approached the car with his hand readily on his sidearm in cased it was needed.

Money rolled down his window. "Is there a problem, officer?"

"I was going to ask you the same question. You've been sitting here for the past five minutes, sir, is everything okay with you?"

"I'm fine, officer, I had a lot on my mind and decided to pull over by the side of the road and think. I didn't know that would be a problem."

"It's no problem at all, license and registration, please, sir," the officer said.

"No problem, officer," Money said as he reached into his glove compartment.

He noticed the officer trying to look over his shoulder to see if anything suspicious was in his glove box. Money tried not to laugh. He knew the officer had already run his tags and struck out when he found out the vehicle wasn't stolen. He calmly handed him the requested information. The officer reviewed it, then turned and looked toward the second patrol car.

Once the other two officers were close to Money's car, the officer asked, "Mr. Rodgers, would you please exit the vehicle?"

"I don't see why that is necessary. Again, I was sitting here thinking. There is no problem."

"Please exit the vehicle, sir!" the officer reiterated.

Money decided to go ahead and not protest. He didn't want this situation to turn into something it didn't have to be. D.C. police would beat your ass in a minute and most of the time it was without a viable reason. Money wasn't going to give them a reason to.

"Sir, I detect alcohol on your breath. Have you been drinking?"

"I had two drinks earlier but I'm not drunk, if that is what you are asking. I went out to dinner with a friend and had two glasses of wine," Money replied.

"Dinner, huh, that's funny, I didn't know they served dinner at Club Mystic."

"Maybe you need to go inside then, so you can see. In addition to being a club, they also have a private section for you and your loved one to enjoy a meal."

"Maybe I will, thanks for the suggestion. If you aren't drunk, Mr. Rodgers, then I'm sure you won't have a problem with taking a breathalyzer," the officer shot back.

"I don't have a problem with that, however, there is no need for me to take one since I am not drunk. I already told you, I had two drinks at dinner. I am not drunk. I am fine. Also, even if I was, I was pulled over to the side of the road. I was not driving. The last time I checked, there is no law against sleeping off the alcohol, if you are drunk. You would think that would be the responsible thing to do. That seems like the responsible thing to do. There are thousands of homeless people who sleep on the streets of D.C. intoxicated every night. I don't see you bothering any of them. Instead, you chose to bother me and I'm not even intoxicated."

The officer couldn't help but laugh at Money's wit.

"Mr. Rodgers, if I knew you were at Club Mystic, it's obvious I followed you to this point. Meaning, you had to drive to get from the club to here which would mean you were indeed driving under the influence."

"So, let me get this straight, you were so convinced that I was driving my vehicle while under the influence that you decided to wait until I pulled my truck over to the side of the road to question me. What sense does that make? Why not pull me over intoxicated once I left the parking lot? Gentlemen, I'm sure you already know this won't stand up in court. Why don't we cut our losses and call it a night."

"Well, I guess we will have to see now, won't we, Mr. Rodgers?" the officer said.

Money knew this situation wasn't going to turn out in his favor. He decided not to press the issue any longer. He turned around and placed his hands behind his back. Whether he took the breathalyzer or not, he knew they would have made sure he never passed it. And none of it had anything to do with the fact he could have possibly been drunk. The test was their way to get him in custody. Once he was in custody, then they'd have cause to search his truck and hope to find something to place a real charge on him.

"As much as I'd like to continue matching wits with you, Nathaniel Rodgers, you are under arrest for driving under the influence of alcohol," the officer said as he placed the hand-cuffs around his wrists.

CHAPTER 21

There was something about Starr that drew O'Neal to her. It didn't help that the chemistry between the two of them was unbelievable. He had come across many different women already in his short lifespan but none of them could keep his full undivided attention like Starr could and definitely not as fast. None of them left a lasting impression on him outside of what happened in the bedroom, and that only lasted until the next one came along. Starr was different. Maybe it was her inner fire, her pizzazz, or persona. Whatever it was, O'Neal wasn't quite sure. What was evident was that he wanted her to be a stable part of his life and that was scary.

"Why are you staring at me?" Starr asked O'Neal as they were sitting on the couch in his living room.

"Is it a problem? And I'm not staring at you, I'm merely mesmerized by your beauty."

"Nigga, please! You better try that shit on one of those other clueless bitches that you deal with. I've seen and heard them all."

"Why does everything have to be about game with you? It's like a nigga can't never be genuine. And tell the truth, naw, it's all got to be about game."

"You damn right and I don't know why you are fronting! I know your type. The only thing you are concerned about is getting the pussy. Once I let you taste this, then the chase is over and you will move on to the next bitch for a new pursuit. Y'all niggas are so predictable."

"The next bitch, huh? You are funny. I'll definitely give you that. First, let's be adults about this, I'm going to get the pussy regardless and we both know that. If I wasn't, then you damn sure enough wouldn't be over here with me right now. So please believe me, if it was about some ass, then there wouldn't be any need to game you right now. Second, I don't let any bitch come to my crib. Sorry, I'm not that open with where I lay my head. If you want to be even more honest, you are the only chick to step foot in my domain. I'm not into relationships. I'm your run-of-the-mill friendly-fuck type of guy and those take place at hotels or at the chick's spot, not mine."

"Is that right? Okay, let's say you aren't full of it. Why am I so different? You swear up and down it's not about game and this facade I see is not an image but rather reality. Why me and not them? I mean we just met. You barely even know me."

O'Neal started to become uncomfortable with expressing himself. He was in unsheltered waters.

"What's up with all the questions? Damn! I feel like I'm in an interrogation or something. Just take the shit as it comes."

"Is that right? Okay, I can easily get my purse and head for the front door if you like and you can take that shit as it come. I keep telling you, I'm not one of these other bitches you used to dealing with. If you are real with yours, then you shouldn't have a problem with answering my questions. I don't deal with secrets and my life isn't a mystery, so yours shouldn't be, either. That includes your feelings."

O'Neal remained silent and stared at her. She gathered her stuff and got up to make her way to the front door. O'Neal didn't stop her. He sat back and continued to watch trying to call her bluff.

Finally he realized she wasn't bluffing. He quickly jumped up. "Hey hey, come on now! See, that right there is what makes you different." O'Neal tried to get to her before she was too close to the door, in case she still wanted to leave. She gave him a look as if she was unfazed.

He continued, "Look, I don't know what exactly it is about you. I mean it's a lot of different things. Mainly though I love how you don't take any shit. That shit right there really gets to me. You aren't the type of woman to take any shit from no one. I need a down chick in my life and not just any ole bitch that is out for self. You seem like the type of woman where a man don't make or break her. You are going to be alright regardless. I respect that. Plus, you are definitely a challenge. Every man loves a good challenge."

"Yeah, but that is only until it's not a challenge anymore," she replied under her breath.

O'Neal's cell phone started ringing. He looked at the number.

"Look, please don't leave. I really want to finish this conversation, but I have to take this call."

"Excuse you? You aren't serious, are you? I know you don't want me to stay here and wait for you to finish talking to some bitch! You've really got the game fucked up. I knew you were off the deep end with the bullshit, but I didn't know you were this far gone," she snapped.

O'Neal became frustrated. "Damn it! Do you ever let up? This is business!" He paused to answer the phone. "Aye look, hold tight a minute," he said into the handset. He turned to Starr. "Now you are starting to piss me off with all this. I'm not going to keep telling you, what is what. In a minute you can believe what you want. I told you, I like you, shit, I like you a lot, but a sucker for you I will not be. I've never been an ass kisser and now isn't the time for me to start, either. If you feel the need to roll, fuck it, go about your business. I have a call I need to take."

O'Neal went into his bedroom.

"What's the deal?"

"If you were busy, you should have told me. Anyway, I don't trust it. There is something that doesn't seem right. These cats were posted up and they weren't even trying to hide it. I mean, I know our name has to be ringing loud up north. It's like they didn't give a fuck. No one is that stupid, O. I think we're being played. I really do," BC said.

"Homie, you know how you get. You are always overthinking shit. You overthink everything actually."

"Yeah, but I'm also usually right when I do. I'm saying, I hope I am wrong but that isn't what I get paid to be. You pay me to watch your back and make sure everything is everything and I'm telling you, these cats up to something and I can smell it."

"Okay. What, feds?"

"I don't think that but you never know. I know one thing; I don't have me still being on the street if they were. I had to kneecap two of them to get the man's attention—it wasn't a game. This nigga was disrespecting us like we weren't shit. That shit was really starting to bother me. And the kicker was he had no pistol. Who does that? Come on, I'm really not feeling this whole setup. I mean, if it pans out, cool, but I really don't trust it."

"Did they at least take the deal?"

"Shit, did we really leave them a choice? Of course they took the deal, and by the way, why was I the last to find out about Joey?" BC asked.

"That was my bad. I got caught up and forgot to place the call through. I meant to send word to you. Well, look, let me get up off this phone. I'm jive been rude. I'll send word up top and see how Money wants to play things. Until then, keep your eyes open. If you see something out of line, go ahead and take care of it and I'll clean it up later. You know how we do."

"Do I ever! Don't worry, I'm on it."

"That's what's up. Get up with me tomorrow and we'll sit down and map this shit out," O'Neal said before they hung up the phone.

O'Neal knew BC often overreacted to every situation, most of the times he was correct in his reactions. If BC was having a funny feeling about something, then it was something concrete and needed to be taken into consideration. The more he started to ponder the situation, the more he thought maybe it was better to eliminate the possible threat and not deal with the headache. However, he wasn't sure if Money would go for that. Though these cats were really testing the waters and everyone's patience, they weren't overly disrespectful. Plus, this was just the avenue they needed to put them on a major supplier level which would bring in even more cash.

"Fuck!" O'Neal yelled.

He was about to pick up his phone to call Money when Starr walked into the room.

"Is everything okay?" she asked.

During the span of his conservation, that quickly he had forgotten all about Starr. The stress of his job could do that to him. It wasn't as if a mistake had caused a sales figure to go down or a client to be upset but rather a mistake could cost you your life in this business.

"Naw, everything is cool. I just have a couple things that I need to map out," he replied, brushing off the situation.

She came over and started to massage his neck. She was just what he needed to keep his mind off the stress.

"I know I'm probably added to that stress, huh?"

"Naw, boo, not really. Actually, you are my only bright spot right now."

"What's wrong?" she asked inquisitively.

"Nothing, just some shit with work, that's all. It's nothing too serious."

"Well, that sounds like something to me. Do you want to talk about it? Maybe I can help."

O'Neal knew better not to discuss work with anyone outside of the family. That was a cardinal sin but a part of him wanted a companion with whom he could share his thoughts regardless of the situation. To him, Starr had those wifey qualities. She was a down chick so he knew she was hip to the game in one way or another. However, instead of freeing his mind totally of the stress by talking about it, he chose not to and bit his tongue.

"It's all good, boo, don't worry about it! I'll figure something out."

Starr knew that when he was ready to totally let her in, he would. So she didn't fight the matter but rather gave him the space he needed and left it alone. She knew that would be more appreciated and maybe the next time would lead him to not keeping it in. She was trained well in knowing which battles to fight and when to fight them.

"Okay, well let's not discuss work. How about you sit back and let me help you to relax."

O'Neal couldn't help but grin at the sound of that. The entire time at the club all he did was envision fucking her.

"And how do you plan on helping with that?"

"Actions speak louder than words."

Starr seductively licked her lips and then strategically planted them over O'Neal's body. The way his body flinched to each spot she caressed, she knew he was no longer worried about anything. She had his full and undivided attention. If that wasn't evidence enough, then the sight of the bulge escaping from his pants was more than enough. She massaged the tip of his dick through his pants which was enticing him more.

She slowly unzipped his pants and pulled it out. Slowly she massaged it while she continued to kiss his neck. Once she made her way down to his hardness, she didn't bother to toy with him. She placed him inside her mouth. The warmth of her mouth sent shockwaves through O'Neal's spine. Knowing she was in total control, she didn't rush a thing. She slowly licked up and down his shaft, then placed all of him inside her mouth.

It was becoming unbearable. He tried everything to fight the urge of exploding. Even when he'd try not to think about how good everything was feeling, all he pictured was being inside her. It wasn't until his cell phone started to ring that everything came to a crashing halt.

"Shit!" he yelled frustrated.

He knew it could only be something related to business, and

pleasure was never to take precedence over business. He had to answer the call.

Starr could sense what O'Neal was thinking "Oh no, we are busy," she said as she continued to explore and twirl her tongue around his dick.

O'Neal knew it wasn't that simple. It took everything in him to do so, but he moved her off of him slightly to stop the festivities.

"I can't. I have to take this call."

"What's up?" O'Neal spat into the phone.

"Yo, we have problems in the house. I just got a call from Ma and she doing pretty bad. Her and Pops got into it and the police were called," Cheese said.

"What else is going to go wrong tonight? Do I need to send someone to bail Pops out?"

"Naw, let's hold tight on that for now. I don't have all the info on that situation as of yet. But I'm sure we'll need to send someone more than likely. I'll keep you posted."

"That's what's up. I'm in the house if you need me."

"Bet. Aye, and you need to quit messing with them Nextels and switch to T-Mobile. I was trying to get in contact with you when I first got wind of the situation, but your shit kept hitting the voicemail first. How many times do I have to tell you their phones are some shit?"

"I might just do that, homie," O'Neal replied.

"Well, let me go, I'll get up with you later when I get more info."

"Bet."

O'Neal turned and looked at Starr. "Now, where were we?"

"We weren't anywhere. I'm through fucking with you for the night. I don't know any man that turns down pussy staring him in the face to answer the phone. At least I don't know any straight man that would do that, that is."

O'Neal laughed off her comment and paid no attention to it. He walked over to her and tried to kiss her.

"O'Neal, stop! I have to get my phone. It's business," she said.

He broke out into laughter.

"I see someone has jokes."

They both shared a laugh, then before they knew it, were back at it again.

CHAPTER 22

Money sat aimlessly wanting to be released. In the bullpen, that's all you could do was wait. In a sense, jail would have been better. At least while confined in your cell, you could pass the time with ideal chitchat with your cellmate. In the bullpen, you tried to stay clear of everyone. It didn't matter who you knew in there. You still sat there and said nothing. It made no sense to tip the police off to whether you were in the life or not. Why do their jobs for them? The alternative, sit down with a closed mouth and wait.

It was going on four hours now and Money hadn't heard anything from his lawyer or been in front of a judge. He figured the police were trying to prolong time hoping to find something more concrete to charge him with. He knew the DUI charge wasn't going to stick and even if it did, the name Nathaniel Rodgers was nowhere in the system. The most he'd get as a first-time offender who pulled his own vehicle over to the side of the road without warning would be probation. Money got up and headed toward the bars.

"What's the status with my lawyer?" he asked the guard.

He kindly ignored the question.

"Look, it's going on, what, four hours now and I still haven't heard a word. This right here isn't going to work. I need to place another call to my lawyer. I know my rights."

The guard continued to ignore Money as if he didn't hear him. Though he knew he was being blackballed, he also didn't want to make the situation any worse. He knew the more he pressed the issue, the more the guard would be an asshole about it. This would result in his stay possibly being even longer. D.C. had its ways of keeping you detained longer than you should have been kept.

Instead of making a big fuss he turned around and went back to his bench to continue to sit and wait. That's when he noticed a pair of eyes guyed on him by another inmate. Money recognized the man from somewhere, but couldn't place where exactly he knew him from.

The man's clothes were run-down, eyes bloodshot red and the sign *going through withdrawal* was written all over his face. It was obvious he was an addict. It had been a long time since Money had done any hand-to-hand deals so it wasn't likely that is where he possibly had seen him. Maybe he resembled someone from his past. He wasn't too sure. What he was sure of was how the man looked at him. It was as if he was staring through Money's soul. The pain in the man's eyes spoke volumes. No matter how much Money tried not to look at him or say anything, it was hard because something about him just bothered Money.

Money knew this wasn't the place to deal with it. Instead he did as the guard did him and ignored the unwanted looks. He had other things to worry about than to concentrate too hard on that. How to deal with O'Neal was priority number one. Money knew it was only a matter of time before it would come down to their friendship, or maybe even their lives.

O'Neal was a grown man and it was becoming clearer that it would be even harder for him to be contained. Money pondered giving everything up and retiring on to something else in life.

Maybe it was time. Why not get out of the game while it was still an option for you. It wasn't as if Money was starving for cash. He wasn't the flashy type so a lot of the bread they had made over the years he had stashed away. He could take his savings and maybe start a chain of restaurants, barbershops, a clothing line or something. Anything seemed better at that point. It would guarantee that his permanent residence wouldn't become a state facility due to someone else's ego. He knew O'Neal would jump at the opportunity to run the show.

Though they always tried to never let it get in the way, ego was a monster in itself to deal with, and everyone knew O'Neal had a huge one. And though he never admitted it, living in the shadow of Money always laid deep in the back of his mind. The whole plan seemed like a win- win situation for everyone.

"Nathaniel Rodgers!" the guard called, breaking Money from his train of thought. "Your lawyer is here."

Without hesitation, Money jumped up ready to be on the move. He was escorted to a private interviewing room so that he could discuss things with his lawyer, JayMarr Dixon.

He was Money's friend from high school and had the book smarts to get out of the hood and the street smarts to survive in corporate America. The only problem was he lived for the streets. Money found a way to give him the best of both worlds. He decided to put JayMarr through college and law school. You could never have too many good lawyers. Especially one whom you could honestly say you trusted. JayMarr's loyalty ran deep. Money knew he would never screw him over.

As Money entered the room, JayMarr stood up and gave him some dap and a brotherly hug to greet him.

"How are you holding up?" JayMarr asked.

"Better the minute you get me out of here. What's the deal on the holdup?"

"It's a stall tactic. As I'm sure you already know, they are trying to buy time to find a charge. The minute we step foot in front of the judge, the DUI charge will be dropped. They didn't do a breathalyzer or even a basic sobriety test at that. I pulled a couple of strings and got the bail hearing moved up. It should be in about an hour, so they should be bringing you upstairs soon. I wouldn't worry too much, you'll be released shortly."

"Good, good! I was a little worried about the search of the truck though. I knew they were hoping to find something for more concrete charges, so I wasn't too sure what measure was being taken to search it."

"There wasn't anything more than a burner in there, right?" JayMarr asked.

"Naw, that was all. Hold up, how you know?"

"That's what you pay me to do. We have someone on the inside at the pound. They handle the searches and seizures for impounded cars. You know the minute I got the call, I placed the call to him to make sure that anything that was found, wasn't found. I needed to know all that was really in there to pay out on."

"My nigga! So how much is this going to cost?"

"For a burner, no more than two g's to be on the safe side, but I'll stamp all that."

"Cool, once you get word, let me know so I can put someone on that drop."

"Okay, well, sit tight. You'll be out of here in a few. I'm going to see if I can get them to take you straight up instead of back into the bullpen, and you can wait in the holding area. That should speed things up a little bit more too."

"No problem," Money replied.

JayMarr headed out the room and instructed the guard he was done. Since his bail hearing wasn't far away, they didn't fight JayMarr's request and took Money to the waiting area. Once Money got upstairs, however, he saw he wasn't alone. He had company. As fate would have it, the same man who couldn't keep his eyes off of Money was waiting there. The minute he saw Money walking down the corridor toward him, his eyes remained glued to him. It was as if he was only waiting for Money to get in range to do something.

The guard sat Money down next to him and then cuffed him to the holding bar. Money was a tad bit nervous because he knew he was securely cuffed to the bench, but wasn't too sure about his counterpart. Maybe since they couldn't find a charge for Money, they'd find another way to take care of the problem. Though it was a stretch, Money's mind was all over the place.

The guard was no longer in the immediate area. He had walked over to shoot the breeze with his colleagues. Money tried to ignore the thoughts that were going through his mind as well as the onslaught of looks. However, that was easier said than done. It wasn't long before Money gave in to temptation.

"Can I help you with something, champ?" Money asked.

The anonymous man smirked.

"Can you help me, huh? Naw, partner, I think you helped enough."

"Excuse me? Do we know each other or something?" Money asked.

"Yeah, I guess you can say that."

"Look here, partner, all these smart-ass comments you throwing out there aren't necessary and soon are going to cause you problems you aren't ready to deal with. So how about we cut all that smart shit out and you say what's on your mind. You've been all up in my grill since I stepped foot up in this camp. It's obvious you've got something you want to get off your chest."

"I'm going to have a problem, huh, man? Look at me, does it look like I don't already have problems. Who gives a fuck about a few more? I damn sure don't." He paused. "You really don't remember me, do you? That's funny, because I will never forget either you or your partner."

That comment threw Money off guard because it was certain whoever the unknown man was he knew exactly who Money was and all about him.

"Slim, I think you've got me mixed up with someone else," Money said, trying to throw the gentleman off.

It wasn't working. "Fuck if I do. Nigga, you don't realize something, I will never forget the man who cost me my family and took my life. I don't give a shit how old you get. I will never forget you. I find it so ironic that you searched long and hard for your ass years ago, but could never find you, only to end up in the one place I wanted to put you."

Money didn't reply. He wasn't going to give himself up, just in case.

"I'll give you credit though, you were smart. You knew better than to kill a cop. Instead you decided to destroy him."

Money tried to concentrate hard on the resemblance but the guy's face still didn't ring a bell. Money assumed he remembered him from his days of bleeding the block when he was on the corner but the way he was talking, that wasn't it. It was something much more, something deeper.

"Look here, old man, you chose the life you live, not me. If you want to blame anyone for your life, start by looking in the mirror first. Plus, I'm far from the boy I was back then, so please believe you need to watch who the fuck you are talking to," Money said annoyed.

"I chose it, you say. Is that right? It's obvious you still don't know who I am or maybe you're the coldhearted bastard I thought you were. Let me go ahead and do you a favor and help you out. Does the name Detective Lionel Taylor ring a bell?"

Everything started to make sense. It all came back to Money fast. Though it had been many years, he could never forget that name. He remembered carefully planning the hit. LT could see the light go off in Money's eyes.

Money didn't know how to reply. Everything the man said was true. All he could muster was, "The game is the game and there is no changing that. You chose to be a part of it just like I did. You played your role, I played mine. It's as simple as that," Money said coldly, then turned away.

"Let me tell you something. I see through you. I can see that it's eating you up inside. You can't bear to look at me. It's killing you, too, because when you do, it makes you take responsibility for your action. It makes you look into the mirror and see what your actions caused. I'm glad too. I want you to take a good look at me. I want you to see what the poison you push every day does to a person, and I don't want you to ever forget this image.

"You see, I accept the fact that I'm lost! My life is already gone. I'm just waiting my time. It happened the minute you stepped foot in my apartment. From that point on, I was dead. Though it wasn't with a bullet, you killed me in other ways. But see, now maybe I can save someone else's life. Now you get to see how dirty your hands are."

Money turned away. Though he didn't want to admit him, it was true.

"Look at me, damn it! You are a man now, remember. You are far from the boy you were back then. A man faces his demons. Turn and face me. See, you bastards push that shit day in and day out but never take the time to see the consequences of your actions. You don't see how it destroys families or how it takes innocent lives, no, you don't see any of that. What did my family do to deserve this? What does anyone's family? Yeah, the addict makes the choice to get high, but the families don't make the choice to deal with the pain that is caused by it.

"My daughter didn't deserve a father who craved to get high so bad she had to hide her personal stuff from me so I wouldn't pawn it. What child does? My wife didn't deserve to live in fear. Yeah, you can easily say when I took the job, I took the risk. You'd be right too. I risked my life to save others, but I damn sure didn't do it at the expense of my wife and child. I used to wish that day you had just put a bullet in my head and killed me that way instead."

Money quickly tried to shift the guilt. "Don't blame me, your own people are the ones that gave you and your family up, but yet you want to put that shit squarely on me."

"And you call yourself a man. You sound like a child right now. If my people did give me up that makes them as guilty as you. Best believe, and they'll have to face their actions, too, one day as you are right now. It might not be with me, but there will come a time because what goes around comes around, and karma is a bitch."

"Look, I'm sorry for what happened to you and your family. I was just doing what I needed to do in order to survive."

"You weren't surviving. You were getting by. A man doing what he has to do to survive is the man that gets up every morning to go to a dead-end job to make sure he is putting a roof over his family's head and food in their stomach. A man who is surviving is one who can have one hundred twenty dollars to last him until his next pay date, and he buy groceries for the week, pays the electric bill, the cable bill and still have sixty dollars left over for gas to get back and forth to work every day.

"Surviving is when you are dead broke but yet find a legal way to make sure your kids don't want for anything and they have everything they need. Surviving is when you only make thirty thousand dollars a year but you make sure your child gets a sixty-thousand-dollar-a-year education. That is surviving. All you are doing is getting by on the lives of others. Your ass doesn't know shit about surviving. Maybe you need to call your momma or something. I'm sure she can tell you about surviving."

"Look, what do you want from me? Even if I wanted to, I can't go back and change the past. It is what it is and there isn't anything either you or I can do about it," Money shot back.

"You are right. You can't do shit about the past. It is what it is and there is no changing that. But what you can do is change the future. There is always something you can do about that. The choice to do so though is up to you."

"Even if I did, the game still will be the game. The minute I step down, you'll have another forty people step up."

"Maybe, but at the end of the day, you can only control your actions and hope that others follow your lead. You'd be surprised at the influence you have. This world is made up of two different people in my opinion: leaders and followers. You might be surprised at how many people follow your lead. And if they don't, you've done all you could.

"For years, I hated you. I wanted you dead. But now, I pity you. I still see the same young boy who was somehow steered down the wrong path today. The good thing is that it's never too late for you to find yourself. It's never too late, just as it's not too late for me to find myself again."

They both sat quietly. What was left to say? LT had said it all. All Money could do was think. LT also zoned everything out. A peace filled his body. He had been battling the demons of his past for so long that now there was no need to. He finally felt at peace within himself. Confronting the man who started the spiral downfall within his life was a revelation. Though he was a victim of the streets and had become an addict at no fault of his own, he no longer blamed everyone for his downfall. He could have decided to be a man himself and get the help he needed a long time ago. He didn't and that blame needed to be squarely on his shoulders.

The bailiff came to escort LT into the courtroom from the waiting area. LT knew that if he would ever resurrect his life, the time was now. It was finally time to start owning up and being a man.

"Good morning, Mr. Taylor. My name is Mr. Justin Lenox and I'm your public defender. I haven't really had time to go over your case, so if you don't mind, can you please catch me up to speed?"

LT couldn't help but shake his head. It wasn't in disgust but rather he wasn't surprised. Why should he have been? He was getting the service he'd paid for.

"No, that won't even be necessary. Your services are not needed. I will represent myself."

"Fine, it's your ass, not mine!" he said without protest.

Before LT could even respond, "Docket #11534, people versus Lionel Taylor. The charge is possession of controlled dangerous substance," the court's clerk said.

"How do you plead?" the judge asked.

"I would like to waive reading, Your Honor, and plead guilty," LT said.

"Counsel, have you conferred with your client," the judge replied.

LT quickly jumped in, "Your Honor, I waived my right to counsel. It's time I start accepting responsibility for my actions. I know I have a drug problem. It doesn't matter how I got to that point but rather taking the steps to correct it and get help with the problem. I could spend the rest of my life blaming any and everyone for what happened, but that won't solve anything. I'm a man and it's time I start acting as one. I've lost my family, my job, and my dignity to drugs. It's time I take back my life and be in charge for once. I don't need counsel to try to weasel me out of accepting responsibility for my own actions."

"I must say, Mr. Taylor, it is not every day I get to hear such a profession of guilt in that manner. I commend you, sir. I pray, however, that your speech isn't a ploy to get a lighter sentence but rather a true testimony to how you truly feel."

"It's not, Your Honor. It's time to stop the excuses. You say you hope it's not a 'ploy,' I say I've already lost everything. How can that be a 'ploy'? There is no punishment that you can give me that matches no longer being able to see my child or the woman I love. Even if not in a cell, I'm still imprisoned every day until they forgive me."

"Understood, Mr. Taylor, understood. I hereby sentence you to Richardson Rehabilitation Clinic, probation for two years, and two hundred and forty hours of community service."

CHAPTER 23

A loud knock at the door awoke O'Neal from his sleep. He turned to look at the clock to check the time. It was a little past nine a.m. O'Neal rolled over and noticed Starr still sound asleep next to him. He wasn't surprised. He had put in a lot of work earlier that night so he knew she was worn out.

O'Neal grabbed his pistol out of the top drawer of his nightstand before he went to the door. He never took any chances on possible unwanted visitors. He was very paranoid about everything. Though he had made a damn good name for himself in the murder game, he didn't care. There was always some aspiring youngster out there who wanted to make a name for himself, and O'Neal wasn't going to be anyone's resume builder.

"Who is it?" O'Neal called out once he reached the door.

"Yo, it's me," BC replied.

O'Neal opened the door for his comrade. "What's going on?"

"This shit uptown is really fucking with my mind. I can't even front. I'm not feeling these New York cats at all. I know a setup when I see one, and everything about them is telling me we are in for that type situation. It's to the point now that I couldn't even sleep last night I was thinking about it and you know how I get when I can't sleep. I need you to trust me on this one. We need to extinguish this situation now while we still can!"

O'Neal trusted BC more than anyone when it came to intuition.

If BC felt something about any situation, usually he was right, so O'Neal was all ears.

"You know I'm going to need more than your intuition to go to Money with. Everyone is game for the deal. Do you have anything concrete or is all this based upon your hunch."

"O, I wish I had something concrete. I really do but all I have is my intuition. I mean, tell me this, back in the day would you have called out the man himself trying to set up a deal, and come out in these streets, bare at that, in case he came looking for you? I mean, no pistol, no nothing and I'm not talking one of you but ALL of you! These cats were out there bare. It's one thing to be caught off guard and we probably did, but fuck that, you stay strapped. I don't care what the situation is. Look at you; you answered the door with the pistol. It's a habit. I don't care if you are going to take a piss. You have your dick in one hand and your other on that steel, just in case. It's like they were purposely trying to get our guard down."

"Come on, we are too far in the game to even try to think like these cats. Maybe they don't know how to properly conduct business. Maybe they don't know the rules of this game. Fuck if I know, and honestly, I don't give a shit. All I care about is if they have that paper and they are serious, this is another avenue for us to make even more bread. That's all any of us cares about. This gives us our line straight to New York. We can finally start bringing in major cash and get on a real supplier level."

"How can you not know how to conduct business? And let's say they don't, then that's someone we not trying to deal with then. Why would you want to? That doesn't make sense. They know how to conduct business. They know the dos and don'ts. I'm telling you, all this is a mirage. They want us to think they are amateurs so we let our guard down. Shit, it's already working on you and probably Money and Cheese too. I'm not buying it. It's too coincidental and a coincidence like that leads me to believe it's for a purpose. These cats are down here to take over. Trust me when I tell you," BC said.

"Okay then, get me something concrete to work with and we'll handle these niggas. Right now you have nothing, but they didn't have any heat when you patted them down. That's not shit! I need more than that before I say yes or no because right now all I'm working with is the little you are giving me. I don't know what you really expect me to say, BC."

"Is there any question about it? I don't think they are worth the headache. I know you looking for a line to New York to set up more paper, but why even take the chance on the setup? I say you run things over with Money and see what he say, I'm sure he'll agree."

Starr came out of the room looking for her new bun. She saw O'Neal was busy in a meeting and didn't interrupt. She turned back around and went back into the bedroom.

O'Neal continued, "Let's do this; I want surveillance on these niggas. If you right, I want to be prepared. I'm not trying to wake up to any surprises. In the meantime let me mull over the situation some. I promise you this though; if these niggas aren't who they say they are, they will get dealt with. You have my word on that."

BC didn't listen to one word of what O'Neal had to say. He had his sights on one thing—Starr.

"Who is the chick?" BC asked.

"Oh yeah, that's Starr. I met her last night at the club."

"Damn, I'm all out here running my mouth. Why didn't you tell me she was in the house? The bitch probably heard every fucking word we said and shit."

"Go 'head with all that. Ease back with the bitches. She's not like the rest of the skeezers. I'm jive feeling this one. Shit, between us seem like it can turn into something jive concrete."

"Didn't you say you met Slim last night at the club? You mean to tell me Slim got you talking like this after one night. You've got to be fucking kidding me! Nigga, is you insane? First of all, none of that shit even matters. I don't give a fuck who it is. She can be wifey for all that matter, you know we don't talk shop in front of no one outside this family."

O'Neal became defensive. "Slim, do you realize who the fuck you are talking to? Nigga, know your fucking role and stay in your lane!"

"Nigga, fuck you! You bleed the same fucking way I do. You know where I'm at with mine so jump out there if you want to or stab the fuck back."

O'Neal didn't respond. BC continued, "I don't give a fuck who you are. If you not going to respect this shit here we do, then don't, but do that bullshit on your time and damn sure not at my expense. If you want to talk to me, you know how to reach me. But I put this on everything I love, if you put my ass out on the line like that again by having company over and talking away, we are going to have more than words. I don't give a fuck if you my man or not."

BC got up and headed for the door. As the door slammed shut upon BC's exit, O'Neal leaned his head back on the arm of the chair. He knew he was wrong but he wasn't the best at apologizing or admitting his faults. BC commanded respect and regardless who you were, you followed suit or you'd know about it. O'Neal knew that and it was one of the things he respected most about him. He wasn't the type to bite his tongue, regardless who he was talking to or the situation.

Once she heard the front door close, Starr came out to check up on O'Neal. "Baby, are you coming back to bed?"

"Not right now! I've got some shit on my mind."

"I didn't press the issue last night because you needed your space, but O'Neal, I want you to know I know what is what. I've dealt with enough niggas in the game to know when I'm dealing with another one. If you are serious about what you said last night and settling, then we need to start things off on the right foot by you knowing you can tell me when things are on your mind. You can talk to me. The reason why I'm not with any of them is because they didn't. They stayed in their closed little shell and took their frustrations out on me. I'm sorry, I can't live like that. I don't do secrets. If it's going to be me and you, then that is just it, me and you. The rest, fuck 'em!"

O'Neal couldn't help but laugh. "Oh, now it's me and you, huh? Last night all I could get out of you was some serious shade. My, how things change after one night."

"After the way you put it on me last night, you damn right it's me and you, unless you have other things in mind. If it was just a friendly fuck, that is fine, let me know. Don't have me looking like a fool thinking it's more when it's not."

"There you go on the defensive. I didn't say anything about a friendly fuck. I told you what I wanted last night and I'm a man of my word. I meant everything I said last night," O'Neal replied.

"Okay, then tell me what is going on. Last night I could tell you were stressed about something, then you are in here arguing with what I'm guessing was a friend."

Starr's presence was the center of the tension between O'Neal and BC yet he still felt compelled to confide in her.

"I don't know if I'm coming or going. If you've been around

the game, then you know the more you put out there, the more people know. However, the less you do, the more you leave them guessing. I'm not a guessing type of guy. I want you to know what is what. It's like we've worked toward building an empire but yet all I'm known for is muscle. It's not understood what role I truly play. I hate being in the damn shadows.

"Back in the day, everyone knew who Mario was," O'Neal continued. "Everyone knew who Santana was. Everyone knew who Carlos was. It didn't matter if you were from D.C., Philly, NY, or Cali, you knew their names and the roles they played. You couldn't *but* know because it rang out. Shit, even Feds knew the players at hand but never mount shit on any of them except maybe a few. Why can't my name ring out the same fucking way?"

"No offense, baby, but there is a huge difference between street playas and the Cardoza cartel," Starr said. "But even with that, how can you want what they had and they strived of doing the opposite. They lived in the shadows. My ex used to run with his crew years ago. He never laid eyes on the man. Though everyone knew he existed, it was if he really didn't. I don't know anyone who has ever met him."

"That's the thing. Yes, you do and that's the problem. Let me ask you something, what do you know about me?" O'Neal asked.

"What do you mean, what do I know? I only know what you told me."

"Don't play me. We both know that is bullshit. You know more than you are letting on and if you are as hip to the game as you say, then I know for sure you've heard something."

"Okay, I might have heard how a few bodies here and there dropped due to your hands. How can anyone not, the way you go about things!" Starr replied.

"Okay, I'll take that. So what are the streets saying about who is running things?"

"The only name everyone really knows is this guy named Money. He is supposed to be Mr. Cardoza's right-hand man. But I'm sure I'm not telling you anything you didn't already know, especially since you are the one dropping the bodies for him."

"You see that's the thing. We all play our role. There is no head of the family, yet he is the fucking face. And like Mario he stays in the fucking shadows too. Fuck that! That's not how I'm trying to live my damn life. I put in the work. I put in the hours. It's damn time everyone knows."

It all started to make sense to Starr. She was beginning to see exactly what was going on.

O'Neal continued, "I mean, don't get me wrong. That is my man, always has been, and always will be, but if it wasn't for me, then we wouldn't be nowhere near where we are. Money doesn't have the stomach for this shit. He was always too smart for his own britches. He craves the bread. I mean, we all do to a sense, but respect means more to me. That doesn't mean shit to him. As long as we are making that paper, he is good to go and he'll do anything to continue to make it."

"So what are you saying?"

"I don't know. Mostly I'm ranting. I know I can't keep living like this. I won't. I refuse to any longer."

"That part I can't help you with. That, you'll have to figure out on your own but I'm sure you will. It seems as if you know what you want to do, but might not know how to go about getting it. Just really think on it. Maybe talk to your friend and tell him how you feel about the situation."

"I thought about that. That's probably what I'll do. It's too much going on right now and everything is hitting me all at once. I need to squash shit with my man BC first," O'Neal said.

"Sounds like you are on the right path. Look, I have some errands to take care of today. Will you be out all day today?"

"Probably, but look in my nightstand. There is an extra key in there to the crib. That way you don't have to wait up for me. I'll see you when I get in tonight."

"Huh?" Starr was stunned.

"I told you, I'm a man of my word. I don't know what it is about you. I really don't, but it's like I can open up to you. I can talk to you. It's like you have a control over me like no other. I've always heard when you meet the one, you'll know. Well, I know!"

"Boy, please! We just met last night. You are moving way too fast."

"We can move at whatever pace you want. The only thing I'm doing is giving you access to the crib. I didn't say move in or anything. Now when you are ready for that, we'll get a spot big enough for the both of us. Right now all I need you to do is pick up a toothbrush for when you are over here because the way your breath smelling this morning... got damn!"

She gave him a devilish look, then turned to go into the bedroom. O'Neal had run across a bunch of women in his life but this time he finally felt as if he had found the one.

CHAPTER 24

Everything went as smoothly as JayMarr had anticipated. The judge had no choice but to drop all charges against Money. The police had absolutely no evidence and struck out with the search of his truck. Even if they had found the pistol he had stashed, the search was illegal and unjust so it would have been thrown out.

No matter how defeated the police were, it didn't stop them from impounding Money's truck and running up storage fees in order for him to get it out as a "thank you." He had JayMarr place a call to O'Neal to make sure a car was waiting for him at the station to pick him up and take him to the impound. To Money's surprise, Lil' Nep was the one there.

"What is your young ass not doing in school?" Money asked.

"O'Neal hit me on the hip and told me to come scoop you. Where to?"

"I need to pick up my truck so head over to the police impound. How much bread do you have on you?"

"Thirty-five," Lil' Nep replied.

"Cool, I'm sure it's going to be at least two grand to get it out."

"No, I mean thirty-five dollars, not thirty-five hundred," Lil' Nep clarified.

Money couldn't help but laugh. "That's my bad, lil' homie. I thought maybe O took care of that and gave you the bread. It's all good. Let me see your phone, champ."

Lil' Nep didn't object. Money didn't want O'Neal or Cheese drawing any attention to him or themselves by meeting him at the impound. He wasn't sure what type eyes were on him, especially after he had beaten the charge so easily. Instead, he decided to call JayMarr.

"How far are you?" Money asked.

"Why, what's up? Do you need something? I know you aren't still at the station, are you?" JayMarr asked.

"Naw, it's nothing like that. I need you to post the money to get the truck out of impound. I'll bring it back by your office later with interest, of course. O'Neal didn't send little man with any cash."

"That's no problem. I'll head straight there now. Are you on your way?"

"Yeah, we are heading over there now. I have to make one quick stop first though. I'm starving. I have to get something to eat up in me."

"Okay, well, if I finish up there before you get there I'll hit you and let you know what is what."

"Sounds good," Money replied.

They both hung up.

Money turned to Lil' Nep. "Lil' man, stop somewhere so we can get something to eat. It doesn't even matter where. I'm hungry as shit and can go for just about anything right about now."

He then handed Lil' Nep his cell phone before reclining the car seat back so he could think. No matter how much he tried to get his mind off things, he couldn't. The man from earlier had really gotten to him. Many men had lost their lives at the hands of Money or someone in his crew. It was all a part of the day-to-day operation. It had even become acceptable.

Even the addicts—how could you have a successful drug business without them? It was a necessary evil but it was their choice. They chose to get high. No one was forcing them to. What stuck with Money so much was that he had taken LT's choice. He knew the police would never rest trying to find him if they had killed him. So instead he had destroyed LT and taken the one thing every man needed—his dignity. Killing him would have been doing him a favor compared to what he'd been through.

Money didn't believe in coincidences. They didn't happen in his world. He couldn't help but believe this wasn't one also. Maybe he was getting the sign he was looking for and the answers to his questions. Maybe it was indeed time for him to walk away. If he was starting to develop a conscience about the consequence his actions had caused, then this definitely wasn't the business for him anymore. The only problem was the lack of an alternative; once he took care of that, then things would be easier.

Lil' Nep pulled up to the next fast-food restaurant which turned out to be Popeyes. Money quickly jumped out the car to get him a two-piece and a biscuit to hold him over until he could sit down and have a real meal. Once he got back in the car, it seemed like a concert hall. Lil' Nep had a CD playing and the music blasting.

Money couldn't help but notice the artist's skills. The voice sounded familiar but he couldn't place it. He couldn't help but jam. Instantly, he picked up the hook and started to sing along.

"Who is this?" Money asked Lil' Nep.

"Why, what's up? You want me to turn it off or something? Is it bothering you?"

"Naw, this shit jive rock. Who is it?" Money asked again.

"Are you serious?"

Lil' Nep became excited.

"Slim, calm it down and tell me who the fuck it is. I need to cop it, matter fact dub it for me instead."

"It's me. It's my demo," Lil' Nep replied.

Money listened harder and realized Lil' Nep was telling the truth. He finally picked up the voice.

"What the fuck are you trying to work for me for? You've got skills. Seriously, if that shit was in stores, I'd buy it. You really have some talent. Why waste the talent in the game instead of doing your music?"

Lil' Nep's smile grew as wide as could be. He couldn't help but feel a sense of accomplishment. If Money liked it, then it must be good.

"I have been trying to. I've been sending out demos like crazy but never get any good feedback. Plus, BC isn't having it. He says that rappers are a dime a dozen and a bunch of bitches fakin' to be gangstas. If I want to fake like one, then I might as well be one. Plus, he only knows what he sees right now, and right now he doesn't see me making any money off rapping—only spending it in recording sessions."

"Shit, you have to spend money in order to make money. That comes with anything. It doesn't matter if it's hustling or working, that is always the first rule of business. BC knows that."

"Well, whether he knows it or not isn't the problem, it's if he catches me doing music, then I have to worry about him putting his foot in my ass. I don't care what it is, nothing is worth that much to me."

"I can respect that but tell me one thing, and please don't feed me no bullshit either or tell me what your brother will say. I don't want to hear none of that. I only want the truth and how you feel. Is music what you love and want to do with your life?"

"Yeah, there is no doubt about it."

"Then that's what we are going to do. I don't want to see you on any packages or running any errands, none of that. From now on, we are concentrating on the music only. I'll talk to BC so he knows the plan so don't worry about him, either. Now you said you have sent out a couple of demos already. Who have you sent them to?" Money asked.

"Shit, most of the major labels: Def Jam, Bad Boy, Warner Brothers, and Interscope. It doesn't matter. I've sent it to them all and haven't heard anything back."

"Well, if New York and L.A. aren't biting, then we'll find a way to make them take notice. I'm going to invest my money in Street Life Records."

"Who? I've never heard of them," Lil' Nep replied clueless.

Money started laughing. "Nigga, you probably haven't. That's because I made the shit up. We are going to start our own label and go from there. I'll get us a distribution deal, a street team and create the buzz, and then we straight. The rest is up to you. I just need you to keep making this fire! Can you do that for me?"

Lil' Nep didn't know what to say. It was easy having a dream, but actually seeing it come true was harder to believe.

"You are serious, right?" Lil' Nep questioned.

"Since I just dropped a shitload of information on you in a short span of time, and all of it is positive and shit you've probably been waiting to hear all of your life, I'll give you a minute to process it and realize that I'm dead serious. Now, what is your answer?"

"Hell yeah, is my answer. I'm in."

"That's what's up. Now, after you drop me off at my car, I want you to meet me at my house around five p.m. so we can go over the details. I'll have your contract drawn up and ready. Also, see how much your engineer wants to run our studio. I'm sure you are comfortable with him so I want to keep your comfort level right.

"Now there is one thing I need you to understand. When I do things, I do them. I put everything into it and I go about it smart. I need to make sure you are dedicated to this. Just because you are starting out as an artist, doesn't mean it has to stay that way. You are our first client and hopefully the start of many good things to come. You help me build the empire and you will grow with it. Believe that!" Money said.

"I'm in. You don't have to convince me. I've already seen and know about what you've been in the streets. If you can do half of that for me in the music business, then that is more than enough. I promise I'll do my part. Believe that!"

They pulled up to the impound lot.

"Good kid, well, we've got work to do. I'll see you at five p.m."

CHAPTER 25

BC was steaming during the entire car ride uptown. The confrontation he'd had with O'Neal really pissed him off. He looked at him as a young brother and loved him like family. He had brought O'Neal up in the murder game. It wasn't as if O'Neal was ever frail when it came down to the bodies dropping. But BC had taught him how to be tactful to avoid police attention, yet still make sure the message was heard loud and clear in the streets.

That is why he couldn't believe O'Neal would be so careless now. He knew how O'Neal could be, but it was as if he wasn't listening to anything and everything was now clouding his judgment. That bothered BC because carelessness led to recklessness and the minute you started to become reckless, you became vulnerable. That was the opening any trained killer would need if they had their sights set on O'Neal.

Adding a woman to the mix wasn't helping, either. It was no secret within their inner circle that O'Neal had a thing for the ladies, but he was always smart with how he went about things. He allowed his charisma and personality to charm his way into a woman's pants but then that was it. After he was done, she was thrown out like the Sunday garbage. This chick was walking around his house, listening to meetings, and O'Neal approved of it. If he was that open with her, there was no telling what else would change or she would change. The more he thought about it, the more pissed BC became. In this game, you learned to trust no one. She could have been a plant for all O'Neal knew.

How the hell do you come to trust a bitch you barely even know, BC thought.

The whole situation puzzled him. It was obvious her pussy had to be golden for him to fall for her this hard and this fast. O'Neal even tried to pull rank on him. Regardless of their positions in the game, he had never stepped out there on BC. There was always a mutual respect between the two of them. That was a hidden rule. O'Neal feared no man but he wasn't stupid, either. BC took murder to another level. He actually took pleasure in it.

No matter how much things were bothering him, BC knew he couldn't continue to dwell on it. Everything would eventually work itself out as it always did. There were more important things at hand for him to deal with that needed his undivided attention. He knew he needed to find a way to get something concrete on the New York boys to substantiate his hunch.

BC picked up the phone to call Tiny. Before he met with O'Neal, he had asked Tiny to try to find out where the New York boys were located. He wanted round-the-clock surveillance in case he got the okay to eliminate them. Now, he needed it for another reason.

"What's the deal? Did you take care of what I needed?" BC said into the phone.

"You know I'm on it. It's quiet up here right now," Tiny replied.

"'Quiet,' meaning what?"

"'Quiet' as in ain't shit going on up here really. These cats are squares for real. I wish you would have told me that up front. Shit! Between trying to rap to these little-ass neighborhood bitches or hanging out on the porch stoop, they don't do shit."

"What about the head nigga, any sign of him?" BC asked.

"Naw, just the same niggas you said who'd be here."

"Okay, where they at?"

"Same spot you bumped head with them the other night."

"What? These niggas haven't relocated?"

"Nope!"

BC continued, "So mean to tell me these cats lay their heads there?"

"That's the only way I see it. One of the cats you shot came outside for a few and posted up, then went back in the building. These cats aren't up to anything. If they are, they damn sure know how to hide the shit."

"Fuck that, I'm not buying it! They are up to something. I can fucking feel it. Just keep watching them and make sure I'm the first call you make if you see anything that doesn't look right. I don't give a shit if you feel like it's the smallest thing. If you notice one bitch that constantly keeps coming around, a mailman stopping to talk to them for a long period of time, or even an old fucking lady having a five-minute chat with them, I want to be the first one to know about it," BC demanded.

"No problem, boss."

"Good, I'll be up there later on. I have a meeting I need to make real quick. After that, I'll get up with you. Make sure you keep them eyes and ears open, homie!"

"I got you. I'm on it," Tiny replied.

BC pulled into the parking garage at the Washington Hospital Center. He got out of the car and headed for the emergency room exit. At the front door, Money was waiting there for him.

Money didn't waste any time with idol chitchat. Too much had happened over the last couple of days so he was very cautious.

"What did you need to talk to me about?" Money asked.

"I need you to talk to your boy. I'm not sure what's up with him but he taking things to another level and you are the only one who I know that can get through to him."

"What's going on?"

"Who is the new bitch he dealing with?" BC asked.

"I know you didn't call me out here to discuss that man's love life. You know he do what he do in that department but he isn't dealing with any bitch that I know of on that scale."

"I wouldn't be too sure about that. This morning I swung past his house and there was some bitch posted up in there. Shit, not only was she posted up, but he was even talking shop in front of her like she was down or some shit. Don't quote me on the name but I think he said her name was Starr or some shit like that."

"Hold up, who! I know you aren't talking about the chick from the club?" Money asked.

"I don't know where he met the bitch from. All I know is that she was posted up in there as if they'd been together for fifteen years or something."

Money shook his head. Things with O'Neal were worse than he anticipated.

"Okay, don't worry about O. I'm on that but do need a favor from you though."

"What the deal?"

"I won't bullshit you or feed you any lines. Straight up, I need you to cut Lil' Nep loose."

"Fuck do you mean, cut him loose," BC shot back.

"Straight up, Lil' Man has talent. He can really make some-thing of himself. I mean outside this street shit. He can make an honest living. He needs to be doing his music. I need you to cut him loose."

"Money, you know I'm as loyal as they come. If you or O need anything, I'm the first one on it. But Money, this is my blood we are talking about. How can you ask me to cut my family loose on a dream?"

"You've always trusted me, don't lose that trust in me now. He is still your blood. I need you to cut him loose of the game. You and I, we are one of a kind. This game called up and we were hooked from the start but your brother has another calling. That music is calling him. That is what he needs to be doing.

"It's not like I'm going to have him out there blind or nothing. I believe in the lil' homie so much I'm willing to put my own money behind him. That is how much potential I think he has. I want to do this straight by the book and cut no corners. We've met a lot of pretenders in the business already when we used to hit up the club scenes back in the day. I'm going to call in some favors and get this thing poppin' the right way, but I need the little one focused. He is willing to put in that work. I just need to make sure it's the right work. Ya dig?"

"Money, I don't know. That is my blood. I know what we have isn't much but it's something and it's real. What is he going to do if no one tries to give him a break or the labels don't believe in him as you do? Then what is he left with?"

"That won't happen, but if it does, then he always has the game to fall back on."

BC knew it was the right thing to do but a part of him wanted his blood to have something stable. With the game, you risked death or jail; that was a given. You knew that was what faced you. You also knew until that day came, you'd have steady paper coming in. But to have to wait on someone to give you a shot, there was no stability in that. You weren't in control, someone else was. With the game, he would never be turned away. The opportunity was already given to him and waiting for him to seize it.

"Let me sleep on it," BC said.

"I can live with that. Now, I talked to Cheese about our out-of-towners and he is setting up the deal now. I want you to handle security on it. I need everything airtight."

"What? You don't know?"

"Know what?"

"I should have known. I thought O would have at least talked to you about that by now but I guess that was too much to assume. That should have been priority number one. Anyway, I don't have a good feeling about these cats. It's something about them that doesn't rub me right. Right now, I have one of my workers sitting on them doing surveillance until I get up there."

"Is that right? Is there anything specifically I need to know?"

"Naw, I don't have anything substantial right now. Tiny says all they've been doing all day is posting up outside or rapping to lil' neighborhood bitches. Also, the lil' niggas I shot out the hospital. He said he's seen them from time to time out there."

"Where they at?"

BC laughed. "They still on Thirteenth and Kansas. My guess is they have a place in the building."

"Okay, keep your eyes on them through the night. I'll send word to put a hold on things until we know for sure everything is what it really seems and I'll talk to O too. I gotta run though. It's not good to stay posted up out here in the open too long. Plus, I have to meet Lil' Nep at the studio."

"You really are serious about my little brother?" BC asked.

"Is money green?" Money said sincerely.

"It is when it comes to you."

"Well, there you go but once the demo is done you'll see for sure."

"Yeah okay, homie! I hear you," BC said as he turned to walk back toward his car.

CHAPTER 26

Money wanted all his cards put on the table. It wasn't fair to Lil' Nep for him to put one hundred percent into the music and he not follow suit by putting the same amount into him. The only way Money could do that was by giving up the game. Money knew that so he set up a meeting with Cheese and O'Neal. He didn't want to prolong the situation. Plus, the sooner he made them aware, the sooner they could plan everything out for life after him.

Money wasn't too sure if he had tails on him after what had happened in court, so he set for them to meet in Virginia. Cops had a thing about being shown up. They took it personal. They might allow you to get the first laugh, but they always tried to be the last one laughing. And most of the time to what expense didn't matter. Though his illegal days were now about to be behind him, there was no way he would lose that when he was so close to a clean break. Plus, he didn't want to bring heat down on anyone else by being careless and not taking the necessary precautions.

They all arrived at Hoffman Center in Alexandria, Virginia at different times, then made their way across the street to the Eisenhower Metro station. Each boarded the last subway car which Money had previously set up to be empty to avoid listening ears. The meeting was at such last notice there was no way the feds could set up to bug the car.

"Look here, we don't have much time, so I'll make it quick. I wanted both of you to know that I'm done with this shit. I'm getting out of the game," Money said.

"What," Cheese replied.

"I know you aren't tripping off that trumped-up charge from earlier. I thought all of that was squashed anyway," O'Neal added.

"Naw, it doesn't have shit to do with that. This shit has outgrown me. I've decided to take the bread I have saved up and go legit. I'm going to start a record label and take shit from there. In order to do it right, I need to put all my time into it."

Cheese and O'Neal started to laugh.

"Come on, Money, seriously, what is this all about?" O'Neal asked.

Money became offended. "Nigga, does it look like I'm faking? Does my face say I'm bullshittin'? I'm dead-ass serious about this. It's time I get the fuck out of this game. I've been in long enough. I have other shit that I want to do with my life and I feel like now is the best time to pursue it."

"Man, come on, you don't know shit about starting a damn label. You've got to be fucking kidding me, right? We on the verge of closing the deal that is going to get us up top and put us on a major supplier level, and you want to just walk away. Money, what's really good with you?" O'Neal asked.

Cheese sat back still speechless and observed O'Neal and Money go back and forth.

"First of all, I'm a grown-ass man and if I choose to start a fucking paper stand, that is what I'm going to do. I'm trying to be civil about the shit and come to y'all as men first. I don't know why you acting like you are beefin' anyway. This is what you wanted, O! Be honest, that's what all this shit has been about.

All you've been doing is bucking left and right at everyone. You are getting what the fuck you want. You want to run shit, you want to be the man. Well, I'm turning that all over to you and Cheese, and y'all can run with the shit."

"Nigga, what the fuck is you talking about? Is someone in your ear with some ole bullshit?" O'Neal questioned.

"I don't listen to petty gossip, so that should be the last of your worries. It's written all over your face. The shit is so obvious, O, be honest about it. I'm not beefin', it's all good, champ. If that's how you feel, there isn't anything wrong with that. Regardless, I'm out so I'm chill. I just wanted to tell both of y'all face to face because I love y'all niggas and always will regardless. Like I said earlier, I figured y'all both deserved to hear my plans from my mouth now versus later."

Cheese tried to break the tension. "Money, I'm not going to sit here and front like I'm down with this because honestly I'm not. But what do you know about the music business? Shit, those muthafuckas carry shit worse than we do in the streets."

"I know how to run an operation. That's all I need to know. Right now, I'm working with one artist and I'll expand from there. I'm like a cat; I'll always land on my feet. If those niggas try to strong-arm me, I have something for that. I'm not going into this dumbfounded or blind. I have the glasses on, homie," Money responded.

"Who is this so-called artist?" O'Neal asked.

"Your fam... Lil' Nep."

"Get the fuck out of here. Now I know you are off some ole bullshit. We all know how BC feels about his little brother. That is the last thing he is going to allow," O'Neal shot back.

"True but me and BC already have squashed that. He agreed

to cut Lil' Nep loose from the game, so he can concentrate solely on the music. That's actually the main reason why I want to get out. I want to concentrate solely on getting everything up off the ground and running. You know I don't like to do shit half ass."

"Hold on the fuck up. That's not BC's call. That's mine. Lil' Nep is one of my workers. You should have come to me about it. I didn't agree to shit," O'Neal said.

Cheese jumped in, "Come on, O, now you are getting awfully sensitive about this. Let the man be, it's obvious he has his mind made up, and you keep throwing more shit in the game ain't going to make it any better." Cheese turned to Money. "Yo, if you serious about the shit, then you know I'm not going to wish you nothing but the best. But you need to keep that phone on at all times because you know I'm going to constantly pick your brain about any and everything, champ!"

"I can't believe this shit. You condoning this bullshit, Cheese! Both of y'all niggas are off some different shit. What the fuck? We made a pact for life. There isn't no getting out of this shit right here. We in it until the end, remember."

"Hold on," Money said, then stood up. "The fuck is you trying to say? Because right now a nigga does not like the way you are trying to come at me about this situation. Now, I tried to be a muthafuckin' man about the situation and rap to both of you like brothers instead off some different shit. Now if you want to turn this into something it doesn't have to be, then whatever is whatever. But best believe I'm out of this shit regardless the fact. I'm done with the game and there isn't nothing anyone is going to do to change my fucking mind. Now deal with that!"

"You know what, Money; everything always has to be your

way. That is never going to change. You can sit here and bull-shit like we are all brothers but in all honesty, you don't give a shit about me or Cheese. It's always been about you and what Money wants. This is no different. The way I'm feeling right now, for real, fuck you! And I put that on everything I love," O'Neal said as the train came to a stop.

He got up and headed for the opening train doors without saying another word. Money and Cheese both let him go to vent. Though he didn't admit it, O'Neal was actually happy he'd now get to run the show. He was hurt at the way it all went down. He never wanted Money to get out of the game, but rather wanted to make a name for himself also in the process.

"Money, don't let that nigga get to you. If this is what you want, then you do what you do. You know we're always going to be here for you."

"Cheese, I put this on everything, that nigga lucky I fucking love him like family. I swear he is."

"O doesn't know how to handle the situation so he lashing out. He feels like he losing you. Give him some time to mull everything over. It will work itself out. I'm more worried about you. Can you handle the funding for the label?"

"Yeah, I'm straight. Right now, it's only Lil' Nep. It's not like I have a full staff or no shit like that. Cheese, you need to hear him. Slim was rocking his CD in the car when he scooped me from the station. He really has some serious skills. Once we finish this demo and shop it around, I honestly don't think it will be long before we get a distribution deal from a major label. After that, I'll let them handle the manufacturing and distributing of our shit and cash the checks until it's time to take it to that next level and handle everything in-house."

"Well, if shit ever does get tight with the bread, at least you'll still have bread coming in from us. Matter of fact, you still haven't said how much you looking for."

"I've never been a greedy nigga. Okay, maybe I have! But naw, I'm content with a hundred thirty a week. That's only thirteen percent of the million a week we bringing in now. Plus y'all have the potential deal up top. That should have more bread coming in to cover the thirteen."

"That's what's up. I'll make sure you get your one thirty a week. Just make sure you send word to Mario's people in Miami. I don't want a problem with them."

"I got you. Look, I need a favor, though. I need you to really watch O," Money asked.

"I told you don't trip off that nigga. He'll come around. Right now he just in his feelings about the whole situation," Cheese replied.

"Naw, that's not what I'm talking about. This nigga mind ain't in the right state right now. He is all over the place. I need you to watch him real close and I mean that. BC said he went over there and the chick from the club was posted up as if she lived there. And O was talking shop all out in the open with her around like it wasn't shit. Prior to that, the little incident with Lil' Nep and bringing him to my crib, it's like he not all there or something. Make sure you keep an eye on the nigga before he really start wildin' out and bring some serious heat on everything."

"Are you sure? I mean, O trip off them bitches, but it's not like him to have one up in the crib. I find that a little hard to believe."

"Yeah, that jive fucked me up, too, when BC first said it but then I had to think, when you ever known BC to lie. Shit, he said the boy even bucked at him over her."

"Get the fuck out of here. He just met the chick!"

"Nigga, you don't have to tell me, I was there, remember? Who knows what or how this chick in his head or what type game she spittin'. With all that is going on, his mind definitely don't need to be all over the place. He needs to be concentrating on this deal and expanding the operation. That's why I need you to watch him. Keep him focused."

"Don't worry about it, Money, I'm on it."

"Shit, the next stop is coming up. Make sure when you set up the deal you stay away from it too. Promote your top lieutenant and send him to make the deal. You need to definitely learn to stay in the shadows now and away from the drugs, money, or any type of deals. Keep it tight and there will never be any leaks," Money advised.

"No doubt."

Money got up and headed for the opening doors. "I'll keep in connected. You stay up, Cheese."

THE WAR FOR A
SOUL

CHAPTER 27

BC continued to eye the New York boys. No matter what his eyes told him otherwise, he wouldn't allow them to shake his intuition. He knew something was out of place. However, he couldn't help but doubt if he was crazy at times as well. Then finally he caught a break and saw his first glimpse of a possible sign.

It wasn't anything big but usually those were the signs that needed to be noticed. BC noticed a dark-skinned woman talking to the head man. This wasn't the first time he had seen her talking to him nor the first time he'd seen her in the area. Her body language didn't give off the impression as if she was trying to get with him—not even as if she was trying to play hard to get. Instead she stood talking with him for three minutes tops and then headed down the street and on her way. Each time she had come past the stoop, it was always from a different way. The more he thought about it, the more he realized this wasn't a coincidence. She was a messenger.

BC finally had what he needed for more answers. He quickly jumped out of the car and started to tail her. He wasn't too aggressive, so she didn't spot him. Also he wanted to make sure none of the corner boys saw him to avoid his cover being blown. By the time he caught up to where she was within eye distance, she had made her way down Kansas Avenue to Georgia Avenue. There was only one place she could have been heading and that was the subway station. If she had driven BC would have noticed the same car long ago and tailed it. But by her catching the subway, it made it easier for her to blend in when trying to get away.

This opportunity might not ever present itself again. He knew it wasn't smart to continue to follow her because her final destination was certain, but he needed something. Even if she only led him to another area to watch, that was something. He made sure to keep a comfortable distance to not tip her to being followed. Once they were on the train, he made sure to keep his eyes glued to her. He didn't want to miss anything. Someone could quickly sit down next to her, carry on a conversation and then be off at the next stop. That was all it would take for her to relay whatever information she needed to and then be in the wind. If so, there was a new target BC would need to set his sights on.

Things wouldn't be that complicated. She sat quietly the entire ride. If anyone sat down next to her, she never said a word to them. She barely even paid them any attention and continued to stare out the window. The train was nearly at its last stop. She got up and made her way to the door as the train pulled into the Suitland station. BC was careful about how he got off the train. Once the doors opened and she had stepped off, then he hurried to get off the train and still keep pace. He kept up as she crossed Silver Hill Road and into the apartment complex directly across the street.

BC's cell phone started ringing. He quickly hit took one look at the caller ID and noticed it was O'Neal.

"What's up?" BC said into the phone receiver.

"I need you on the deal, ASAP. It's taking place in two hours."

"What the fuck? O, you said you were going to give me time to make sure everything was everything. I need you to cancel the shit ASAP. I'm on something that might prove to be big as shit. I'm following a lead…"

O'Neal quickly cut BC off. "Look, I don't give a shit what you are following. All that is insignificant to me right now. I sat back and thought about it and I don't give a fuck who these niggas are. I'm not tripping off of them. If they not who they claim to be or can't produce what they say they can, then we'll eliminate them. But until then, this deal is going through and it's going through now. So, I need you to drop whatever it is the fuck you are doing and get your ass to the spot."

"Fuck that! Put Money on the phone. I need to rap to him about this shit. I've told you, you not being smart about this shit."

"Nigga, fuck Money. He not with us anymore. He wanted out of the game, so he doesn't have shit to do with us and the shit we doing. I'm that nigga calling the shots now and I say we are going through with the deal."

BC didn't know how to react. He didn't understand exactly how serious Money was about working with Lil' Nep but now he knew. However, that was besides the point. He also knew Money was the only one who could talk any type of sense into O'Neal.

"O, look, I know we haven't been on the best terms as of lately, but I need you to put all of that shit aside and listen to what I'm telling you. Something isn't right about this whole situation. Now, I'm possibly close to figuring this whole twisted puzzle up and I'm not about to let you fuck that up. Hold off on shit for twenty-four hours. That's all I'm asking for."

"I'm not feeling that. Shit, we have strung these cats on long enough, if you ask me. It's time for us to quit all the bullshit and get this money. Now, if you are with me on this, cool; if not you can stab the fuck back and join Money in retirement!"

"Is that right? Nigga, how about this, I'll make sure I address that shit right there when I see you. Until then, you do what you do."

Disgusted, BC hung up the phone. He couldn't believe how bold O'Neal had become. Power was the ultimate drug and once you got a taste of it, it was a possibility that you would never be the same again. As much as BC wanted to say fuck it, his conscience and loyalty wouldn't allow it. O'Neal was going to have to deal without him. He might be pissed but he'd be thankful for BC's defiance later on.

The unidentified woman finally reached her destination. She'd walked all the way to the back of the complex to the last building. It had been a while since BC had been in the area but he knew it well from the old days. Though newly renovated, this was known drug territory. BC needed information and waiting for her to come back out the building wasn't going to get him what he needed.

BC waited a couple of minutes before he headed inside the building. He stood at the front door quietly hoping to get any indication of which apartment she had gone into. There was nothing. He started to make his way up the steps when a hard knock came to the back of his head. Dazed, BC went down to one knee. Never did he catch a glimpse of his assailant. The blows continued to come constantly to each part of his body until he couldn't move anymore.

In pain, he felt the unidentified assailant drag his body into one of the vacant apartments. BC's vision was blurry. He wanted to put up a fight and resist but he no longer had his bearings. Once inside the apartment, he felt two people pick him up and put him into a chair where they tied him up.

The woman whom he was following appeared in front of him. She looked at him with a devilish grin.

"I'm going to make this very simple for you. The amount of information you give me will dictate the amount of pain you go through. You give me what I want and I'll promise to kill you now and get it over with. If not, then I promise you, you'll deal with a level of pain you've never dealt with before in your life. To make things simpler, I only have one question for you: Where is Money Green and how can I find him?"

"Bitch, can you count, that is two questions but I'll make things easier for you… Fuck you!" BC replied.

She couldn't help but laugh. BC wasn't the type to crack under pressure and it didn't matter what kind of pressure. He'd take the desired information to his grave, if need be. A blow quickly followed to the back of BC's head. In pain, BC tried to laugh it off, not wanting to show any signs of possible weakness.

He continued, "Y'all might as well go ahead and get this party started now because I'm not telling y'all muthafuckas a *got damn thing* and I put that on everything I love. So you can tell whoever the fuck you are working for to kiss my ass, and you put a muthafuckin' bullet in me now because I'm not telling you or any of your bitches shit! You better believe that. You really want to do both of us a favor, tell your boss to show his face so I can tell him to kiss my ass. Matter of fact, you can join him. Once he is done, then you can proceed to as well."

She looked at one of the men in the room with her and they began to take turns beating BC's ass. Constantly, left after left and right after right, they continued to rain on BC's face and body. His nose was broken and blood gushed from his mouth. He didn't care. The minute they started to let up, he continued, "Are y'all done yet? Shit, I've got things to fucking do with my time so let me save you some time. Fuck you, homie! I have a high tolerance for pain. Y'all bitches don't scare me."

She knew this would be pointless. She turned around and headed to the back bedroom. While she was gone, the onslaught continued. They left him severely beaten and battered. It didn't matter; he would not break. His determination and will power was unprecedented. BC knew his fate. He knew he was a dead man no matter if he gave Money up or not. He figured if he was going to die, he wasn't going to die being the one who gave his man up. Especially since Money wasn't the one pulling the strings anymore.

Finally the constant blows stopped. Both of BC's eyes were swollen and shut. His mouth was bloody and ribs were cracked. They had beaten him so badly he never even realized the familiar foe who had entered the room. The man behind it all had finally appeared in front of him. BC questioned himself on how he didn't see it coming. How didn't he figure it all out? There had to be warning signs that he missed that would have opened the door to this entire mystery. BC was mad he was eyeing the setup and not what it really was, an all-out war.

"It's been a long while, BC, far too long. I'm sorry that we had to meet up under these circumstances but it is what it is, right?" Big O said.

BC started coughing. "That's how the game goes now. I see you are still the same bitch from years ago. You have bitches now doing your dirty work for you. I always knew you were soft and hid behind your man, but I thought you had more balls than to have a bitch putting in work for you. Actually, naw, I'm not shocked. They say birds of a feather flock together. I guess that goes the same for bitches, y'all flock together too."

Big O added a chuckle. "That was real cute, my nigga, real cute! You know that's not my style, homie, not in the least bit. As much as I'd love to shoot the breeze with you, we do have some business that we need to get back to."

"You might as well not even waste your time with the talking then and get back to the beating at hand," BC replied.

"A real nigga until the end, huh, man! I really do respect that. You are a true G. BC, if there is one nigga in this game I respect, it's you! I want you to know that."

Before BC could reply, the dark-skinned woman put two shots into the back of BC's head ending his life.

"A true soldier until the end," Big O said.

Big O took out his cell phone.

"It's done," he said into the handset, then hung up.

CHAPTER 28

O'Neal and Cheese sat in the car patiently waiting for the New York boys to arrive. O'Neal wanted to check out the meeting place to make sure everything was safe and no cops were in the area. He made sure they arrived early. However, as time started to grow closer to their arrival, he began to worry. He could sense something was wrong.

Cheese, on the other hand, was pissed about even being there. The fact that this was a major deal didn't matter to him. There was no need for personal attention until they had established a good business relationship with these cats and even then there still wasn't a need for one. No one knew anything about them. They could have been feds for all they knew. If so, there was no doubt they would have purchased themselves a one-way ticket straight to the pen.

No matter how much Cheese protested, O'Neal wasn't hearing it. He had a one-track mind and nothing else mattered to him. He wanted to have his hand on everything and personally pull the strings. He wanted it broadcasted that he was now the man in charge of the whole show.

"Where are these niggas at?" O'Neal said.

Cheese started shaking his head. "I told you, we should not even be here, O. This whole situation should be telling your ass something."

"Nigga, all it's telling me is you are bitching. Shit, that's all you've been doing all fucking day. I keep telling you, I'm not stuntin' these niggas or any nigga at that."

"O, you aren't thinking smart about this at all! It's not about what they can do to us but rather who they really are. How the fuck do we know that they aren't undercovers? We don't know shit. We out here in the open brokering the fucking deal like we go way back with these cats. This is something we need to put Joey on. If after a while they pan out, cool, but for now, we need to cover our own asses."

"Yeah, yeah, we are here now, so all that is pointless. It is not like we are out here with any product or anything. All we are doing is meeting these muthafuckas. I want to know who I'm doing business with. Plus, if they were feds, we'd know by now. That's what we have people on the payroll for, to find out information like that."

"When have you known the locals to ever know shit about anything before it happened? They are always a day late and a dollar short. I'm talking about federal. That is another league right there," Cheese said.

"You know who you sound like? You are starting to sound like that nigga Money and it's getting on my nerves. Nigga, be your own fucking man. Have your own fucking ideas!"

"Good, that means I sound like I have some sense then. It would be nice if you joined me. Ten years, nigga! We've been doing this now for ten years and we haven't even come close to sniffing a damn police station. Nothing! Money is the nigga we both need to be thanking for that. I'm glad I'm talking like that nigga because he is the reason why that shit happened. He knew to be smart regarding this business and what—and more importantly what not—to do.

"We don't need to change shit up now. We are doing fine

keeping things close and making this paper. Right now, you are all over the place with everything and you don't even know it. I don't know what the fuck is up with you but this shit has to fucking give. You are my man and I'll put that on everything I love, but if this is how shit is going to be, then maybe I need to join Money in early retirement too," Cheese said.

O'Neal started laughing. "I should have known. You aren't any different. You going to just turn your back on me, too, like the rest of them niggas. Is that what you are telling me? First, this nigga Money just walk away like we don't mean shit to the nigga. Then this nigga BC stands me up and doesn't show up to the deal and now you."

"Are you listening to anything you are saying? You are talking about the three niggas who would ride or die for you. Did you ever stop and think about the fact that if we bucking, it must be for a reason? Nigga, you aren't thinking clearly and not listening to anyone. We are out here naked right now and at what cost? Over four keys! Joey could have handled this deal.

"If your thing was meeting the man, cool! I can dig that but let them show who they are first. Then we check the shit out and make sure they are who they say they are and finally, we wait to see if they can do what they say and move the product they ask for. We go about it smart. If they feds, all they get is Joey. He'll do the years like they nothing and won't think twice. But us, we out scot-free, we still in the clear."

No matter how much sense Cheese was making or how much O'Neal wanted to admit Cheese was right, he couldn't. He wouldn't allow it. He couldn't help but feel as if the men he looked at as brothers were now betraying him. Betrayal was its own monster in itself.

Cheese's cell phone rang. "What's up?"

"Cheese, we've got a problem. The truck never showed."

"What the fuck do you mean the truck didn't show?" Cheese questioned.

"It never showed. We are still waiting at the spot to pick it up. It hasn't gotten here. This is unlike them. They have never been late on a shipment before."

"Okay, do this, give it a few more minutes and if they still don't show, then make your way back up here. I don't give a fuck how long a drive it is or how tired you are, the minute you reach back in D.C., you fucking find me. Do you hear me?" Cheese hung up the phone.

Cheese turned toward O'Neal. "O, hit BC on his hip. Tell him he needs to meet us at the hideout ASAP. We out!"

"Now you giving me orders!" O'Neal responded.

"Nigga, did you hear shit I fucking said? Our entire shipment didn't arrive. Right now, I don't give a fuck about how you feel or what you feel right. This shit isn't a coincidence. On the same fucking day our shipment doesn't arrive at the drop-off point, these New York boys are nowhere to be found. They have been calling all around town for this deal and they don't show. I'm not buying any of it. If you want to bitch, fine, bitch on the way back to the spot because whether you like it or not, we are out. Now hit BC on his hip."

Cheese quickly took the car out of park and sped off. He refused to sit out in the open and be sitting ducks. He checked his rearview mirror to make sure they were not being followed. O'Neal didn't protest. Instead, he did exactly what Cheese had asked. However, BC's phone was going straight to voicemail.

"All I'm getting is his voicemail. Maybe he's screening calls or something or he still in his feelings with me over our beef."

"Yeah, okay, try him on my cell then because that definitely doesn't sound like BC."

O'Neal took Cheese's cell and tried the call again. He got the same result. The call went straight to voicemail.

"Shit, I'm getting his voicemail again. He must don't have his phone on."

"Fuck!" Cheese shouted.

O'Neal handed Cheese back his phone. He couldn't help but think the worst. It was unlike BC to ever have his phone off. BC knew how important every call was. He made sure to keep his battery charged and extra batteries available. It didn't matter the situation, that phone would be on, and both of them knew it.

Cheese called the only person he could think of who would be able to fix things. This was something neither him nor O'Neal were prepared to deal with so early. He started to dial the number.

"Yo, I need you to meet us at the hideout. The shit has hit the fan."

"When?" Money asked.

"We about fifteen minutes out now," Cheese replied.

"Sounds good. I'm on my way," Money said, cutting to the chase.

The entire ride to their hideout spot was silent. All O'Neal could think about was his right-hand man. He knew someone had gotten to him. How, he'd never figure out. No man in this world is invincible but BC was the only one close to it. BC had niggas scared to even think about trying him. They knew the minute the thought crossed their minds BC had already anticipated the thought and they were six-feet deep, long before they could carry out their plan. His intuition was his best asset. He was always able to sniff out the setup.

O'Neal beat himself up over not listening to him. BC was so adamant about not going through with the deal and now it was looking as if what BC had predicted was finally coming true. O'Neal jumped with pistol in his hands pointed toward the front door as it opened. Once he saw it was Money, he eased up.

"Nigga, kill all that shit," Money said to O'Neal. "What the fuck is going on? Y'all niggas look like y'all on edge up in here."

"First things first, our shipment never arrived in South Carolina. Joey said it never showed up at the drop-off point," Cheese said.

"You said, 'first thing'…damn, there is more?"

"The deal with the New York boys was today and they never showed up. Also BC is missing in action."

Money didn't waste any time. He took out his phone and called the man who he knew would have all of the answers.

"Is this a free line?" Money asked.

"*Si, senor!*"

Money carefully thought of the proper words to use.

"I've just received word from my associates that their delivery never arrived. Can you shed any light to this situation?"

"My friend, we go way back. Is there anything that I need to know?"

"With all due respect, I'm not sure what you are referring to, so please be candid with me and say what is on your mind."

"I find it a little troubling that once you decide to leave the business that not only does a shipment disappear, but the drivers of this shipment end up found dead and in the cabin of the truck.

I also find it a little troubling to find out there was a deal in place with friends from the north, and I was never consulted by anyone in your camp on this matter," Mr. Cardoza said.

"Ten years! In ten years, I've never missed a payment, late on a shipment, or failed to deliver exactly what I stated I would deliver. I've always been a man of my word and a man of integrity. I stand by that and I hope you do as well."

"It's not you I question, my friend. It's your associates. Which is the very reason why I suspect you are the one placing this call in the first place—versus them."

"I can vouch for them. We have no idea as to what's going on. All I ask is for time to find out exactly what has happened and to handle it the proper way."

"I don't care what you do. The minute the shipment left Florida, it no longer became my responsibility. I'll expect payment by Friday."

Before Money could respond, Mr. Cardoza had already hung up the phone. Cheese and O'Neal both were on the seat of their pants hoping to hear Money say all was taken care of.

"The drivers were found in Georgia a little outside Florida without the shipment. Whatever you thought was going on, it's ten times worse. Not only do you have no product but you still need to come up with the two-point-seven million for it, plus another two-point-seven for another shipment."

"How the fuck is we supposed to come up with over five million dollars with no product to move to make it?" O'Neal questioned.

"I don't think you truly understand the severity of this situation. You haven't been given a choice but rather an ultimatum," Money answered.

CHAPTER 29

It had been over two weeks since LT'd had his last fix. The first couple of days were the hardest he had ever endured. His body ached. However, he didn't give in. This time, his determination would outweigh his desire to make the pain go away. If he felt the wall crashing in again, all he needed to do was picture and dream about reuniting with his family. That was all the motivation he needed in the world because there was no way in hell Denise would come back to him if he continued to be the same man he used to be.

LT could see himself holding his daughter again. He could see the two of them having a father-daughter talk. It had been so long since the last time he had seen her. There was so much they would need to catch up on. The only vision he had of her was one of the precious four-year-old he had last seen years ago. She was now thirteen. Several times he thought about going past his old home, but he never wanted her to see him high. He didn't want her to see the rundown addict he had become. He always prayed that any memory of the man she last saw was erased. However, he knew that wasn't the only memory gone. She probably had no real memory of him at all.

Then there was Denise. If there was ever one person who deserved to hate him, it would be her. The person who loved him the most, he, in turn, hurt the most. He knew things were probably damaged beyond all repair but he didn't care. The hope of being able to call her his wife again was enough to drive him down the road to recovery. He knew this fight was one he would go at alone.

LT didn't have family who cared enough to check up on him. The ones he did have he already had screwed them over when he was high. There weren't any friends. All he had was himself, his will, and his memories. Hopefully, that would be all he would need. His days now consisted of group therapy, one-on-one sessions, and workouts.

Group sessions turned out to be harder than what he first had anticipated. LT still wasn't quite at the point of opening up himself. Normally he would sit through the sessions and listen to others confess their past digressions. Today would be something different. He felt compelled to open up and let out a mountain worth of problems.

"Hello, my name is Lionel but everyone calls me LT."

"Hi, LT," the group said in unison.

LT continued, "Usually I sit back and stay quiet. I listen to everyone talk and tell their stories. Well, I'm an addict. It took me a while to face it, but I can say that I am truly an addict. I've lost about any and everything to drugs. I've lost my daughter, my wife, my job, the little bit of friends I had, and any other sense of family that remained. Luckily, the only thing I didn't lose was my mind. At least I didn't lose it totally.

"There was a time there where I had lost it for a while. When I say that, I mean there where times when I craved that high I would do about anything to get. Most of the time I was doing things that if I were in a right state of mind, I would have known I had no business doing them. It didn't matter. Achieving that high was the ultimate goal. I always knew that there would be consequences for my actions. I didn't care, though. Shit, I didn't care about anything but getting high. Oops, I'm sorry, I didn't mean to cuss," LT apologized.

"It's alright, LT. This is your time to talk and express yourself. I'm sure there are other people here who have gone through the same things as you have and need to hear that they are not alone. Right now is your time to make a difference. If cussing helps you do that, then you can say all that you want," the counselor said.

"Okay, well, as I was saying I didn't care who I hurt. As long as I found a way to get that high, that was all that mattered to me. I would steal from any and everyone if that was what was needed. I have gone as low as stealing from my own child. My precious little girl, I stole from my daughter. Every time I think about it I cry. What four-year-old should have to hide their belongings from their father? That doesn't even sound right."

He felt himself becoming vulnerable. He tried to hide his emotions, but he couldn't fight the tears any longer. It was obvious to everyone that his emotions had gotten the best of him.

"Take your time, baby, we are right here with you," a woman said.

"It's so hard. When you are high, life has no meaning. You have not a care in the world and nothing to worry about. But the minute you come down from that high, all you are left with are your thoughts, your fears, and insecurities. That was enough to push me back to get high again. I don't want to revert back to the person I used to be anymore. I don't. I can't. I need help."

"That is what we are here for. What makes you feel as though you will revert back?" the counselor asked.

"My past is proof enough. It's hard to change nine years. That is all I've done for the past nine years. In the past I would lie and say that I can handle things or I would lie to myself and say I'm not a junkie. The drugs didn't have a hold on me but instead I had a hold on them. The only thing I was doing was trying to kid myself. I know that now. I only pray that I haven't been an addict so long that I have lost myself as well in the process."

"You have already proven that you haven't lost yourself. It's inside you," a woman said.

"LT, use your wife and your child as your motivation. Let them be your drug. You say that in the past when things started to get hard and you were faced with the problems and issues of life, you turned to that next high to try to substitute for it. Well, let your family be your substitute. Allow them to help you deal with those type situations," the counselor suggested.

The woman chimed back in, "One thing that helps me tremendously is I write my mother and father letters. They haven't responded to any of them but it's a way for me to express my thoughts, concerns, and fears to someone other than the group. That way, it didn't feel as if I was going through things by myself. It also gives me some sense of family. I know that might sound weird but it does."

"What do you say in your letters?" LT asked.

"Mostly I ask for their forgiveness and hope that one day they can actually find a way to forgive me. I apologize for all that I've done in the past. I let it be known that in the event they are not able to ever forgive me that is something that I would have to deal with. I might not like it and definitely don't want to think about it. But I let them know that I have no expectations. My only concern was for them to know how sorry I was for all that I'd done.

"What's really wild is that even though I haven't gotten any response from them, I still feel at peace. The minute I owned up to my faults, it felt as if a huge weight had been lifted off of my shoulders. All the hurt and pain I had caused, though I can never make it go away, I made peace with it and know that I'm a stronger person now to deal with it and not cause it again."

"That sounds like a good idea. Maybe I should send Denise a letter."

"I don't see why not. But if you do, make sure you are doing it for the right reasons. Do it to express yourself and your feelings to her and not as an avenue to win her back because your words won't lie to her. She will be able to see right through you and know what your true intent is," the counselor chimed in.

LT's mind was made up. That was exactly what he was going to do. He went straight to his room and grabbed a pen and pad and got to work. He didn't know what to say, so he wrote from the heart.

Hi, Denise,

It has been a long time. Man, I don't even know where to begin or even how to start. You would think this would be easy being in written word versus face to face but it really isn't. They say it takes a real man to admit when he was wrong and to face his mistakes. I'm sorry, baby, it took me this long. I don't want anything from you. I need to express myself and who better than to you. I know I wasn't much of a husband and for that I apologize. I damn sure wasn't much of a father either and I'll make sure to send Alexis a letter as well. It wasn't that I didn't know how to be but rather I didn't know how to face the demon of drugs.

I always assumed since I never chose to be an addict, it would be something easy to kick. The drugs wouldn't run my life. My, how wrong I was, I'm sure I don't have to tell you that. And however absurd or asinine it might seem hearing this, I never intended on hurting you. By the time I was realizing what I was doing, it was too late. The drugs already had their hold on me; hook, line, and sinker.

I tried over and over again to tell myself I wasn't, I could kick it. But I couldn't and when that was evident I was ashamed to tell you. I was ashamed to ask for help. I always thought the definition of being a man was being able to handle whatever situation that arose and deal with it. I didn't think a man went to others for help or seek others' help.

I am man enough to say today, I was wrong. Getting help is what a responsible adult does. I know that now. I am proud to say I've been sober for close to two weeks now. Though that might not sound like shit and I haven't been faced with the temptation of the street to go back to drugs, it's a start. I feel this letter is a part of that start. Though our life as husband and wife might be over, it's the start for me making amends for the man I was. It's a start for me correcting all that I should have done back then. I feel like the same philosophy applies to getting help with my addiction, it's never too late. It's never too late to apologize and make amends.

Denise, I apologize for the man I was and the husband and father I wasn't. I can't go back and change the past and probably wouldn't if I could. Because then, I wouldn't be the man I am today. The trials and tribulations I've gone through are what have made me into what I am. However, I would change the pain and hurt I've caused you and Alexis. Nine years is a long time, I know, but again, it's never too late for some things. This hopefully is one of them.

Sincerely Yours,
Lionel

CHAPTER 30

BC's funeral was packed. It was hard to believe the man who was so feared by many was also loved by more. Mourners from all over the city came out to pay their respects. After the burial, Money set up for the immediate family and street family to have a private repast ceremony back at the funeral home. Security was tight, in case. These were war-time situations so he didn't want to make it easy for whoever was the mastermind behind everything. When you were most vulnerable was always the best time to strike.

Lil' Nep was taking things as good as expected. He had looked up to BC. That was his big brother and actually father figure so you wouldn't have been surprised if Lil' Nep simply lost it but he never did. He remained composed throughout. O'Neal, on the other hand, was a wreck. He hadn't had one good night of sleep after they found BC's body. He blamed himself for BC's death. Had he only listened to BC they would have taken action against the cats from New York long ago, and his man would still be alive. It didn't matter what anyone said. No matter how much anyone tried to console him, it wasn't going to work.

O'Neal's only comfort was knowing that whoever was behind this would soon suffer the same fate of his fallen comrade. O'Neal already had a contract out for information for whoever had pulled the trigger. The price didn't matter. Vengeance now filled his veins. It was so bad that O'Neal would even pay out on information that would put him next to someone who had information. His ultimate goal was revenge.

Money noticed O'Neal in the corner of the funeral home staring at the wall. Starr was with him at first, so he had decided to leave him be. But now he was alone.

"How are you holding up?" Money asked.

"I can't even call it. I can't stop thinking about everything," O'Neal replied dryly.

"Where is your girl? I haven't seen her in a while."

"I think she said she had to run. I'm not too sure. I remember her saying something like that before we left the house. I hope you didn't come over here to start with me about bringing her to the repast because if those are your intentions, I don't want to hear that shit right now."

"Naw, it's nothing like that, homie. I put that on everything I love. I know I'm hard on you about her but I was only asked because I saw her over here with you earlier and hadn't seen her for a while. That's all, it's nothing big," Money said quickly. He didn't really care about Starr's whereabouts. He was only trying to break the ice.

"Are we good?" O'Neal asked.

"What are you talking about?"

"I know I've been a little hard to deal with lately. I just want to know if we are good now. You are my man and I need you to know that. Especially with all that is going on right now. It's like, shit, I can't even really explain it. It's like the walls are coming crashing in on me and I feel all alone. I mean, yeah, I have Starr but it's not the same. She can't replace fifteen years. Shit, you and I go back farther than BC and I do. You know I need you in my corner. I need to know we are straight."

"O, you know you are family to me. Nothing will change that. I don't care what we go through. We can come to blows and tomorrow it's as if nothing happened. We are back to normal. You are my brother from another mother. Don't ever forget that. I know we aren't always going to see eye to eye. This isn't the first time we've bumped heads about something. We will always be good. That is no matter what!"

"That's good to know because I've really needed someone to talk to. Lately, I've been real fucked up. I can't shake these thoughts. It doesn't matter what time of day it is. I could be trying to get some sleep or whatever and I'll see this nigga callin' me for help, but I never make it there in time to save him. I'm always a step late and a dollar short. This shit is fucking haunting me and I feel like I'm losing my mind."

"Dawg, I'm going to tell you something and I really need you to listen to me. You can not keep blaming yourself for what happened. That blame doesn't belong on your shoulders. I really need you to relax and stop blaming yourself."

"That is easy for you to say. If you weren't battling me, you probably would have seen this shit coming. BC saw it. Even Cheese saw it. Everyone saw it but me. All I had to do was listen to any of y'all. Money, BC doesn't beg for shit. That isn't him. That man practically begged me not to deal with them dudes. He called the setup from the very beginning. He knew it and I ignored him and fought him all the way—all because I saw the opportunity to bring in more money. Who does that? When your man feels that strong about something, you have to listen to it. Fuck the money! But did I? Hell no!

"Money, I swear, I put this on everything I love. I will not rest until I find the muthafucka who pulled the trigger, the muthafucka who is pulling the strings, and every and any muthafucka who had anything to do with my man being in the ground." O'Neal started to become emotional. Tears started streaming down his face. He tried to collect himself and continue but couldn't. He was overwhelmed with emotion.

Talking and being able to express his feelings made things seem as if a huge weight was being lifted from off his back. Money didn't know how to react or what to make of O'Neal's actions. In all their years he had never seen this sensitive side of his friend. The way O'Neal went about anything with business you would expect him to be this coldhearted rock, regardless the situation. Instead, he showed the humane side of him. Losing someone that close to you would do that.

"Come on, O, pull yourself together before you have me up in here bawlin'. We have word out in the streets for these niggas. They will turn up. I even put word out to some folks I have up top to keep their ears to the ground and let me know about anything that falls. Sooner or later they will turn up. It's not like they can run or hide but for so long."

"I know, let me chill out. I know you probably like what the fuck is wrong with this nigga. Let's change the subject because if we don't, I'll probably go on and on. What's the deal with Mr. Cardoza? Are we back in good graces with him since we covered the price for that lost shipment?" O'Neal asked.

"'We'? What do you mean 'we'?"

"Nigga, you know what I meant. I know you took care of that situation, why are you breaking my balls?" O'Neal replied.

"It's a joke, O, nothing more than that. I don't know what to make of them right now. Everything seems as if it's cool but I can't help but feel as if they were trying to set things up for y'all to fail. How the fuck was you supposed to come with the bread? But then again that might have been the whole plan because there is no way we would have been able to go up against Latin America. Maybe all this shit had to do with me getting out of the game. I really don't know, homie. All I know is that I don't trust things at this moment."

"So are you saying we don't need to be doing business with them anymore? Trying to find another supplier isn't the easy thing to do. Mario's ass control South Florida."

"I'm not saying that right now. It all depends on where the deceit lies. I find it hard to believe Mario would jeopardize guarantee money over nothing. Either it's not him or there is more to this story. But whoever is behind it, knows too much. They know about us, Mario, and probably the whole situation. Either it's in our shop or in his; that much I can say."

"That jive puts us in a bind then because it's coming close to time for us to re-up and I can't afford to have another shipment snatched."

"It doesn't put you in one. You have no choice but to set up the deal. But make sure you are smart about it. Change everything up, I mean everything. From this point on, you only deal with Mario himself. You make sure he knows this. Since the problem could possibly be on his end, I'm sure he'll understand your apprehension. This will keep whoever guessing.

"Instead of meeting one of his drivers, send one of ours down to Miami to pick up the shipment and bring it home. It doesn't even make sense to chance it. Especially since I believe the problem is on his end. I trust the man to a certain degree but I damn sure don't trust his people. This would be the perfect job for Joey. It's going to be one hell of a drive but we all know he can handle it. In fact, Cheese probably needs to go with him. This is too top priority not to have one of you making the trip too."

"That's a lot of road to have Cheese traveling with all that product," O'Neal replied.

"I know but what choice do you have. There is no way Joey can do the sixteen hours down and back without having to pull over and rest. I know you don't want him pulling over. You have to have another driver. I don't want to send Cheese, but what choice do you have. This actually would have been perfect for…"

Money tried to catch himself but it was too late. O'Neal's mind quickly reverted back to BC. He put his head down as the tears started to stream.

"You never really appreciate a person and all they do for you until they are no longer in your life anymore. It's like that song Notorious BIG did back in the day, *You're nobody, til somebody, kills you*. That shit is so true."

"It is but not with BC. He knew how you felt about him regardless what y'all were going through. That was your man fifty-grand and nothing can change that."

"Yeah, maybe you are right," O'Neal replied. He paused, then continued, "So how have things been with you?"

"Shit, everything is jive hectic right now. I finally got a show set up for Lil' Nep and got a rep from Sony to attend it."

"That's what up right there. So you really are trying to do this music thing."

"Yeah, if things go as planned we surely are going to try to take the world by storm. I haven't told Lil' Nep yet about the Sony rep. Shit, the more I think about it, I don't think I told him about the damn show, either. I'm really slipping."

They both shared a laugh and noticed Cheese and Lil' Nep making their way toward the two of them. It was obvious something was on both of their minds.

"Yo, they found them," Cheese said.

"Who?" Money asked.

"Them New York niggas. They still in town," Lil' Nep replied.

O'Neal jumped up.

"The fuck is we waiting for then. I want these niggas' head on a fucking platter."

"It's all good, baby, Tiny got them niggas in the warehouse," Cheese informed.

Without another word being said, everyone headed for the door.

CHAPTER 31

When they arrived at the warehouse, they were shocked to only see one of the boys from New York. They were under the impression that Tiny had caught up with all of them. If not, then hopefully the head man. He would definitely be able to put them in the right direction. Instead they ended up with one of the boys who handled the muscle.

"Damn, Tiny, I see you got your fair share of licks in, huh, man," O'Neal said as he approached the both of them.

Both of his eyes were swollen and nearly shut. It looked like Tiny did more than get in a few licks.

"I'm sorry, O. I couldn't hold out. You know BC was my man," Tiny replied.

"It's all good, homie. I'm not mad at you at all. If I was in your shoes, I probably would have gotten a few in myself."

O'Neal turned his attention to his prey. He started to scratch the stubble on his beard. He pulled out his pistol and held it in his hand.

"Look here, playa, I'm not even going to fill your head with a bunch of bullshit. I'm not going to tell you if you tell me what I want to know, I'll spare your life and allow you to live. That isn't going to happen, playa, but what I will do is put two quick shots to your head and end any possible misery that you already haven't experienced.

"From the looks of things, looks like Tiny had some damn

good fun beating that ass until we got here. Now, I'm a little more twisted than him. I'll pluck body parts off of you. I will tear into your ass piece by piece until there isn't nothing left of you and won't think shit about it. But you can stop all of that by telling me all that I want to know."

"Nigga, do what you must because I don't know shit and even if I did, I'm not saying shit," he replied.

"I see you've got your chest already stuck out, huh, my man?" Cheese started laughing.

"These niggas, I tell you, they some funny muthafuckas," Cheese added.

"Who you telling, homie," O'Neal replied. "Tiny, do you have a blade on you?"

"Let me see." Tiny checked his pockets. "O, today must be your lucky day because I damn sure do have one." Tiny handed it to him.

He looked the New York boy in his eyes.

"You see this here? Back in the day, niggas didn't use pistols. They would take their shank and plug your lungs with it until you took your last breath."

Before anyone knew what was about to happen, O'Neal took the knife and stuck it into the boy's thigh muscle. He began to scream in pain.

"Even in jail, the preferred weapon is a shank. You can never go wrong with it. You don't have to worry about stray bullets that are intended for someone else hitting the wrong person or anything like that. Where you stick it, that's exactly where it goes."

Before the kid could catch his breath, O'Neal stuck the knife into his other thigh. This wasn't the scene for Lil' Nep and it was evident. He turned and faced the door not wanting to see any more.

"O, I think the boy has something to tell you now," Money chimed in. He saw Lil' Nep's reaction and though this was one of the niggas who had something to do with his brother being killed, he knew some things he still wasn't quite ready to see. "Isn't that right, son? Don't you have something you want to get off of your chest?" Money asked.

"What do y'all niggas want to know?" the boy replied.

O'Neal shook his head. "Man, they sure don't make them how they used to. I tell you that. I want to know who your boss is and where I can find him."

Without hesitation, the boy quickly replied, "His name is Wes and I honestly don't know where you can find him. We were all told to go into hiding."

"By who," Money asked.

"My orders came from Wes so I can't say. I'm guessing whoever paid us to do the job," he replied.

Tiny followed up with a swift right and left hand to the back of his head.

"Tiny, kill all that!" O'Neal said.

"My bad, I couldn't help it. This nigga put his hands on my man."

"Look, B, I've said over and over again I had nothing to do with your man getting killed. That is not on me, son," he said in his defense.

"Okay, let's say you are telling the truth, then what job were you paid to do?" Money asked.

"All we were supposed to do is lay eyes to the boy Money. We were supposed to set up a meet with him to cop some product and then report back. That was it."

"So Money was the target?"

"Not in that sense, if so, we knew nothing about it. The way it was brought to us was to set up the meet for the connect and the rest would be handled by whoever."

"But you said you were supposed to lay eyes on Money. Why lay eyes on him, kid, if you were only setting up a connect?" Cheese asked.

"Do you do business with a nigga you've never seen before? Though his reputation travels you can never be too sure. How does a nigga stay in the game as long as he has and never been indicted or arrested or nothing? From what Wes said, there was no paper on him at all. He said he wasn't trying to find out that Money was actually a fed."

"Nigga, please, try that shit on some niggas that don't know any better," Cheese replied.

Money didn't say anything. He knew he was the target regardless what the boy said. It was obvious he was too low in the chain to know the true plan. He was only being used as a pawn. He knew there was no more to gain from him so he didn't bother to continue interrogating him.

"Who put out the order?" O'Neal asked.

"I told you I got my orders from Wes."

"No, the orders for the hit on my man?"

"I don't know. My guess, whoever is running the show."

In one swift motion, O'Neal took the boy's left ear off.

He began to scream out in pain. Blood gushed everywhere.

"It's obvious there is some type of break in our communication and you are not understanding me fully. I'm guessing it must be because you can't hear me. Hopefully, we will not continue to have this problem.

"Now I'm going to ask you one more time, who put out the hit on my man?"

Tears filled his eyes. "I don't know. Wes never said. I only came down as a favor to him. I never met the guy. I don't think Wes did, either. He usually got his orders from T. Lee."

"How do you get in contact with Wes?"

A light went off in Tiny's head. He remembered going through the boy's pockets before he had tied him down. He wanted to make sure he was unarmed and he'd found a cell phone.

"Hold up, O," Tiny said. He ran over to where he had put the phone and grabbed it. He flipped it open and looked for the name "Wes" in the phone book. "Jackpot! He got the boy number in his cell."

"That's what's up. Now we are getting somewhere. Bring me the phone." O'Neal looked at the boy. "I want you to tell him that you have some urgent news you need to tell him about Money. Tell him you got wind to where he lay his head at. Tell him you want him to meet you at the playground in the school-yard across the street from Anacostia subway station."

The boy didn't refuse. He did exactly what he was asked to do. He knew O'Neal meant business and wanted his misery to end fast. He couldn't take it any longer. The minute he hung up the phone, O'Neal happily obliged him. He sprayed four shots into the back of the boy's head.

Everything was set for Wes to be at the schoolyard in an hour.

"Tiny, when you spot the kid, point him out, then we'll pick him up. If we have to pluck these niggas one by one, that is exactly what we are going to do."

"That's a bet. Let me get some in with the boy," Tiny replied.

"Lil' Nep, you have any heat?" O'Neal asked.

"No," Lil' Nep replied.

"I have another in the car. Take this one."

"Naw, he good," Money replied.

"The fuck do you mean he is 'good'? The nigga just said he bare. He's not going out there with us like that. Anything can happen. Who is to say this nigga comes solo? He might have company."

"That's my fault for not being more clear, he isn't going. I told you before, we are out! I thought you had the nigga who killed BC so I didn't object earlier because I thought he was going to get some type of closure and that was my fault. It stops here though."

"Man, who the fuck is this nigga?" Tiny said.

Money turned toward him but didn't say a word. Cheese quieted Tiny before he said the wrong thing.

O'Neal started to laugh. "I'm starting to wonder the same fucking thing, Tiny, because this isn't the nigga I would ride or die for. I don't know who this nigga is in front of me right now."

O'Neal scratched his temple with the barrel of the pistol.

"Nigga, you question where my heart is at again and I'll kindly remind you."

"Now I want to know, who the fuck do you think you are talking to?"

Before O'Neal finished his sentence, Money had his pistol drawn and pointed at O'Neal. He no longer trusted his best friend's action. O'Neal wasn't himself and Money wasn't willing to bet that O'Neal would check himself and realize the situation. Money knew better. He knew O'Neal was the type to react and think about what he had already done after the fact.

"You going to kill me now, Money? Now I'm the enemy. Is that how you feel? Brother, right?" O'Neal asked.

"Money," Tiny said under his breath, now understanding why Cheese stopped him. He had never laid eyes on the myth before and had no idea it was him even though he worked for him.

"Look, both of y'all put the pistols down and let's talk about this. We just buried BC today and I'll be damned if I go through that again with either of you, especially not at the hands of one of you. We are bigger than that," Cheese said.

"Lil' Nep, get in the car. We are out," Money said.

He ignored Cheese. With time O'Neal might calm down and they would be able to talk about all that happened. But Money knew now was definitely not the time. He knew O'Neal hated being embarrassed and it didn't matter by whom.

CHAPTER 32

"What just happened back there?" Lil' Nep questioned.

Money quickly shook it off. "Nothing you need to worry about. So do us both a favor and don't worry. Trust me when I tell you, it's nothing serious. Plus, right now I need your mind focused on this show I set up for you."

"Show, what do you mean show?"

"Didn't I tell you I was going to come through for you? I'm a man of my word. I set it up for you to perform at this club for their open mike night."

"Are you serious?"

"What do you think?"

Lil' Nep didn't hide his excitement. All of his dreams were finally starting to take shape. He was used to recording songs. That was nothing new but doing a show—he was now in uncharted waters.

"That's what's up. So what day did you set everything up for?"

"Oh, now you are full of questions, huh?" Money joked.

"I'm just saying, I want to make sure I'm on my A game. That's all. I want to make sure I'm well prepared. This is my first show so I understand how big an opportunity this is. I'm not trying to go out there not prepared and make either of us look bad. Fuck that! Before I hit that stage, I want to make sure I have my routine down to a science. That's all."

"I hear you, lil' man. The show is this Saturday night. So I need you to decide what song you are going to rock. I want you to bring music for at least three songs in case you rock the first one and they ask you to do more. You never know these days. Plus, who is to say that everyone scheduled to perform will even show up. If they don't, they'll need replacements. You rock the first one, I'm sure they'll be willing to let you rip a couple more. They have to do something to fill time slots. If they don't suggest it, then we will. I don't see them denying us, especially if the crowd is feeling you and is asking for me. Yeah, we are going to take these niggas by storm."

"That does make sense. I'm on it. As a matter of fact, drop me off at the studio now so I can get to work. I want to crank out a couple of new hits specifically for this show. It doesn't feel right going up there and rocking that old shit. This is a new beginning, a new chapter. I want to go up on stage and hit with some shit never heard before."

Money was already two steps ahead. He could tell that the light bulb in Lil' Nep's mind was shining loud and bright.

"Is that right? Do you already have something in mind?"

"Yeah, I actually do," Lil' Nep replied.

Without Nep saying a word, Money already knew what the topic of whatever he came up with would be.

"Regardless what you do, I'm sure you'll make BC proud."

Lil' Nep started to think about his brother. All day he tried to stay strong and keep his mind off of the pain. But he couldn't deny that he would pay anything to see the expression on BC's face while he was on staged ripping the mike. The slogan for the MasterCard commercials that came on TV described it best— *priceless*. BC's opinion had always been the one that mattered the most to him. If he approved and accepted him as an MC then Lil' Nep knew that anyone else would; if not, he didn't care. BC was always his toughest critic.

Lil' Nep quickly changed the subject to take his mind off of his brother. "So what are you going to do about O'Neal? I can't lie, though you say it's nothing to worry about, that nigga has me shook. I'm not trying to go head up with that nigga. I don't think you should be trying to, either."

"I'm not worried about him, champ. Trust me when I tell you, there is nothing to worry about there. He is more talk than action when it comes to the two of us. That is my family. We are no different than whenever you and your brother went head to head about something. At the end of the day or night, it was over and done with and all love again between the two of y'all. Brothers fight, that's what they do. We aren't any different. O'Neal and I are the same."

"I've never pulled a pistol on my brother. You did. That is totally different than BC putting his foot in my ass and calling it a night. He has never pulled out on me and never would," Lil' Nep shot back.

There was no denying Lil' Nep was right. This was a totally different situation. Money didn't want to give Lil' Nep any ammunition. It didn't matter that he wasn't too sure himself about what to make of O'Neal. Money knew he was now unpredictable. One minute they were making up, the next they were going at it again. Money didn't want to believe that his life possibly could be in jeopardy at the hands of his best friend. But at the same time he wasn't going to be naive about the situation.

"Look here, I need you to promise me something. I need you to promise me no matter what happens, you stay clear of the game. I don't care what it is; I don't want you having anything to do with the game or anyone in it. If you are, you are all the way and that's how I need you."

Lil' Nep was confused. "Why are you talking like that?"

"Let's not be naive about things. We are at war right now and though I'm no longer in the day to day, my name will always be associated with the family. That will never change no matter how much I want it to. I accept that but that is the life I chose. You didn't. I don't want it to get to the point where you are so far in like me, you can't get out.

"This right here is what you need to be doing and that only. You have a gift and you need to let that gift shine. Your brother believed in you enough to let you go, I believe in you enough to see you grow, so I need you to respect us enough to follow through and bring this dream to light. Do you have that? So come on, right now, I need you to promise me."

"You have my word," Lil' Nep replied.

"Never forget, a man is only as strong as his word. Make sure you keep yours to me."

O'Neal struck out with Wes. He never showed up to the meeting he was supposed to be having with his soldier. O'Neal figured someone must have tipped him off about the setup. That didn't disturb him that much, because at least now he had a name and more information All he had to do was have his foot soldiers hit the streets hard with it and turn something up.

Once he realized they had been stood up, O'Neal asked Cheese to drop him off at his crib. He was tired of hiding out and refused to do it any longer. It had been a while since he had time to chill with his girl. He missed her and craved a night alone in the presence of her company more than anything.

On the way there, O'Neal decided to phone ahead so Starr would be at his house waiting for him. To his surprise, she was already there. Her excuse was because she wanted to make sure the place was clean for whenever he decided to come home. O'Neal didn't care what the excuse was; as long as she was there that was all that mattered to him. He had missed her so much over the last couple of days. Seeing her at the funeral and spending some time with her then didn't help matters. Instead it only took things to another level. Cheese, however, protested the idea.

"I really need you to think about what you are doing. We are at war right now and we are on the wrong end of the stick. Right now is the time we need to be laying low, at least until we know who we are at war with. Going home is the last thing you need to be doing. Come on, O, this is a time where we need to be smart about everything we do and how we do it. That is all I'm saying."

"Nigga, I'm not trying to hear all that shit. I'll be damned if I go into hiding over these bitch-ass niggas. They bleed the same way I do. My heart does not pump any Kool-Aid. There is no sugar in my tank. If a nigga wants to bring the drama to my door, best believe I'll have something waiting for their ass. Fuck that!"

"Sometimes I wonder if you confuse the difference between having heart and being smart," Cheese said. "Nigga, being smart about shit don't mean that you don't have heart. I don't get you. It's like you think staying low means you are a bitch. It doesn't. All we are doing is holding tight until we find out whose head we need to hit. When we find out, then we do what we do and handle that shit on a gangsta level.

"Open your eyes and really look at how much of a disadvantage we are at right now. These muthafuckas know everything about us and we don't know shit about them. You want to be out in these streets blind. Nigga, don't you get it? We are walking in the fucking dark right now. If your ass walking around in the dark long enough, sooner or later, you will bump into the wrong thing and end up getting hurt. Staying low, you avoid that shit. That is being smart!"

"Take me to my crib," O'Neal coldly replied. "I'm not trying to hear all that shit."

Cheese shook his head.

"This nigga Money is right, you are out of fucking control. I'm starting to think you fucking sniffing that shit we pushing or something. At least then this bullshit you are on could be explained. It would make some type of fucking sense."

"Who the fuck do you think you are talking to?" O'Neal asked, getting defensive.

"Nigga, you really letting this power shit get to your fucking head. We are the ones who have been there for your ass since day one. You can swell up on them cats out in the streets, but don't bring that shit to me. Money already made it clear how he felt about it too. The fuck is wrong with you?" Cheese quickly replied.

"Nigga, fuck Money! I have something for his ass later. Right now I have these damn New York boys to worry about. You keep at your mouth like you've lost your mind and I will quickly add your name to the list too."

Cheese started laughing.

"Slim, you really are off the fucking deep end. You are so far gone I can't help but to laugh. You want to go home, cool. I don't give a shit. You are going to do what the fuck it is O'Neal wants to do regardless what anyone else has to say. It's always about what you want. Everything is about O'Neal."

"Yeah, whatever." O'Neal replied.

Cheese pulled up in front of O'Neal's crib and didn't say a word. Cheese didn't even bother to put the truck into park. He sat waiting for O'Neal to get out. They were both so engulfed with their argument neither was paying much attention to their surroundings. Both missed the two masked men making their way toward the truck.

O'Neal opened the door to get out.

"Yo, Cheese peel out!" O'Neal yelled as he finally noticed what was about to take place.

He quickly jumped back in. Before Cheese could even get his foot on the gas pedal, bullets were already in the air and headed toward the truck. O'Neal got as low as possible. He noticed the truck wasn't moving but only coasting. He looked up and Cheese's head was on the steering wheel. He'd been hit.

O'Neal quickly took his hand and pressed down on the gas pedal without a care in sight. He knew if he didn't try to get out of there, he was a dead man. The truck sped off down the street. O'Neal took his hand off the pedal and looked over the dashboard. He noticed the truck was about to hit a parked car. He quickly swerved out of the way.

The shooters were still in range and firing nonstop at the back of the truck so O'Neal still couldn't move Cheese's body out of the way to take total control. Instead, he put his left leg over to the driver's side and pressed down on the gas pedal. Once he hit the intersection, he turned onto the next street and out of fire. He didn't stop. He wasn't sure if they would be following far behind in pursuit to finish the job.

O'Neal continued down the street until he reached the entrance to a back alley. Without hesitation, he turned down the alley. Once the truck was out of plain sight, O'Neal stopped the truck. He tried to shake Cheese to see if he would awake but it was too late. He was already gone. The shots that had hit him in the back of his head had ended his childhood friend's life.

CHAPTER 33

O'Neal didn't know what to do. He didn't have anywhere he could go. He couldn't go home. There was no telling who was there waiting on him. It was a difference being the hunted versus the hunter. O'Neal was finding that out the hard way. He was a wanted man now. O'Neal thought long and hard about what to do and decided to go to the only safe haven he could think of. He knew no one would ever think to find him there and even if they did, they had no way of knowing how to get there.

O'Neal pulled up into the drive and contemplating showing up. It probably would have been best if he would have called ahead prior to coming. He wasn't too sure if Money was still beefing with him over their earlier argument. It was too late to worry about any of that now. The circumstance had chanced drastically so Money would have to get over it. O'Neal went up and knocked on the front door. Money opened the door. He noticed the blood all over O'Neal's clothes.

"What the fuck happened?" Money questioned.

Though O'Neal was covered in blood, he wasn't hit. He was covered in Cheese's blood. When he had moved his body into the back seat of the truck, that's when it had gotten on him.

"These niggas just tried to hit my head. Cheese tried to warn me but I wouldn't listen. I had to fucking go home. He tried," O'Neal ranted.

Money opened the door all the way so O'Neal could come in.

"Naw, I don't think that is a smart idea. I don't know. Right now I don't know what to make of anything. Money, you don't get it, these niggas were at my fucking crib. How the fuck did they even know where I live? The more I try to make sense out of this shit, the harder it is."

"Standing out here isn't going to get us any closer to the answers we need. Come on inside the house and let's talk about this," Money reiterated.

The tears started to well up in O'Neal's eyes.

"There is something I didn't tell you."

Money could sense something serious was wrong. It was unlike O'Neal to cry out of the blue. He looked around and noticed who was missing.

"Where is Cheese?" Money asked.

O'Neal turned and headed back toward the truck. Money didn't know why but something told him to follow him. He wasn't sure if O'Neal was about to leave or what. If he was, Money wasn't about to let him to. They both needed to sit down and figure out what the next move would be and this was something that they needed to do together.

O'Neal opened the car door to the backseat and stood there and looked. Money looked at O'Neal as if he was crazy, then moved in closer to see what exactly O'Neal was trying to show him. Once he saw he was lost for words. There lay the body of Cheese across the backseat.

"No! No! O, NO, tell me that isn't what I think it is. What the fuck? How the hell did this shit happen!" Money yelled.

They had buried BC earlier that morning, now Cheese was gone. It couldn't be.

Money collected himself because he knew going off on O'Neal

wouldn't get them anywhere. He needed to know exactly what had taken place. "O, I need you to start from square one and tell me what the fuck happened. And I don't care how small a detail it might be, don't leave nothing out."

"Money, everything happened so fast I didn't really have time to see or process anything. They hit as soon as Cheese pulled up to my crib. I got out of the truck and that is when I noticed them. I jumped back in and told Cheese to get out of there but before he could, they had already hit him."

Money could tell by all the holes in the back of the truck what O'Neal was saying was the truth.

"I almost didn't get out of there myself. If I hadn't put my fucking foot on the gas pedal, I probably would be laying in front of my crib on the curb next to Cheese right now with a fucking chalk outline around me."

"They had to have known your ass was going home. Why else would they just sit on your house? Plus, you said they were making their way up to the truck as you were getting out. That means they've been doing surveillance on our whips or…"

"Or what?" O'Neal asked.

"Someone is snitching. I should have known, think about it. How the fuck they know Cheese truck? He rarely even pushes it. Someone is feeding whoever information about us. I don't give a fuck who it is; they aren't this got damn good. We have a leak somewhere. That is the only thing it can be. It has to be a leak somewhere in our organization."

"Even if so, I don't see how they would have known to catch me at the crib. I didn't even tell Cheese to drop me off there until we were already in the truck. No one knew I was going home but Cheese and we know he wasn't a snitch."

"What happened with the boy Wes?" Money asked.

"Shit, we struck out there also. This nigga never showed."

"Are you sure he didn't, or you just didn't spot him?"

"I'm positive. There was no one on that damn playground. There is no way I could have missed him unless he showed up early. Even then, why wouldn't he wait until it was time for him to meet his man? Naw, you are right. I think someone in these niggas' ears because he had to have been tipped off. That is the only way I can see him not showing because he knew it was a setup."

"Yeah, but who, we were the only four in the damn warehouse. Did y'all say anything to anyone?"

"No! Money, I wish I knew. It seems like the closer I get, the farther away I realize I actually am when it comes to figuring this shit out."

"What about Tiny? How much do you know about the kid or better yet, how much does he know about you?"

"It's not Tiny. I'll vouch for him. Plus, he knew where the hideout spot was. If it was him, why not hit us there instead of my house. But to answer your question, he doesn't know where I lay my head. If I saw him, it was always in the street."

"Okay, well, did you at least get a good look at the hitters?"

"Naw, these niggas were masked up and even if they weren't, I saw them coming at us with pistols drawn. I wasn't paying attention to their damn face. The shit happened so damn quick, I shouldn't even be here, really, nigga. When I say they were on top of everything, they were. If they were maybe a split-second faster, they would have got me," O'Neal replied.

"Okay, well, for right now, I need you in a hotel until we can figure this shit out. I don't want you calling anyone, O, and I mean that. It's obvious we have a leak somewhere who knows a little bit too much and is selling their soul right now. Until we find out who the fuck it is or what we are up against, I need your ass safe and laying low. I'll be damned if I lose you too. Fuck that! Do you hear me? I'll take care of everything else," Money commanded.

"No, I'll be alright. I don't want you mixed up in this shit. I'll be fine. They caught me slipping once, but they won't catch me slipping again. I can promise you that much."

"O..."

O'Neal cut Money off, "Money, look, I don't need you fighting me on this one. I'll lay low for a few but I will handle things. You have a show to worry about. I'm not trying to drag you back into this street shit. I know I get besides myself a lot at times but I'm really proud of you. I'm proud of what you are trying to do. Shit, who knows, maybe later on down the line I'll give this shit up, too, and join you.

"But for right now, you handle your business with that music and make Lil' Nep's dreams come true and let me handle this street shit. You and I both know that is what BC and Cheese would have wanted.. I know lately I've been fucking shit up, but I got this. I'll figure everything out. I have to. My niggas didn't die for nothing."

"Champ, I need you to listen to me. I'm in this with you for life. Even though I'm out, I'm always in it. They are here looking for me just as hard as they are looking for you. I just haven't been found yet. But best believe they aren't going to stop looking for me until they find me. How can they? The only way I can truly do Lil' Nep any good is to team up with you and squash this war now before it gets out of hand and out of our control," Money replied.

Money extended his hand. O'Neal shook it in agreement.

"The truck is hot so you don't need to be pushing it. Take one of my cars and I'll get on the phone to JayMarr so he can tell me what to do about Cheese body."

"My bad, I didn't feel right dumping him anywhere. I know that was probably the smart thing to do but it just didn't feel right," O'Neal said.

"And it wasn't, you did the right thing. Now go ahead and get out of here. I don't want you taking any chances out here, O, so I need you to go across the line and check into a hotel in Virginia. That little motel on Route 1 by Fast Eddie's is the perfect spot. You have a couple of fast-food spots you can hit to get something to eat while you're there. That way you don't have to go too far out the area. Text me what your room number is after you check in. I'll get up with you Friday. That gives us a couple of days to let things die down.

"In the meantime, I'll check around and see if someone in-house is asking about you. Hopefully, that will put us closer to who our leak is and we can go from there. Also I'll get the word out on info on the boy Wes and this mystery bitch," Money said.

"That's what's up."

CHAPTER 34

Hey there, Lou,

How have things been? I know I'm probably the last person you thought you would hear from. I've gotten in the habit of sending Denise a letter each night. Today, it came to me that she wasn't the only person that I needed to apologize to. She wasn't the only person that my actions hurt. So, I'm sending you this letter mostly to apologize for those actions.

It took for me to get locked and sentenced here to verbally admit that at some point along the line, I lost the cop you took the time to teach me to be. I lost the man my mother raised me to be. I totally lost my identity and myself in the process. I realized this long ago but never admitted it. But even if I had it would have still been far too late. I was already gone and deep in denial.

I can admit it now. Shit, it seems like the only time people ever admit the wrong they've done or cause is always after they've done whatever it is they did to cause it. The counselor here says that is a part of life. I don't doubt it. I'm learning how to deal with that part though instead of turning to drugs to help me forget. It's all a process. Everything is really, but with time, one day I'll be there. I have to not rush and take it one day at a time.

This place isn't what I thought it would be. It's not that bad. I sat around and thought about what it would be like when I'm no longer here anymore. Because sooner or later that day will come and it will be something I have to deal with. I know that I'm not ready for it now.

I'm far from it. That's why I try to absorb everything they teach us here or listen to all the stories of everyone's downfall. Those are the things that will make me a stronger person. Those are the things that will help and have me better equipped to deal with the situations life presents.

It's scary because with each passing day, it brings me a day closer to leaving. Last night that was all I could think about. Here I have a circle. I have people that I can come to and talk to and share the things on my mind. Also, listening to what they've gone through or how they handled a certain situation and finding out the consequences of their actions is also another great learning tool. One guy here has been in rehab three times and each time he got out it was always a different thing that happened that caused him to fall off the wagon. By him sharing in a group, it opens my eyes.

Well, I don't want to go on and on about this place. I do that enough with Denise. The real reason why I'm writing you, Lou, is because I finally found him. I wanted to tell you. It took close to what, nine, maybe ten years, but I found the nigga who started my downfall. And the trip-out is, after I found him I realized that he wasn't even the one who started it. I was. The whole time, whenever I looked in the mirror I was staring at the bastard then.

I realized I valued the wrong things in life first. My job came before my family. I even conned myself into thinking that good I was doing in the community, by doing my job, no one else could do. It was so bad I had myself believing it to the point where the job had to come first. It was a must. That's how serious it was.

I feel like such the fool. I wasn't superman. I wasn't any different than the next officer. We all do good in the community. That is the nature of our job. It didn't have to be me taking on the prize cases, at least not all the time. We are a police force comprised of many officers.

But all I saw was myself. That was the only thing that mattered and that right there was the start down the wrong path and until now, I never recovered. It wasn't when they pushed that poison in me but then I probably wouldn't have even been on that case if I had put my family first.

That is so frustrating, too; seeing exactly where you made your mistakes but by then it was already too late to correct them or stop them. Before I even took the Cardoza case, I had already worked three other long-term cases. You actually asked me to take some time off and get away from work for a while. But no, my hardheaded ass didn't want to take your advice. I wanted to do what I wanted to do and that was all that mattered. Do you see the pattern? It's always all about Lionel Taylor.

I'm learning, Lou. I can honestly say that I am learning. I wish that things didn't have to get to this point for me to learn so much but I guess I can't help that. I can only play the cards that I dealt myself.

Well, I didn't want to bore you with a long drawn-out letter. I wanted to send you something mostly to apologize and to let you know, you once believed in me but it didn't matter. It didn't help. It was because I didn't believe in myself. The whole world can believe in me but I have to believe in me. One day I'll make you proud again and it won't be for bringing in a big case or anything police-related. I'm going to make you proud because I'll be the best man that I can be and turn my life around.

Take care, Lou. Until the next time,
Lionel

CHAPTER 35

O'Neal hated the whole idea of being in hiding. He was growing restless. All he could do was sit around and wait. That wasn't him, nor was it in his nature. He was always on the block and in the middle of everything in one way or another. This time though, he couldn't do that. He had the proof already of how serious this situation was.

There were beefs before in the past, but none to the point where his head was almost hit. Definitely not any to where they lost anyone close. Most people wouldn't risk going up against them. It was perceived in the streets that if you did, that was a guaranteed death wish. But now, O'Neal couldn't help but to think they were looking like chumps in the streets.

These people had succeeded where no one else had. They were able to get to BC, Cheese, and came close to getting O'Neal. The only one who they hadn't been successful with was Money. O'Neal realized why. Money always preached the importance of hiding in the shadows and now O'Neal saw exactly how that paid off. If no one knew who to hit, then how could they ever get close to do so? Any attempt would have had to come from someone within your inner circle which would consist of two to maybe three people. That alone limited the possibilities.

No one in the streets knew Money. Most people knew him as Nate. Everyone else only knew of the myth or the name of Money but everyone knew the respect that name carried. O'Neal knew it was time for a change. He needed to learn from what was to be a proven successful theory.

O'Neal hadn't been out of the hotel since he had first checked in. When it came time to eat, he'd ordered out. It had been a couple of days and he figured some sunlight would do him some justice. He wasn't going to go far, only to the 7-Eleven which was within walking distance. His face wasn't known in Virginia so that wouldn't be a problem. However, just in case, he made sure to be carrying.

O'Neal walked out of his dingy room and headed for the parking lot. Something didn't feel right but he wasn't sure if he was overreacting or not. He couldn't help but to think he was being paranoid. Then his suspicion proved him wrong. His first instinct was correct.

One of the men who didn't succeed in the first attempt on O'Neal's life was back to finish the job. O'Neal was on it this time. Before the assassin could react, O'Neal already had released four shots into his body. The assassin dropped to the ground. O'Neal walked over to him and released one final shot to his head to make sure he had ended his life.

A car in the parking lot sped off toward the highway. O'Neal started to fire at it. He didn't care who may have witnessed the shootout. All that mattered to him was stopping that car from getting away. Unfortunately, he was unsuccessful. Soon the car was out of sight.

O'Neal knew he didn't have long before Virginia's finest would be on the scene and he would be led away in handcuffs. He ran to his room and collected all of his stuff. He had given a fake name when he checked in so he wasn't worried about being tracked that way. He grabbed his car keys and headed for the highway also.

He didn't know where to go. He whipped out his cell and called the only person he trusted.

"Hello."

"Hey, baby, where are you?" O'Neal asked.

"In the house," Starr replied.

"Okay, good. I'm on my way over there."

"Is something wrong?"

"Not over the phone. I'll talk to you when I get there."

She didn't protest. Both of them ended the call.

During the drive to Starr's house all O'Neal could think about was how they had found him. He made it a point not to tell anyone where he was staying because he didn't know who he could trust. He called Money to make him aware of what had gone down. There was no answer on his cell phone. It was going straight to voicemail. O'Neal couldn't help but to think the worst. He hadn't talked to Money since the night Cheese was murdered. He needed to find out something so against his better judgment, he called Tiny.

"What up?" Tiny said into the phone.

"What's the word on the street?"

"Who dis?" Tiny questioned.

"Look, nigga, I don't have time for you to try to register the voice. Answer my fucking question," O'Neal snapped back.

"My bad, O'Neal, I didn't pick up your voice off the bat. The streets aren't saying much. I was a little nervous though once I found out about what happened to Cheese, then I hadn't heard shit from you the last couple of days so I didn't know what was what."

"Have you heard anything about Money?"

"Like what?"

"If that is your reply, then you just answered my question. I hadn't heard from him in a minute and I got a little worried."

"Naw, I haven't heard anything about that nigga. I wouldn't worry too much. I never hear shit about him. He keeps his name out of folks."

"Any update on the nigga Wes?"

"Naw, I don't have any leads on this cat at all. I'll find him, you better believe that. My nigga didn't die for nothing."

"Okay, well look, I'll get up with you later on or something. I don't want to spend too much time rappin' on this phone."

♣♦♥♠

O'Neal pulled up in front of Starr's house and sat in the car for a minute. He didn't know what to do. It seemed like he was a step behind and too slow, yet the answer to everything was staring him in his face. But he couldn't see it. The frustration would have to continue until he could figure it out.

The minute he stepped into the door, Starr came at him with a shitload of questions.

"What the fuck is going on, boo? And don't feed me any of that 'don't worry about it' shit, either."

The emotions of things really took over. Before a word even came out of O'Neal's mouth, tears were rolling down his face. Starr's demeanor changed.

"Baby, what is wrong?"

"Right now I'm walking around in the dark and bumping into every fucking thing."

Starr was confused. "What are you talking about, boo? Right now you aren't making any sense."

O'Neal calmed himself. "Where do I start? I've had two attempts on my life this week and each time it seems like they get closer and closer. These muthafuckas know more about me than I probably do. I haven't heard from Money. This nigga phone is going straight to voicemail. That is the same exact thing that happened with BC when I was trying to get in contact with him and look how that turned out."

"I wouldn't worry too much about him," Starr replied sarcastically.

"I'm not in the mood for none of your shit right now. This is serious. I know you don't like him but that is my man. Here it is he could be dead and in a dumpster or something and you want to bitch. We are at fucking war right now."

O'Neal tried to calm himself again but it wasn't working. "This is a nigga I have known over ten years of my life so can you please, spare me all that extra shit."

Starr decided to get off of Money. "So what happened?"

"Somehow they found out where I was hiding out and I don't know how. I didn't tell anyone. Money made it a point to remind me not to."

"Look, I can't sit here and not say anything. I know you don't want to hear it but I've never been phony. Your own man is setting your ass up. Boo, based upon everything that has happened and all that you've told me, think about it. Who would have known about the shipment? Who knew how to get to BC or you? You said it yourself, no one knew where you were hiding but yet they found you. I bet you told one person. I bet his ass knew exactly where you were and what room you were staying in. You might not want to hear it or listen, but your man is setting you up and I'll be damned if I allow him to succeed.

"Look, baby, I know I can be this bitch when it comes to a lot and I know I'm not the best at expressing how I feel, But I love you and I don't know what I'd do if I lost you. I don't, so please don't ask me to shut up or not say nothing when I see what is happening. I hear what is being said around the block and I know what you tell me. I know you and Money haven't been right in quite some time now, and I find it awfully funny around the time y'all started going back and forth all this shit is happening.

"If you want to be dumb and blind about the situation, fine, go ahead ,but do it on your time and not at the expense of my heart. You do the math; with you out of the way he can do things how he wants when he wants."

"Baby, if that is the case, then why would he step down? Why would he get out of the game if he wanted me out of the game? That doesn't make sense. It doesn't, I'm sorry, it doesn't."

"It doesn't make sense because you don't want it to. I've played the game he is playing, so I can see right through him. Shit, I played it with getting you. I knew I wanted you the minute I saw you in the club. I only acted as if I didn't to make you try harder. It's all the same. Him acting like he was getting out of the business was to throw you off of his true intentions."

O'Neal's cell phone ringing interrupted their conversation.

"Where the fuck have you been?" O'Neal asked.

"I was in the studio with Lil' Nep. You know he has a show tomorrow. I just got word from JayMarr about you. What the hell happened?"

"Nigga, I don't even know. I was about to head up to the 7-Eleven and then I saw the nigga making his way toward me. I didn't ask any questions, I just let loose. I've been trying to wrack my brain and figure out how the fuck they even found me. No one knew where I was."

"Where are you at now?" Money asked.

O'Neal started to become suspicious. Though he didn't want to believe what Starr was saying, he couldn't help but question things now.

"Hold on, how did JayMarr find out what happened?" O'Neal asked.

"The same way he finds anything out. Why all of a sudden are you starting to act brand-new?"

"Look, I'll get up with you later. I have some shit to sort out right now. I might have a lead on the mastermind behind this whole situation."

O'Neal hung up the phone before Money could respond. He couldn't believe it. Starr was actually right.

CHAPTER 36

All day Money battled whether or not he needed to attend Lil' Nep's performance. It didn't matter that he had set up a meeting with record executives from a major label. There was no telling who else would be there mixed into the crowd. The smart thing to do would be to stay clear of the whole scene and allow JayMarr to handle the execs. If they liked the performance and wanted to do business, JayMarr could set up a meeting for another time to work out the details.

As much sense as it made not to attend, Money wanted to. He didn't want to miss Lil' Nep's first performance. The two of them had been working so hard to get everything off the ground and running. He wanted to witness Lil' Nep shine bright in the limelight. He wanted to relish in this moment and treasure it. Money continued to go back and forth with what to do all day. Once Lil' Nep found out exactly what Money was contemplating he wasn't about to make matters any better.

"Money, I'm not going to sit here and lie to you. I think this is some bullshit. Your whole reasoning for not coming doesn't even make sense. You don't have shit to do with this fucking war. You got out of the game. I need you there with me and you know that."

"If there is one thing it took the hard way to learn, even when you are out, you are still in. I'm guilty by association so I have to be smart about this whole situation. Right now, I don't know what is going on and until I figure everything out, it probably would be best if I stayed clear. Who knows who is going to be in the crowd? Who knows who knows about the show? No one and that is what bothers me the most. We don't know shit right now, not a damn thing. Yeah, the more I think about it, I do need to chill out.

"There will be other shows. This is the first of many. I'm going to sit this one out but best believe, once shit calms down, I'll be right there by your side. That is for sure."

"That's what's up then. We *both* are sitting it out then. If you aren't going, then I'm not, either. It's not only you in this but me too. If whoever knows about the show, knows about you, then they know about me, too, and my ties to you and that BC was my brother. So I'm just as much a sitting duck up on the stage as you'd be behind it," Lil' Nep replied.

"Nep, I can assure you, you are far from a target. No one knows who your little ass is. You are the only one who has to be there. It doesn't make a difference whether I'm there or not. This show is for you, to showcase you and your music. We've worked too damn hard preparing for this show. What the fuck am I thinking? This is not a request, I'm telling you. Your little ass is doing the show and that is that, so you can kill all that you are spitting right now."

Lil' Nep simply looked at him and didn't back down.

"Right now, Money, I don't give a shit what you have to say. I honestly don't. There isn't anything you can do to me that my brother hasn't already done. I stand behind everything I said. Either we are going to be there rocking the house together or we will be in this house together. The choice is yours. All I know is regardless the situation, we'll be together."

Money knew Lil' Nep meant what he was saying. Right now all he had was a hunch to go off of and that wasn't enough to ruin Lil' Nep's dream.

"JayMarr will be here shortly. Go get your shit so we can be out."

"My nigga!"

♣♦♥♠

Once JayMarr pulled up and they were both out of the door, JayMarr noticed Money was coming along for the ride as well. He quickly got out of the car.

"What are you doing?" JayMarr questioned.

"He going, what does it look like," Lil' Nep replied getting defensive.

He wasn't about to allow anyone to talk Money again out of going.

"I can see that, but for what?"

"Don't you start with this cautious shit too!"

"You got damn right, I am. Do you know what's going on out here? We just buried your brother and will be burying Cheese tomorrow. It's a fucking war zone right now. Money, you already said that you are the one they were calling out and looking for. Why even chance it?"

"It's all good, Jay. We'll only stick around for the performance and be out. I've always been good about peeping my scenery. If something seems out of place, then we'll roll. I'm not going to leave the little one out in the open alone, either. You never know what these folks' mindset is. They might try to hit his head trying to get at me or snatching him up for info on me. Trust and believe, I've thought this through."

JayMarr had more on his mind than he was saying but wasn't too sure whether he wanted to be open about it. Money could detect his hesitation.

"Come on, Jay, I can read you like a book. Don't hold back now on me, champ. Speak what's on your mind."

"Look, the word around the street is you are the mastermind behind the hit on Cheese and BC."

"What! Niggas will start anything fronting like they know something. Let them muthafuckas talk," Lil' Nep replied.

"Yeah, I wish it was that simple. O'Neal is the one putting it out there. Right now, we really need to be lying low and mapping out a plan of what to do. This is your head we are talking about."

"What the fuck? You've got to be kidding me. Is this what shit has come down to? My name is the one being thrown around in the streets as some backstabbing-ass nigga. I was with Lil' Nep when all this shit fucking happened. In the got damn studio. Man, fuck this!"

Money took out his cell phone and called O'Neal. He didn't answer. Then the light bulb went off in Money's head like a lightning bolt. It all made sense to him now. Money had an idea who was behind everything.

"I don't know why I didn't see this shit before. I know exactly who is behind all of this but there is still one piece missing, why. That part I'm still not too sure about. Yo, head over to O'Neal's pad. I need some answers and that is where we'll find them."

"Money…," JayMarr questioned.

"Nigga, just do what the fuck I said," Money reiterated.

Though he thought Money was out of his mind, JayMarr

didn't protest. They went over to O'Neal's house. Once they arrived, everything looked bleak. There were no signs of anyone in the house.

"What now?" JayMarr asked.

Money tried to call O'Neal again, still nothing.

"Do you know where that bitch Starr lives?"

"I don't even know who that is," JayMarr replied.

Money turned to Lil' Nep. He shook his head no.

"Shit!" Money exclaimed.

"Nigga, you've been tight-lipped the entire way here. Are you going to fill in the blanks for the rest of us?" JayMarr asked.

"Not before I have them all filled in myself, just head to the club. Look, Nep, we in there, you doing your tracks, and then we out. Is that clear?"

"Look, Money, I know I was giving you a lot of shit earlier but you were right. Right now shit is real out of line, maybe it is best if we sit this one out. I don't even feel up to it. Too much shit is on my mind."

"I told you, I need you to concentrate, man. Shots like this don't come along too often. I didn't want to tell you but I have some industry folks who will be in attendance. That is why I need you there to rock out. I didn't tell you everything because I didn't think you needed that type of pressure on your mind right now. I wanted you to be focused and relaxed so that you could get up on that stage and do what you know how to do and that's turn that crowd out."

Lil' Nep didn't respond. None of that mattered to him. It was hard losing his brother but what helped him cope better was Money. He looked up to Money as a brother figure and knew he had his back and best interest at heart. BC had taught him how to survive in life and on the streets, but Money was showing him that he could do and be anything he wanted in life. Lil' Nep valued that.

"Nep, look at me, I need you to focus, baby. The prize is in front of us now and in reach of our grasp. It's sitting right there for the taking. I need you to find a way to block all this bullshit out of your mind, let me handle that. We are going to get through this. You hear me?"

He nodded his head in agreement.

They pulled up to the club and exited the car. Though he tried his best to hide it, Lil' Nep was visibly shaken. Money knew there was no way he could pull off the type of perform-ance he needed in order to impress. He stopped him before they went inside.

"Fuck it, we'll find another label. I keep forgetting you are still a young nigga and right now I know you have a lot on your mind. We'll do this another time, okay?"

"Naw, I'm up to it. Once I get up on stage, I'll be fine. I can turn it on and off like a light switch, baby. I will be fine."

"Nigga, I'm not new to this, so save that shit for someone else. I know better. We'll do this another time. It's written all over your face right now. Jay, go inside and let them know we had to pull out and I'll get up with them Monday morning to try to set something else up. If they aren't interested, then fuck it. We'll move on to another label. I can't send him up there like this."

"I'm on it. Y'all go ahead and get back in the car. I'll only be a minute," JayMarr said.

Money was about to reach for Lil' Nep to calm him down when he noticed a familiar car. He could never miss it, especially since he was the one who'd bought it. It was the same car he told O'Neal to take the night he left his house and went in hiding. The tires screeching let everyone know what time it was. Money quickly pushed Lil' Nep out of the way as bullets flared toward the both of them.

In a split-second it was all over. The car continued to speed off down the street. Lil Nep was hysterical. He quickly checked to see if he was hit. All was fine.

"Money," a voice called from a distance.

Lil' Nep's ears where still ringing. He could barely make anything out. He turned and saw Money lying on the ground motionless. He and JayMarr met at Money's body at the same time.

He'd been hit twice in the chest. JayMarr quickly dialed 9-1-1. People from inside the club started to make their way out once they heard the shots to see what exactly had happened.

Money looked at Lil' Nep. "Remember your promise, no matter what, you are out of this shit. All I want you doing is concentrating on that music. You have the gift."

"Stop talking like that, you are going to be okay. JayMarr is calling you an ambulance now. Don't give up on me. I need you to fight. Come on, Money, fight!"

"Remember your promise, I believe in you. I always have and always will," Money said. And then he was gone.

The tears started streaming from Lil Nep's eyes. He no longer had the two people who meant the most to him. He had always dreamed of becoming a rapper, but this wasn't the cost he was willing to pay in order to achieve it.

CHAPTER 37

O'Neal walked into the house in disbelief. He couldn't believe what he had just done. Though he knew it was something that needed to be done, he still couldn't believe he'd actually carried it out. The whole ride to the club, he tried to convince himself this was something that needed to be done. He had no choice, Money forced his hand. But once it was done and over, he wish he could go back in time and change the outcome and possibly do things differently.

The whole time, Starr sat nervously waiting in the living room for O'Neal to return. The minute he walked in, O'Neal could sense the relief in her face.

"Baby, are you okay?" Starr asked.

"No, I'm not. I can't believe what I just did."

O'Neal tried to collect himself and his emotions but they were still all over the place. He was in denial. "What have I done?"

Starr didn't know what to say. She didn't know if she needed to be comforting or give him the hard truth. What she didn't want to do was act phony and lie to him in the process.

O'Neal continued, "I can't believe I actually did that shit. I can't. I have to go. I have to go see if he is alright. I have to make this right. He has to be okay. He has to be."

Starr jumped in the way before O'Neal could reach the door to leave.

"No, you need to sit down and calm down. You did what you had to do. Don't go making matters worse. You getting locked up is not going to solve anything right now. It's survival of the fittest out there. You know that. This is the jungle and only the strong survive. It was either you or him. Now what is done is done, calm down," Starr said sternly.

"That is easy for you to say. You didn't just kill your fucking best friend, either," O'Neal sarcastically said.

"That is true but my best friend didn't try to kill me, either. Come on, we have already talked about this. If you didn't do what you did, then sooner or later he would have succeeded in getting to you. He has already taken two shots at you. I know I was going to be damned if I sat back and allowed him a third. How many shots were you going to give him before he actually succeeded? Come on, baby, think about it. If it was anyone else, would we be having this discussion? No, we wouldn't and you know it."

No matter how much sense Starr might have been making, O'Neal still felt as if he had gone about the whole situation wrong. All of their childhood memories started to come over him. The tears started to stream down his face. He had killed the only man he truly trusted. He could have at least given Money the benefit of the doubt to talk things over with him. Investigate and make sure the allegations were true, but instead all he did was react. Even if they were true, they could have worked things out. When did they get that bad to the point that they couldn't talk to each other anymore?

Starr could sense she was losing him. "Baby, talk to me. Say something, please!"

"What is there to say? I've lost everything that ever meant anything to me. In a span of a fucking week, BC is gone. Cheese… gone, and now Money. What do I have left?"

"You have me, baby, you have me. I told you I'm not going

anywhere. As long as we have each other, everything will work itself out."

O'Neal bit his tongue and didn't say what came to his mind. Though he loved Starr, he knew she could never fill the void that was now left in his life. However, part of her statement was true. She was all he had left now and he didn't want to lose her also.

"Where is Tiny?" Starr asked, trying to change the subject.

"I don't know. I told him to go get rid of the car and I'd get up with him another time. Why?"

"I was just asking, it's not that serious! Right now you are on edge and need to relax. Why don't you go into the bathroom and take a shower. That will help to relax you, at least for the moment, and went you get out, then I'll take care of the rest."

"It doesn't matter how many showers I take, I will never be able to wash away what I just did. I'll have to carry that with me until someone finally puts me out of my misery."

O'Neal walked off and headed into the bathroom. He stripped himself of his clothes and turned the shower on. However, he didn't get in. Instead, he sat on the toilet and cried. All he could picture were Money's facial expressions once he realized they were rolling up on him and he pulled the trigger. Money had stared O'Neal straight in his eyes. It was as if he was in disbelief that his best friend would betray him. Why would Money have that type of look on his face if he indeed was the mastermind behind everything? It didn't make sense and the more O'Neal tried to block it out, he couldn't help but realize the mistake he'd made. No matter how much Starr tried to comfort him, O'Neal knew he was now alone in this world and had only himself to blame.

The sound of talking in the bedroom broke O'Neal out of

his self-pity. He grabbed his pistol off the sink countertop and went toward the door. He listened closely but couldn't make out what was being said, only that there was definitely another voice in the room. O'Neal couldn't help but think Starr was in trouble. He quickly bolted through the bathroom door with his pistol drawn but was greeted with a gunshot to the shoulder.

O'Neal's body flung back into the wall and he dropped his weapon. The pain rushed throughout his body. He looked up to see who his assailant was and couldn't believe who was in front of him. It had been so long since O'Neal had last seen him but he would never forget his face. It was Big O.

"Look, O, this is between you and me. Please leave her out of this," O'Neal pleaded.

Big O couldn't help but laugh. "You and your man are definitely total opposites. I mean, I wouldn't have ever figured you to be the type to bitch up, especially not over a female. I thought I taught you better than that. You supposed to be this hard-core gangsta, right? Hard to the core, huh, O'Neal? You damn sure had me fooled.

"Now you see, your man BC went out with respect. This nigga didn't give a shit what anyone did to him, he wasn't giving up shit. He didn't care about shit. You couldn't help but to respect the nigga. I actually wanted to give him a pass, but the boss wasn't having that. But your bitch ass sits here and begs for the life of a chick who you don't even know."

"Look, say all you want! You can't do anything to me I haven't already done to myself. I'm already dead; all I'm asking is to leave her out of it. She has nothing to do with this. Santana doesn't even have to know," O'Neal pleaded again.

"Nigga, Santana has nothing to do with this. You see, that was always your problem. You could never see shit! You see, she has everything to do with this. Your dumb ass is too fuck-ing blind to see it. I guess pussy will do that to you. Is that the case, Starr?"

Starr took the pistol from Big O and started to laugh.

"It sure is. It does it every time! Shit, mine was so damn good I was able to turn him against his own man," Starr said.

Both Starr and Big O started to laugh in triumph.

O'Neal was in disbelief. He couldn't believe what he was seeing.

"How the fuck could you? I fucking trusted you. I loved you! How the fuck could you do this to me? Why would you?" O'Neal questioned.

Starr's whole demeanor changed. Her face straightened and her eyes began to redden.

"How could I, huh? I'll tell you how. It was easy. For the past nine years all I was left with was a child who I had to raise without his father and the memories of the man I wanted to spend the rest of my life with. He was the love of my life and you and your little bitch-ass friends took him from me. Y'all took my life from me.

"Chico loved both you and Money like little brothers. He brought you into this game and the way you repaid him was by turning on him. You think you know pain. Nigga, you will never know what true pain is until you have walked in my shoes. I had to wake up every day and look at a child who looks just like his father. Every day he reminded me of what I no longer had. And you sit there and question me about what I did. You'll never understand. But today, your ass has a glimpse. You know what it feels like to be betrayed. You know the feeling of being played. You ask me, how could I? I say, easy, and I loved every minute of it," Starr coldly replied.

O'Neal couldn't respond. How could he? There was nothing

for him to say. She had said it all. In actuality, a part of him was thankful everything would be over with soon. The only thing he regretted was not being able to see either of their faces when he got his revenge for what they caused. He knew he'd never live to see that day.

"What goes around comes around, bitch!" Starr said, then emptied the clip into O'Neal's body.

CHAPTER 38

Dear Alexis,

How are you, baby? I know you aren't a baby anymore but you'll always be my baby. I'm not sure if your mother has been giving you my letters but I hope she is. If not, I understand why. I can't be too mad at her.

I wanted to let you know that Daddy is doing pretty well. I feel as though I'm getting better every day. I miss you so much. I wish I could have been, or should I say I wish I was, more of a father to you. I could have been, I just chose not to be. That's why I had to change my statement.

At first I wasn't going to write you because a part of me felt as if you were too young to read this but you've gone through what most children haven't. Because of me, you had to grow up before you should have. For that I apologize. I wasn't in my right state of mind. I was a junkie! Drugs took my mind. I wasn't strong enough to stop it. Even though I knew it was wrong, I was too weak to be a man and get help.

I'm getting help now. It's going to be a long process but I'm in it for the long haul. I have to be if I'll ever be a part of your life again. That is if you let me. I know the choice is yours but I have to be prepared if you do. I know I can't be a part of your life and still be sick.

Not a day goes by that I don't think about you. I miss you and your mother so much. It's hard to even describe. I'm not even going to try. I know you probably think I forgot all about you, but I never did. I

never have. I could never forget about either you or your mother.
Though I didn't show it the right way, the both of you mean the world
to me. Y'all are actually all I have.

A knock on the door disrupted LT from finishing his letter.
In walked one of the orderlies.

"Mr. Taylor, you have visitors."

This was a first. No one had visited LT since he was sentenced to serve his rehabilitation there. He didn't know who it could be.

"Are you sure you have the right Taylor, Kevin? You do know there are three of us here."

"Yes, I know, Mr. Taylor. I'm positive," he replied.

Though LT figured it would be a wasted trip he followed the orderly to the visiting room area. He walked into the room and he couldn't believe his eyes. It was as if a mirage was in front of him.

LT walked over to the table. He was overjoyed.

"I take it you got my letters?"

"Yes, I got them," Denise replied.

He turned and looked at Alexis. He couldn't say a word. All he could do was smile. He could sense she was very uneasy about the visit. He was speechless. He prayed for the day he would be able to see either of them again and now when that day was here, he couldn't find the words to express his feelings.

"You know, it's a lot easier talking to you in letters."

"I guess so but some things are better said in person."

"I can respect that. There is no need to say that I messed up, but I did. I wasn't much of a husband to you or much of a father to you. I was actually writing you a letter when they came and told me I had a visitor. Anyway, I can't begin to apologize. I can't. I've done too much to only apologize."

"Lionel..."

"Please, Denise, this is hard enough. Let me finish what I have to say. For so long all I've done was make excuses for everything. I blamed everyone else for my actions and I wouldn't face reality. But this is the first time; I haven't been high in a long time. This place has really changed my life. It's really shown me another perspective on life. I'm being better equipped to deal with the pressures of life.

"I know you've moved on with your life probably and I've accepted that. And if that is the case, I might not ever get my wife back, but at least I can have my friend. I miss our friendship. I miss talking to you and sharing my ups and downs with you. I was a fool for ever thinking that I could do everything on my own. I know I can't."

He turned and looked at Alexis. "I want to be a part of your life. I know I can't get the nine years I've lost but I can be a part of your life now and promise to never underappreciate that again. You mean the world to me. God blessed me with you in my life. There are people in this world that will never experience the unconditional love of a child. There are people who will never know that feeling. I do and I'm willing to do whatever it will take to earn that right back. Yes, I said 'earn' because it's a privilege that I didn't appreciate. I know this so I have to earn that right again.

"And even if after I've said all that I've had to say and neither of you still wants to give me a chance, I'm still going to do what I have to do to be the man that I need to be. Because the person I need to change for the most is myself. If I don't do it for myself, then I'm not doing it for the right reason at all. I just hope that I'm not by myself. I pray you give me that chance."

Now it was Denise's turn to be at a loss for words. They both sat there and stared at each other. LT knew it was a lot of information to process, so he was happy she was even thinking about it and not telling him where to shove his apology or his letters.

"I don't know. I mean, what do you want me to say, Lionel? It's been over nine years and you want us to pick back up like nothing has changed."

"Everything has changed, so that is not what I want. I want to take things one day at a time, if possible. That's all I can ask for. It took me nine years to get things to this point; I know it's not going to take nine minutes to overcome all of it. That takes time, and I want you to know that I'm willing to put in that time and do whatever it takes to make it work."

Denise shook her head no. A part of LT couldn't help but feel as if he had a chance. A part of him felt let down because he actually had his hopes up. He knew he shouldn't have allowed them to get too high but everything was a little unexpected.

"That's okay, Denise. I understand. Regardless, I'll always love you and I'll always be a friend to you. You've taught me so much about life and about myself that I will forever be thankful to you."

He didn't even bother to ask Alexis how she felt. One rejection was enough for him. Instead, he started to get up and make his way back out of the visiting room. He didn't want to cry in front of either of them. And though he was very disappointed, he was thankful for at least having the chance of seeing both of them again. It had been a long time since the last time he had so for that, he was very thankful.

"It was nice seeing both of you," LT said.

"Daddy, do you always give up that easy?" Alexis said. "I thought you said you were a changed man. A changed man doesn't give up on what he wants the most. At least, I know my father wouldn't."

"Baby, I will never give up on either of you. I didn't want to be overbearing. I'll never give up. You can tell me no a thousand times and you'll have to tell me one thousand and one because I'll continue to ask."

Alexis started to smile. She got up and went and hugged her father. LT couldn't help but cry.

"I forgive you, Daddy. I forgive you."

Denise followed suit and walked over to the both of them.

"We'll get through this the way we should have nine years ago—together! But don't ever deceive me again, do you hear me?"

"You don't have to tell me twice. I love you too much to lose either of you again."

"I've never stopped loving you," Denise said.

CHAPTER 39

It had been over a month since Lil' Nep had buried Money. The streets weren't the same anymore. The District was now a battleground, everyone fighting over territory. There had been a few rumors surfacing about how O'Neal was killed but nothing substantial. A part of Lil' Nep wanted to find out the deal to have the answer to questions that would forever be in his mind. Instead he had a promise to keep.

Lil' Nep had decided to take some time off from everything after the murder. He was questioned nonstop by police, but JayMarr had stepped in and pulled the heat off of him. The police knew Lil' Nep knew more than what he was letting on, however, they had no proof so they had no choice but to give loose.

Though he was going to abide by the promise he had made to Money, Lil' Nep still had one thing of unfinished business he had to attend to in order to make that happen. Lil' Nep had JayMarr set up the show that he had to cancel on. A part of him never wanted to do music again but he wasn't about to let Money's death be in vain. He had given his life to give Lil' Nep a life.

Lil' Nep stepped up on stage and looked out into the crowd. It didn't matter what anyone thought. He knew the two people whose opinion mattered the most to him both would be proud. Though they weren't there with him in person, they were there

in spirit. Their presence was felt throughout the venue. Lil'
Nep gripped the microphone, closed his eyes, and then let the
words flow:

At 5:02, April the twelfth in 1991
Congrats to Mom and Dad for having a baby son
Maybe someday we'll realize why demise
It's something we know is coming but still it's a surprise
We dying slow but it takes time for us to notice
We might not see it for years but avoiding the ripper is hopeless
Hate to question your methods, Lord, but why is it like this
I wish it was a way to explain it all to my kids
But so be it, I wish my brother didn't see it
At least not before me 'cause I hate grieving
There is not a chance that I'm not leaving
I've got to cope with the fact that one day I'll stop breathing
That's not a joke so I smoke till my fingers burn
To kill the stress since dust I came dust I'm returning
The answer's yes so I live it up by the day 'cause tomorrow's no
guarantee
Everyone has got a number that's called up eventually
So you can pretend to be immortal but dog you're not
It's one life you have to live and when it's faded that's all you've got
So when it's over, it's over ain't no beating it, nigga
And living in the life only decreases your chances of cheating it,
nigga
Is there an after, Lord, that's something I just have to ask
Or is it eternal darkness when living has come to pass
Six feet, dirt, and grass are all piled up on your casket
With tombstones to remind the world of how long we lasted

Born Dying

It's madness living with the fact that we are going to die
So life to me is nothing but a race against time
But that's a race that ain't nobody winning
That's the truth, plus we trapped up in this life of sinning
We only human, God, was this the way you planned it out
Or maybe these were just the cards we were dealt that you were hand-
ing out
I know my time is close to me with every second ticking
All I can wish is you would exclude me when you are number picking
Who am I kidding?
My contracts are signed and sealed
There ain't going to be no renegotiating when it comes to this deal
That shit is real, so when it is time for me to go
I want my niggas to remember me with a pound of blow
I mean that and I can't lie I'm kind of scared to leave
I never had a chance to meet wifey or plant my family seed
The Lord knows I smile at life but sometimes I can't keep from crying
I guess it's all a part of knowing that we are Born Dying, my God!

ABOUT THE AUTHOR

Harold L. Turley II was born and raised in Washington, D.C.
An author and performance poet, he lives with his
children in Fort Washington, Maryland. Turley first
thrilled readers with the critically acclaimed novels
Love's Game and *Confessions of a Lonely Soul*.
He is also a contributing author to *A Chocolate Seduction*
and the upcoming *It's a Man's World*.
Visit the author at www.myspace.com/haroldturley2.

EXCERPT FROM

Confessions of a Lonely Soul

BY HAROLD L. TURLEY II
AVAILABLE FROM STREBOR BOOKS

Chapter 1

N o one knew what to expect. No one knew what to think. All anyone could think about was the fact that I was alive talking, laughing, and joking last week. Now today, they were here to bury me. Life was unpredictable like that at times.

My mother, accompanied by her husband, my brother, my sister, and my in-laws, walked into the church. They were deep in mourning. My mother dropped to her knees at the sight of my closed casket. Pictures of me filled the church. No parent wants to live the nightmare of outliving one of their children.

On top of that, I was her eldest. Each step closer to the casket brought back a different memory. She remembered the first day she brought me home from the hospital. My first step. My first day of school. My first grade-school crush. The day she caught me having sex. The day I graduated from high school. The day I graduated from Towson University. My wedding day. Finally, probably her most treasured memory, the night I performed in front of twenty-one-thousand screaming fans.

The tears poured down her face. She no longer tried to hold them back. Being the strength of our family, her emotion was just what most of the family needed. They needed that sense of it was OK to cry. It was OK to mourn the loss of a friend, relative, or confidant. Finally, she approached my casket, laid her arms across it, and did the only sane, rational thing that entered her mind. She prayed.

"Dear Heavenly Father, please look after my son as he makes the journey from the flesh into the spirit. Please guide him throughout and never leave his side as You've never left mine. Look after my family, Father, during our time of grief and give us the strength and the will to see us through. In Jesus' name, I pray. Amen," she whispered as she lay still on my casket.

She felt a calm come over her spirit. Though she was deep in mourning, she knew that everything was in Christ's hands and she'd be alright. She wiped the remaining tears from her eyes and took her seat. The rest of my immediate family followed to pay their final respects. Finally, they sat down and watched as the church began to fill with friends and distant relatives.

At one, Reverend Young started the ceremony. Even in death I found a way to be late for something. The funeral should have started at eleven- thirty but it seemed as if the steady stream of people never stopped. The church was packed to capacity. I would have never thought I would have touched so many lives.

Reverend Young approached the podium. "Good afternoon, church! We are here today to celebrate the life of DeMarco Montreal Reid. Not to mourn his death, but to celebrate the *life* of a man who devoted his time and energy to bring laughter in the lives of anyone he came in contact with.

"I can remember the first time I attended one of his many sold-out shows. He had the audience literally in tears from laughter. What I remember most about the event was the way he used comedy to educate us on HIV, AIDS, and other social issues. He used his platform to educate, not merely for his own personal gain. That spoke volumes to me.

"He taught me that neither HIV nor AIDS are a death sentence. Simply twists and turns brought on by *life*. I can still hear him saying it now, 'Life is such a strong, powerful, but yet unappreciated word. Life!' He had the ability to bring many emotions out of anyone. He'd make you laugh. He'd make you cry. He'd make you angry. He'd make you happy. But most importantly, he'd make you think. He reminded us not to live for our future but rather in the present, since the future isn't promised to any of us.

"A lot of you are probably wondering, why? Why did the Lord have to take him away from us at such an early age? If you've come today seeking an answer, it will not come from me. Go to the Lord and He will not only provide you with the answer, but also give you the strength to see you through.

"Now I promised Brother Reid I wouldn't preach to you today. When he came in my office and laid down all these rules of how he wanted his funeral to go, I thought he must have been out of his mind. I just knew he was a couple cards short of a full deck. Then, I had to remember the type of man Brother Reid was. I hate to disobey his wishing but when Christ puts something on your heart you want the world to know.

"Go to Him! When you are up late at night and wondering why Marco is no longer here, call Him! When you are lying on the couch watching TV and you think about one of the many memories Marco left you with and the depression starts to set in, GO TO HIM! When life seems as if it has you down and the struggles of life won't let you back up, GO TO HIM.

"No matter what the cause, no matter what the occasion, no matter what the question or the situation go to Him and *He* will provide you the resolution. He will solve the problem! He will ALWAYS be in your corner. He ALWAYS will be on your side. Church, just please… GO TO HIM!"

Reverend Young stepped back from the podium to the sound of "Amen's" and "Hallelujah's" throughout the church. Everyone was so caught up in her mini-sermon that no one even noticed the large overhead projection screen coming down.

"Let the church say amen!" I yelled to the audience on film. "I better not say that too loud. I don't want ReShonda suing me for using the title of her book. Hold up, I'm dead. What can she do? Let the church say AMEN!"

I cracked up with laughter on screen. Some of the audience joined me. They knew I was referring to the author, ReShonda Tate Billingsley, who wrote a very powerful novel called *Let the Church Say Amen*.

I calmed down and continued, "Everybody, cheer up! I know this is my funeral and all, but damn, my body isn't even cold or in the ground yet.

"Let me first apologize for not allowing anyone to say a few good things about me and speak on how I touched them and yada yada ya. No, I've always been different and I'm not going to stop now, not even in death. I don't want any of you crying. The ushers have instructions to escort anyone out of here who they spot crying.

"I'm just playing, but seriously, I'm in a much better place now. It's a little hotter down here than I thought. Okay, let me stop! Seriously though, it's nice up here. Me and Tupac are going to my Welcome to Heaven after-party over at Nat King Cole's jazz club tonight. The drinks could be a little better. All they serve is water or wine, no Remy.

"The wine is strong, I'll give them that, but you know how a brotha loves him some Remy. I can't complain too much, because Jesus sure does know how to throw a party; and the fish, man, the fish is off the hook. Talk about a fish fry, man, it's another level up here.

"Ma, you were right about Christ. Jesus is a black man. I wouldn't have known for real but then he got on the dance floor and it was official. My man can really cut a rug. I thought I'd lost my mind when he started the Electric Slide line over at Nipsy's club last night."

My cousin, Tia, burst out laughing loud enough for someone across the street to hear her.

"Tia, it's not that damn funny sweetie!" I said.

She stopped, astonished, wondering how I knew she was laughing from beyond the grave.

I continued, "I'm willing to bet my last dollar that Tia was the first one to start laughing hysterically. It doesn't matter where we are or how corny the joke is, Tia will find a way to laugh as if Eddie Murphy was on stage doing his rendition of *Saturday Night Live* or *Delirious*."

People in the audience started nodding their heads in agreement.

"We could be at a funeral and everyone is in there crying but she will find a way to laugh about something somebody said. Hold up! We're at a funeral right now. Humph!"

The crowd all laughed.

"But seriously folks, Tia, your laughter is needed throughout the world. You have the gift to be able to see the bright spot in the darkest of clouds. You never let anything get you down and always find a way to find the positive out of every situation. I love you for that."

"I love you too, boo," Tia replied as tears began to stream down her face.

"I hope all of us can follow Tia's example on how to deal with a crisis or a tragedy when you deal with my passing. Some of you will miss me, mostly because I owe a lot of y'all money but make this a happy occasion. I was able to do what the Lord placed me on this earth to do. Don't think about the fact that I won't be acting a fool at any more family reunions. Instead, remember the times I was able to share with all of you. If all else fails, be happy that I'm up here with Tupac and Marvin Gaye cutting a rug at Club Nazareth every Tuesday and Friday night."

People were really laughing now. My funeral seemed more like a show at a local comedy club instead of a funeral at church. People were laughing so hard they were gasping for air.

"Okay, I better stop before my mother tries to kill herself so she can come up here with her switch. Mama, don't do it! You can't come back if you do. There you go. See that smile on your face right now? That is how I want you to remember me, with that same smile. I want you to remember me as a man who would do anything to put a smile on someone's face, no matter what the situation.

"I know Reverend Young found a way to preach, even though I specifically told her not to. She probably broke out with the 'Look to the Lord' sermon she always uses; if she did, I also want you to look toward one another as well. Be there for each other and don't judge one another's faults. We are all family and without family we have nothing.

"When I lost Kalia, I no longer had the desire to live. My family tried to give me the strength to keep going but my eyes were closed and I didn't have the desire to open them. It wasn't until Lia spoke to me that I snapped out of it. After that, I saw the light. I had what I needed in order to move on and get past her death. Each one of you helped me to realize that it was alright to mourn her death, but also continue to live my life as she'd want me to. Because of you, I couldn't and wouldn't allow HIV, AIDS, or depression to destroy another family as it did mine."

Everyone looked around in confusion, wondering what I was talking about. As far as everyone knew, no one in our family had either disease. They believed that I had a very close friend who had AIDS which caused me to increase HIV and AIDS awareness through my comedy. That's what I had told them.

"Today, it's time for the truth. I've never told a soul what I'm about to share with each and every one of you. I vowed to take this to my death bed out of respect for my wife but now is the time. One of the reasons why Kalia committed suicide was because she found out she was HIV positive."

Everyone just sat there silently; they were stunned at the bomb shell I had just sprung. It couldn't have been true; not Lia. She would have come to someone. She would have told somebody but she didn't. I knew that was on the minds of many throughout the sanctuary who knew Lia well.

"She decided that instead of facing the challenge of fighting this disease, she'd take the easy route. I sat up countless nights wondering why she never just came to me. Why didn't she let me help her through it? I needed her just as much as she needed me. I also think she didn't want to see me suffer because she gave me the virus."

Mr. Robinson yelled, "That is bullshit! Turn this shit off! I'll be damned if I'm going to sit here and listen to him lying about my daughter like that. She didn't have AIDS. She would have come to me. She would have told us. He is lying because she was miserable with him. That is probably the real reason why she killed herself. It is because of his cheating, not no damn AIDS. She killed herself because of that bastard."

Kenny stood up.

"You call my brother a bastard again and I swear on my life, I'll beat the shit out of your old ass. If my brother says he got AIDS from that bitch, then that's where he got it from."

"Kenny! Sit your ass down. Both of you need to watch your mouth in the Lord's house and show some respect. I'm not going to sit here and listen to either of you being disrespectful at my son's funeral. Right now all of us are shocked and left with a lot of questions that finally someone is trying to provide the answers to. If you can't sit back, listen, and pay respect to my son on his day, then please leave," my mother said, eyeing both Kenny and Mr. Robinson with pain and disgust in her eyes.

Mrs. Robinson added, "Phil, please calm down and just listen to the boy. We have known Marco for over ten years and have never known him to be a liar. Please, just listen to what he has to say."

Everyone settled themselves down while Reverend Young rewound the tape...

Printed in the United States
By Bookmasters